Blood of My Brother II: The Face Off

By

Zoe & Yusuf Woods

RJ Publications, LLC

Newark, New Jersey

The characters and events in this book are fictitious. Any resemblance to actual persons, living or dead is purely coincidental.

RJ Publications
ywoods94@yahoo.com
www.rjpublications.com

ISBN 0-9786373-7-2
978-0978637378

Printed in the United States

March 2016

5 6 7 8 9 10

Dedications

by Yusuf

I would like to dedicate this book to the woman I love, my wife forever. Thank you for always being understanding with me. Please know that I treasure everything you do as a mother, woman, and a wife. For every moment that you're away from me, I wish that I could hold you tightly and this is the way that my heart feels only seconds after you have left the room. On everything…I love you until the end of time; no matter what we face your love will live through me. *And to my children, you're the reason I live.*

Dedications

by Zoë

My inspiration through out this entire project; husband I dedicate this book to you. You never do anything half way, and I admire that about you. Since 94' when we first met, our souls connected in a way that cannot be described. We have come through storms and we have been strengthened. Our faith, determination, and love for life and our family are why we've worked so hard to be successful. I do see that ambition in your eyes baby, I know that you are so great in every aspect, intelligent, and loving. The blessings have just begun. You've opened my eyes to things that I could not have imagined experiencing in this life. I know the rhythm of your heartbeat, the greatness of your love… I feel you, I breathe you, I adore you, we are one.

Acknowledgements

Through Allah's blessing I would like to extend my pen and in gratitude allow a few of the many solid good men I have been blessed to encounter; the opportunity to use my platform to momentarily say a few words to their loved ones.
Real recognizes real and I'm setting the bar!

Triple O.G. Trice says: I'm sending my deepest and most humble love to each of my children and to each of my brothers in the struggle.
Butter 'Riverside Delaware' says: A special Hello goes to my son and daughter, Daddy's most precious possessions and to everyone else that kept it real in Riverside.
Artie 'Delaware's Bad Boy' says: I'd like to use this moment for my future Aetega Jr Arkeal Arteez.
Cearful Speight says: A big up to my two sons Lorenzo & Nagid, my legacy.
Jay 'Jasir' Hines says: To my mother and the greatest gift Allah has ever given me, my lovely daughter and to the memory of my brother "Manny." You will continue to live through me.
Francisco 'Flaco' Bigio says: An unconditional love goes to my son Luis. The sun seems to shine through you. And to Yusuf, continue to set the trends.
Tabyis Pagget says: There's no place like home so shout out to 7th St. we're in here and as always we love the baby's, especially my baby's.

Ruff Inc says: To Allah, I give all praise and thanks, surely without him nothing is possible. To my loving mother Santra Harris & Stepfather Erncost Kegler, my definition of heroes. My undying love to my children Taria Burton and Brendon Jones, please allow my obstacles to play as a road map for your lives.

Zoë would like to acknowledge Ms. Sharon P. You're the best friend, thank you for consistently being there. I appreciate everything. To my father, Mr. Van Ness, I love you so much. You've been there to listen, love, and advise, the way a parent should. I am so proud to be your daughter. My brother Tony, I will never forget where we came from and the times that we were there for each other. I miss you more than words can say. Though miles separate us now and a lot has changed, my love for you never will. Please continue to take my only nephew under your wing and guide him in the right direction. There are many wrong paths for a young man to go down but have faith, don't give up and don't be afraid to talk to Grandmom, I know she's watching and listening. And finally, I must give an acknowledgement to our daughter Brooklynn. Sweetie you've been so helpful and I know we've passed out a lot of promo items, you get out there and represent Blood of My Brother like no body else (smile), and it seems like we've traveled all over the place but one day you'll realize why all this effort is essential. To you and my step-children, college will be waiting for you.

I guess they've said it all so please enjoy my story as we take it to the next level.

YNZ Productions, we're in the building!!!

Yusuf T. Woods

Introduction

When the streets are calling for blood and the soul of a hustler has been captured, power, money, betrayal, and revenge will change the lives of many. The saga continues in the rough streets of Philadelphia. Stakes are at a much higher level as the pieces to the puzzle are put together and Roc realizes that the very ones he entrusted are after more than territory, more than money...they want his life!

Blood of My Brother II: The Face Off unfolds into an even deeper war as the fury of Roc will be felt by many. The overwhelming desire to become the next Kingpin has put Solo in a fight for his life and has set the streets of Philly on fire. Witness the dangerous moves that are made to become the greatest and hold the title of the most powerful. Family, friends, enemies...no one is who you think they are!

This story can only be told by a person who has lived it.

1

"I'm sorry about your brother's condition Roc….but unfortunately there's more," stated Manny.

Roc closed his eyes unsure of how much more he could take and then asked, "What now?"

"Boggy struck again," he replied.

"How many blocks?"

"4 and 7."

Enraged, Roc pulled the phone out of the wall letting it crash to the red oak floor in his new six-bedroom, three-bath, and ocean view home in New Jersey. The disappointment over the fact that his younger and only brother's coma status had not changed in almost a year was tearing him apart. Adding to that, Boggy now had control over another one of his most powerful blocks and Roc was fighting hard to remain calm. He understood that his anger would only be counterproductive in this time of war, but who said that the rules would be easy to follow?

The noise from Roc tearing the phone out of the wall caught the attention of his beautiful wife, Gizelle. She came rushing into the master bedroom with their eleven-month-old son, Larry Odell Miller Jr. who was named after Roc's deceased father. Gizelle looked at Roc and then at the wall where fragments were all over the place and questioned, "Baby, what happened? Are you all right?"

Shaking his head, Roc answered, "They're forcing my hand to show them something they have never seen before!" Roc squeezed his hand, making a tight fist as his veins pulsated on the side of his neck. Then he slammed his fist into the other hand. Gizelle stood at 5'8" with a beautiful golden, caramel complexion and lovely hourglass figure. They had been together for over ten years and she knew Roc better than he knew himself. Yes, Roc was a great father and husband, but there was also that dark side of him and once awakened, she knew life itself wasn't safe.

"It's Boggy again," Roc said in a low voice. Gizelle closed her eyes at the sound of the name of Roc's once best friend and top soldier. The scene of that life-changing night instantly flashed in her mind as if she didn't fight so hard to replace it. At the time, Roc and Boggy had just been going to war for sometime against a new up-and-coming team calling themselves "The Get Money Clique". Their mysterious leader known only by the name of Solo made one mistake, when he looked Boggy in the eyes and refused to kill him. It was at that moment that Boggy swore to make *that* the worst mistake that the masked man would ever make.

Boom! Boom! Boom! Echoed in Gizelle's ears, as the vision of Boggy pulling the trigger on Lil Mac sent a chill down her back. Quickly she reopened her eyes to look into Roc's eyes, which had still not regained their original color. "Baby, I know the things that Boggy is doing are not him. There is love in his heart for you. I know this. You two have come too far together to finish apart. Please think about that before you make your next move." Gizelle again kissed his lips softly and then left the room, feeling that Roc needed this time alone. Roc paced back and forth wondering if he should have ever stepped a foot into this father's room and got that gun.

~ · ~ · ~ · ~ · ~

The powerful scent of his father's cologne filled his nostrils while the words entered his thoughts. "Son, never let a man stop you from feeding your family and if you're not man enough to keep what you have then you're not supposed to have it!" With those words fresh in his head, his dad's gun in the pocket of his black hoody that was pulled down low over his little eyes, Roc recalled walking down Fifth Street and Brown one night, a block he now owned. He dipped down an alley where crackheads were everywhere. Watching every movement around him closely as his stomach moaned from hunger. A few moments later, he noticed a white man hiding his money from a pretty light-skinned woman. As she exited the car, she threw her ass from side-to-side while walking across the street, giving him a good view of what he was about to receive. Roc eased right next to the car, checking to make sure that nobody was watching. He abruptly slid into the back seat with the gun leveled at the man's chest.

Terrified, the man's heart raced rapidly when Roc demanded the money. Without resistance, the man handed everything that he owned over to Roc. When his emotions got the best of him, he tried to scream. Before the sound could fully escape his mouth, Roc pulled the trigger several times leaving the man slumped over on the steering wheel. The sound of the horn caught the attention of two cops that were just a few cars behind. Roc barreled out of the car, leaving the door wide open. From the interior light, the cops could see the bloody body as Roc headed their way.

"I got him Eric," yelled a rookie cop named Rayfield who grabbed Roc by the back of his hoody. "Freeze…police!" Roc never stopped pushing his powerful legs, moving from left to right quickly trying to get away. He threw his hands into the air as he came out of his hoody, leaving it in the hands of the cop. The money was in one hand, the gun in the other. Eric, who was an overweight forty-year-old cop, screamed to his partner, "Watch out, he has a weapon!"

"What?"

Officer Rayfield's legs were too strong for Roc; no matter how hard he ran, the distance between him and the cop got shorter. A second police car pulled up to the scene. Roc now could feel the breath of the cop on his back as he just missed his T-shirt by a few inches. The only thought going through Roc's mind was that he had to feed his brother, Lil Mac, in the morning when Roc threw his right arm under his left one and pulled the trigger. On contact, the bullet cracked the bone in the officer's left leg as he fell face first to the ground.

Picking up speed, Roc was in a panic not knowing where to go. He started down a dead end when someone called out, "Come in here…hurry up!" Roc quickly slid under the sixty by forty wooden board the kid held to the side for him to enter into the abandoned building. They raced out the back when police lights lit up the night. Stopping five yards over, they entered a dirty, roach-infested house.

~ · ~ · ~ · ~ · ~

Still pacing, Roc smiled thinking back to those memories. As if Boggy could hear him now he said, "Indeed we came from rags to riches for real, old friend. Please know I'm trying to let you live, but I feel you're going to make me do this to you." Roc took a seat on his tailored leather comforter while lighting a Cuban cigar. He took a deep puff letting the smoke escape his mouth. "But the question is, is it really worth it?" he asked to himself before continuing to reminisce on the times that were easier.

~ · ~ · ~ · ~ · ~

Out of breath and looking at another person's blood on his hands, Roc asked the kid "Who's here?" to which he answered "Chill, ain't nobody here. It's just us. My Mom is somewhere getting high and my dad is in jail for murder." The kid turned on the water nozzle and suddenly remembered that the water had been shut off. Roc looked around at the roaches and dirty pots that were everywhere and swore that he wouldn't let this happen to his family.

Taking a half gallon of water from the refrigerator, the kid said, "Come on, we got to get that blood off of you. Hey, what's your name?"

"Odell Miller…and it's okay, you can leave it."

"Leave what?"

"The blood," replied Roc looking at the dried-up blood on his hands.

"If you say so. I'm Vincent…like my Dad but the hustlers call me Boggy."

"Thanks for saving me, Boggy. This is yours." Roc handed him $150 of the three hundred he had just robbed.

"Thanks man, but here…I don't need all that. I eat off the land." Boggy passed back fifty dollars and kept the rest.

Roc looked at the money puzzled and then asked, "How do you do that?"

"Tomorrow, I will show you."

At that moment, an undeniable bond was instantly formed and Roc and Boggy's friendship began. Roc aggressively stepped into his father's shoes and began running to the store for every hustler on 5th & 6th off Brown Street with Boggy right by his side. When over half the block witnessed his shoot-out, word began to spread, making Roc well-known in the hearts of hustlers.

"Odell, come here…take this kid and get me a cheese steak and some fries and keep the change," said Money Man Holmes.

"But this is a twenty dollar bill!"

"I can count baby boy, but what would I look like if you're taking care of me and I don't do the same? That's not what men do. See out here it's a different world, son." Money Man Holmes moved his hand out wide in a circle and watched as Roc's eyes followed it taking in everything around him. Content that Roc understood, he continued, "And we take care of each other, Odell! Look at me when I'm talking to you…always."

"I'm sorry."

"Now that's better. Son, I've been to a lot of places in this world and you know what I have learned?"

"No. What Mr. Holmes?" Roc asked, happy to be receiving some wisdom.

"That no matter how far we make it in life, the people you take care of and that take care of you is all that you will ever have. You got that?"

"Yeah, we are all we got."

"You damn right…now make sure my food is hot."

"You got it!"

Roc did this for months, saving most of the money he made and only spending what was necessary for rent, food and clothes for his family. One Friday, a big dice game was in full swing with all the top hustlers, players, and pimps like Stevie Blue, Sammy "Big Block Gators", Fresh to Def Billy, Poppin' Tags Shorty, Money Bags Merrick and Money Man Holmes. If a person could smell money, they were there.

"Hey shorty, get over here!" Roc dashed to the game pulling out his pen and pad. He took over thirty orders with every player handing him a twenty or bigger, all saying to keep the change. Ron G watched from a distance as Roc stuffed a few hundred dollars into the front pocket of his hoody sweatshirt and walked off.

Boggy and Roc stepped out of the corner store with two large bags in each hand. Roc flagged down a local hack driver, "Yo, let us get a ride down to the end of the block and I'll take care of you Keith."

"For you shorty, come on…no problem."

Roc passed Boggy the bags into the back seat when out of nowhere Ron G appeared placing a Rambo style knife to Roc's neck and demanded, "Give up the fucking money kid before I put this knife through your wind pipe!"

"What money?"

"Don't play with me, nigga. It's in your front pocket." Ron G was 6'1" and 165 pounds.

"Just give the money up kid, don't make him hurt you," yelled Keith.

Boggy quickly tried to exit the side door to help Roc when Ron G pushed the knife in a little deeper.

"Aaaahhhhhhh!" A small flow of blood trickled down the side of the knife.

"You stay in the car vic!"

"Okay, okay. You can have it, but it's not my money. It's the hustlers," Roc explained.

"Fuck them! They can get it back when I buy some more of that good dope." Roc slowly eased both hands into his hoody, pulling out the money with his right hand. Ron G's eyes grew as soon as he saw the money up close. Then they quickly closed, *Bang! Bang!* Roc pulled the trigger of his dad's 22 four times, all hitting Ron G in the stomach. The knife hit the ground seconds before his body. Roc then jumped over the body into the car, "Keith pull off, let's go!"

"Son you just killed that man. I have kids and I don't want any part of this." Roc fired two more shots into Ron G's frame then swung the gun around to Keith's head and screamed, "Now get moving!"

Boggy just sat back and smiled as he watched Roc in action. Keith pressed down hard on the gas, the sound of spinning wheels made the hustlers look in the direction of a green *Nova* racing down the street. The car came to a stop in front of them with the door flying open with Roc and Boggy getting out on each side with bags in their hands.

"Keith, what's going on?" asked Stevie Blue.

"That kid just rocked the stick up boy Ron G to sleep. I'm out of here." Keith's car disappeared down the block.

"This kid's not going to be making it hot around here. There is too much money being made so he has to get the hell out of here," yelled Poppin' Tags Shorty who was watching the cops pull up at the other end of the block.

"Take it easy on the kid partner, now what happened young blood?" Money Man Holmes questioned as he slid into the middle of the crowd so that they couldn't be seen.

"The man put a knife to my neck and tried to stop me from feeding my family and I'll never let a man stop me from doing that!" The hustlers looked back and forth at one another, knowing the words but couldn't place where they'd heard them from before. "Where did you learn that?"

"From my dad," Roc answered.

"Who's your dad?"

Roc stood up and looked Money Man Holmes straight in the eyes and said with pride in his voice, "Larry Odell Miller."

Through out the crowd whispers filled the air, "Oh shit that's Silky Smooth's son." "Yeah Silky was a good dude." "You're right I remember Larry killed Ray Ray, Big Jeff, Cool Phil and a whole lot of other suckers." and "Yes, Larry was a real man."

"Where is Top Dollar at? Do you know him?" Money Man Holmes asked, testing the young one.

"Yeah that's my dad's best friend. He used to come around the house and then he stopped," Roc said.

"I hear he's out of the game now, but you no longer have to worry about feeding your family like this anymore." Holmes removed the bags from Roc's arms. "Top Dollar may have stepped down, but you have just stepped up and gave the game a new player." One by one, the men gave Roc a hug and some money with words of wisdom to live by as they passed.

"Kid, always be the man you say you are and never think for one second that they don't see it when you're not." "Son in this life, your word means more than money so if you tell someone you're going to do something…do it. If you speak it, you better mean it." and "Remember this as long as air enters your lungs: first, the "Man" is not your friend… ever! When it comes to dealing with our kind, we police our own land. Second, anytime real money is involved there will always be jealousy with it so you'll need loyalty," Money Man Holmes paused and looked at Boggy who stood right at Roc's side. He then continued, "So when you're blessed to possess it, do your best to keep it and if it's ever separated, give them a way of warning. Show them some good faith for the love in your heart for them and if all else fails, try to get a level of understanding before you kill them."

~ · ~ · ~ · ~ · ~

"If only it were that easy old head." Roc rolled from the chair stopping in front of his full length mirror staring at his reflection after reminiscing about how he became the man he is and thought, *"I'm a successful self-made millionaire with a nightclub that is doing very well in hand with several other small businesses. I have a lovely wife and a healthy son that one day will take over all this legal money. On the other hand, my life is war."*

Roc lowered his head, realizing what would happen if he was to answer the call from his soul. Talking to himself, he said, "I can't believe the man who has been by my side for twenty years, now wants me dead because I stopped him from killing my brother. Boggy, it's impossible for him to be Solo." Just thinking of their name made Roc's blood boil. The clique had been on the low lately for about a year, but Roc swore that if he heard *anything* that sounded like Get Money, they were sure to die a slow and painful death.

Slipping into deep thought again, Roc asked himself, "Is all this pain that I've endured…the killing, and having people mark me for death really worth it?" Moving away from the mirror, Roc approached his black marble desk and opened the gold case that sat in the middle of it. He then picked up his father's old 22 handgun from it and held it tightly in his right hand. Roc studied the weapon that had the power to take life. From there he analyzed his appearance: the three-thousand dollar gator shoes and his twenty-thousand dollar Rolex that accessorized his ten-thousand dollar Giorgio Armani suit. Finished, Roc looked back at the gun and asked, "Are you worth losing all of this over?" With the same devilish smile that Ron G witnessed, Roc answered his own question, "You're damn right, I'm a gangster and my word means more than money. It's time I fulfill my promise." Roc opened his cell phone and pushed six to speed dial one of his top assassins.

"Assalamu Alaikum, Mohammed."

"Yeah Boss?"

"Your wait is over, it's time."

"I'm on it."

2

Boggy, Chris, Bo, Minky and Haffee had just finished packing the last fifty keys of the shipment when Minky started to remove his mask and rubber gloves and said, "Yo…I'm high as gas in here. This mask and shit can't be working; Boggy you got to get some naked bitches to do this. I got to see my P.O. and I can't have no hot urine."

"Man, shut the fuck up and stop crying all the damn time!" Bo remarked, throwing a key of cocaine and hitting Minky in the side of the face.

Minky jumped to his feet, "Man stop playing with me all the time…" *Knock, Knock.* The sound of the door stopped Minky in mid-sentence.

"While you're up, get the damn door!" Bo demanded, laughing.

Minky looked to his boss who said again, "Get the damn door!" Minky opened the door to see Boomer, Joe, and Show step in.

Boggy stood up to greet some of his top block runners. "Now that you're all here, please tell me what it feels like out there on my streets Show?"

"On my end, I can handle another five on top of our weekly ten now that Roc's block is out of the way. You should see this shit, I got fiends smoking under cars…they're everywhere!"

"Haffee, give the man what he's asking for and Show, I don't want to hear no shit on the other end of this," Boggy stated, never releasing eye contact. "Joe, and you?"

"The block number is increasing each day in South Philly. But the junkies are still people that just get high so they're on some geographical stuff; mad that some North Philly cats just came and took over two corners and started eating," Joe answered.

"In a minute I want them to be calling us greedy. To do that, how many you need?" Boggy asked.

"For now, give me the same five."

"Okay, yo Haffee…give this clown ten and Joe, put a smile on my face by the end of the week. I don't care if your crew got to do double shifts. If we can't see a quarter M off a block, we don't need it or the management that's running it. Is my point understood?"

"Completely."

"Last but far from least, Boomer, how are we living?"

"You know how I do, just keep taking the blocks from Roc. Keep me in charge and all I got to do is put the water to the pot and it's gone. Whatever remains once they're done I can handle it."

"You hear this Haffee? Your man Boomer's a real go-getter."

Haffee held up one finger as he finished his phone conversation. "Yeah that's him, but you definitely don't want to speak to him about this. Just stay put and I'll be there in twenty minutes," Haffee said, disconnecting the call as he headed out the door.

Overhearing the conversation, Boggy asked in a concerned tone while cocking back his 45 automatic, "What happened, Haffee? You need me?"

"Nah, I'll handle it, but if I was you I would lie in for the night, Gizz just killed one of Roc's head lieutenants on block six. There's going to be retaliation over this…I can feel it."

"Man, fuck Roc. I wish he would step up and be a man and stop just letting me take his shit and fight back.

This game is not fun if the King don't fight to keep his crown," Boggy said smiling.

"Watch what you wish for, we don't want that. We need to keep getting this money and leave that man alone." Haffee locked eyes with Boggy, making sure he understood the meaning of the statement before walking out.

"Well, tell him the door is always open anytime he wants to come into my building and play. Now the rest of you niggas, get your work and get the hell out of here."

Moments earlier… Mohammed placed his cell back into his pocket as he once again checked his surroundings while he blended into the darkness. On a small block in West Philly from the shadows he watched the drug flow move steadily in and out of a yellow house on the end of the block. Thoughts of the war in Iraq entered his mind as his body temperature began to rise. Suddenly he was right back there on the front line ready for action, only this time the face of his enemy was clear to him. He placed black kiwi polish thickly under both eyes before double checking the ammo on his twin black-handle, grip 45 automatic. Satisfied, he lowered the hoody of his camouflage outfit down over his eyes and spoke into the wireless headset, "Shamone, Disco, do you see that?"

"Yeah," answered Disco, "I see him, but I can't get a clear shot from here."

"I'm going in closer," replied Shamone as he eased out from under a porch that was four houses up from the target. Shamone was the son of Mohammed's brother Abdullah who was killed in the desert storm war. After Mohammed returned without his father, Shamone begged him to teach him how to out live his new enemy. The news of the U.S. invasion in Iraq awakened his call for revenge. Shamone quickly enlisted into the United States Army and after six months of hard basic training, he was declined due to a late finding of an irregular heartbeat.

Searching for somewhere to redirect his anger, Shamone began to rob government banks to get even. Then Mohammed returned to the States dishonorably discharged for acts of over aggression on his fellow soldiers. That's when he introduced Shamone to Roc and they've been putting in work together every since.

"Just cover me," said Disco who was cocking back his gray tech nine. Disco unscrewed the dome light in the stolen corvette before exiting the car. Mohammed stepped out into the opening a few feet behind two crackheads. "Men, I just received from our Intel that there are only four men left inside and one of them is the traitor we've been tracking for over a year but tonight he meets his maker. Be ready, we move on 'go' in thirty seconds."

Chris stepped out onto the porch into the clear night air making sure that the product made it off the block safely. Once the last car's taillight disappeared out of sight, he sparked up a blunt of pepperhead as he watched three smokers approaching the step. He stated, "I'm telling ya'll niggas now, if you don't got straight money don't even come the hell up here."

"My money's right, I got twenty."

"That's what I'm talking about, here you go. That's the new work we got and it always feels like another one," Chris replied.

The other customer immediately asked, "Can I get four for 35?"

"Man is you retarded or stupid? I said no shorts. You better take this and get the hell out of here." Chris handed the man three quarter-size rocks, putting a smile on his face before he dashed down the steps. Chris turned to the last person who was standing still with his head down and looking at the ground.

"Now what's up? What you want?" The man did not answer. "Come on man, don't just stand there looking at the ground. This ain't no damn bus stop." The man slowly raised his head and said," I want your life but I'll take Boggy's first."

"Oh shit....Mohammed!" Chris' eyes looked as if he had just seen a ghost as he tried to run. Mohammed wrapped his massive hand around Chris' neck while his 45 automatic pressed into the middle of Chris' back. Disco and Shamone were on the top step in a second. Disco rushed to one of the doors and Shamone posted up on the other.

Chris's eyes started to water as he became light headed. Mohammed whispered in his ear, "Listen, when I let you breathe again I don't want to hear you make a sound...do you understand?" Chris tried to shake his head yes but Mohammed's hand was too tight so he moved his eyes up and down. When Mohammed released his hand Chris fell to the floor.

"Get your ass up," Disco said while pulling him to his feet with one hand.

"How many people are in there?" Mohammed asked, patting Chris down and discovering a chrome, 9mm in his waistline. Chris put three fingers in the air. "Is Boggy one of them?"

Chris moved his mouth slowly and said, "Yes."

"Target confirmed," Mohammed gave Shamone a light head nod. Shamone then hit Chris with a crushing blow to the back of the neck with the butt of his gun knocking him out cold.

Disco quickly placed a pair of stainless steel handcuffs around his wrists before tossing Chris over the side of the porch. "Don't go no where, you'll be needed in due time...I promise, hahaaaa."

Inside the three-story row house Bo, Minky and Boggy sat in the living room watching American Gangster on a 54" plasma TV. There was a cloud of blunt smoke in the air as they passed a bottle of Absolut back and forth.

"Man I'm hungry as a hostage…where the hell is Chris at with that damn food?" Boggy asked.

"I don't know but I'm starving," answered Bo.

"Minky get your ass up and see if you can spot that nigga at the corner store! He should have been back by now," said Boggy. Minky was irritated as he got up off the sofa and thought, *"Why do I always have to be the one running around and shit. Minky do this, Minky do that. This is going to stop…I bust my guns too. This clown should have been back, he's probably out there trying to get some head."*

"Boggy, look at this nigga walking all slow and shit. Yo! Hurry the fuck up," Bo screamed as they both laughed at a now pissed off Minky. As Minky approached the door, he noticed that the handle moved slightly to the left. "Here he comes now Boggy, the ass done forgot his keys," Minky said as he unlatched the top lock and then the bottom one. "What took you so lon…" Before the words could finish leaving his mouth, several shots cut through his upper body. Minky's lifeless body crashed to the floor.

"Oh shit," echoed off the walls as Bo and Boggy knocked the coffee table over while scrambling for cover. Mohammed stepped over Minky's body and continued firing. His first two shots just missed Boggy's head by a hair, blowing the red, oak wood china closet into pieces. Bo made it into the kitchen using the door frame as a shield. He dropped low while raising his Mack 11 to return fire. He let off five wild shots in every direction trying to cover Boggy who raced for the stairs. Woods chips flew everywhere as Disco's tech nine ripped through the stairwell banister cutting Boggy's shadow in half.

"You're out numbered and over powered so surrender soldier," demanded Mohammed. Bo renewed his clip and fired off eight shots that forced Disco and Mohammed to take cover behind the sofa. Bo slid under the table into the dining room. Disco caught the move out of the corner of his eye as he saw Bo inching closer. Disco put his finger up to signal Mohammed to stop firing.

"Chill I got him," he whispered into the earpiece. He moved to the opposite side of the sofa as Bo moved closer. "Shamone, shoot at the top of the doorway and when he pops his head out, I got him."

Boggy took the steps three at a time and stopped at the top just as a bullet missed his leg. "Surrender, it's ride or die nigga." He gripped his two 9 mm automatics from his waist as four shots echoed in the background. "Let's get it." Boggy spun around and then rushed back down the steps firing from both hands. Bo popped out into the opening of the living room firing in the direction of the shots. Shamone jumped behind a green and gold leather chair for cover.

"I got your ass now," said Disco, leaping out in the open catching Bo off guard. *Boom! Boom! Boom!*

Surprised at what just took place, Mohammed wanted to get even. "Allah Akbar," leveling his gun off when, *Boom! Boom!* He got caught in motion as Boggy placed two bullets into the center of Mohammed's chest forcing him to land right next to Disco. Boggy hit the last step then turned and dashed for the kitchen back door as Bo rushed passed into the living room.

Boggy gripped the back of his shirt, "Come on, we're out."

"No Boggy, we've got to finish this." Bo tried to proceed pass when Boggy slavishly pulled him back in front of him.

"Don't go near him, it's a trick…he keeps a vest on." They headed for the door, when bullets crashed into Boggy's shoulder, 'Aaaaaaahhhh, you bastard."

"Come on Boggy," screamed Bo as he bent down and helped Boggy back to his feet.

Dry wall stones covered their head as the wall exploded in the spot where Bo's face was just seconds before. Shamone let Disco's tech fly in five shot pauses pinning them on the left side of the kitchen and cutting off any chance of escape because every bullet made a bigger whole in the door. Mohammed cautiously made his way up off the ground. Then he motioned for Shamone to move in.

"Boggy, you good?"

"Yeah this shit ain't nothing. I've been through worse."

"Well we've got to do something because here they come."

"Once again it's time to ride or die and that's what I live for," responded Boggy while looking at his iced-out chain with the words *Ride or Die* on it before he let off some rounds in their direction. He then took off at full speed to the back of the kitchen and raised his gun. *Boom! Boom!* The glass shattered with him right behind it as he dove through the second story window. Bo didn't waste any time as he did the same thing having to adjust his eyes to the darkness as he landed next to a large bush.

Quickly, Bo searched the area for Boggy, thinking he heard something to his left, he dashed in that direction. Moments later, Shamone appeared at the edge of the missing window, letting bullets fly after Bo as he turned the corner.

"Damn Mohammed, Roc's going to be mad they got away."

"He knows it's only a battle, we're born to fight but the war is yet to come."

"You got that ri…" In mid-sentence three bullets slammed into Shamone. One nipped his ear with the other two making contact in his chest, forcing him to fall out the window and plummet to the ground. Two more shots backed Mohammad deeper into the large kitchen.

Police lights were visible in the distance as Boggy eased his way out of the bush. "I learned a lot from you Mohammed," he said, disappearing into the night.

3

Sam Clinton stepped out of his freshly waxed black 600 Mercedes Benz checking his appearance off the reflection of the car. The double-breasted light gray suit with white pinstripes was as sharp as ever. The jacket stopped just at the tip of his rose-gold Rolex. Sam fixed a piece of hair that was out of place and then started to walk up the steps of the 39th Station. His soft gator shoes echoed down the hallway as he stopped at the third door on the right that read *Captain Citric.* He tapped on the door three times, "Damn it who is it?" Sam didn't respond he just walked right in; he was one of the best criminal lawyers on the east coast, if not the best. When he stepped in a building of law he knew it was his domain so he walked with an air of confidence.

"Captain Citric, how are you doing today? I believe you have a client of mine here and he's been here since last night. Apparently he's not been brought up for bail yet and this will not be tolerated. His name is Chris Black."

"Chris Black is not here. If he was I would know about it so try down at the 30th or 20th Street Stations," replied Captain Citric arrogantly, never looking up to speak to Sam while continuing to read the newspaper.

"Well let's refresh your memory. He was found unconscious, handcuffed and bleeding with a fractured jaw at 3:20 this morning. It was at 1311 in South Philly. A paramedic by the name of Zack Vaughn treated him after he responded to a call placed by one of your detectives; I believe it was Detective Michael to be exact. So…may I see him now?"

"I don't give a damn about your fancy words, I said he's not here damn it and I mean it. Now you can tell your boss that a lot of things are going to keep happening to his little thugs if detective Rayfield isn't returned safely. Now get the fuck out of my office," Captain Citric yelled. Sam smoothed out his pants and then fixed his white silk tie before taking a seat in a chair. He flipped open his cell phone and pushed speed dial. "What are you doing? Can't you hear?" Captain Citric interrupted. He was a 6'2" man who weighed at least 280 pounds and towered over Sam when he rushed around his desk stepping right in front of him. Sam remained calm as he put a finger to his lips telling the Captain to be quiet.

"Hello Marie, can you please put Mr. Earl Dash on the phone. Oh I didn't call the house because we spoke earlier and he said he would be there all day. Yes I'll hold." Hearing the name of the head district attorney, Captain Citric started to sweat. "Hello Earl, it's me Sam. Sorry to trouble you but I'm having a problem down here at the 39th Station again."

The district attorney replied, "Sam who are you with?"

"I'm with a Captain Citric."

"Okay, I will handle it and don't worry, that's done and you're in."

"Okay, thank you." Sam disconnected the phone and then stood back up to face Captain Citric. "Now are you going to take me to see Mr. Black so that I can say you were a good fellow and cooperated with me?"

"Cut the bull! You weren't talking to anybody. Mr. Dash wouldn't deal with your kind, now for the last time get the hell out before I throw you out."

Sam turned and headed towards the door when the sound of Captain Critic's phone rang and stopped his stride.

"Yes?" Captain Citric said as he pressed the speaker phone button.

"Captain, D.A. Earl Dash is on line three."

"Hey Mr. Clinton stop right there, will you?" Sam just smiled seeing that things were falling into place just as they had so many times before when people thought they had power they didn't. "Yes sir, right away. Whatever he wants he's got it," Captain Citric held the phone out in the air and spoke to Sam Clinton, "I'm sorry for inconveniencing you in any way." He then put the phone back to his ear, "No sir it will never happen again." Captain Citric slammed the phone down with the strength of half the muscles in his body, sending the phone flying across the floor.

They rode the elevator to the fourth floor and Captain Citric opened the interrogation room door to see that Detective Michael had his hands wrapped around Chris's neck saying, "Tell me who killed Disco boy or I swear to God you're going to go with him."

"Hey, hey…what the hell is going on in here? Detective Michael, get your hands off of that kid!"

"Captain, but…" Before the detective could say anything else the Captain cut him off, "I'm stopping all of this bullshit, let that kid go. He's free to leave now." Detective Michael was ready to protest until he saw Sam Clinton.

"Detective Brian and Detective Michael please step away from my client," Sam demanded. At the sight of Chris, Sam rushed to his aid. His face was badly bruised with his left eye shut and blood flowed out of the right side of his face. Sam helped him up, "Can you walk Chris?"

"Yeah I'm all right. These two faggots couldn't hurt me if I let them," he replied.

"Captain you're going to let this man just walk out of here when he's the only link we have in this murder case?"

"It's out of my hands Detectives and I don't want to hear anymore about it."

"Damn," screamed Detective Michael.

"Don't worry he'll come back, they always do," Detective Brian commented.

"I don't know Brian. Every time it seems like we're getting close to having something on one of Boggy or Roc's men to apply some pressure to see if one of them will crack, a high priced lawyer frees them like they got their own damn keys." Detective Michael picked up a chair and threw it against the wall. He desperately wanted answers that would lead him to finding out what happened to his missing partner Detective Rayfield and he knew that if anybody had that information, it was Roc and Boggy.

Outside the station, Haffee spoke on his cell phone waiting patiently for Sam and Chris. "I'll talk to you later, here they come," he said to the person on the phone while seeing Chris's face. Haffee quickly ran up the stairs to meet him, "Man, are you okay? Who did this to you…Roc and them? I swear somebody's going to die for this."

Chris answered, "Believe it or not the cops did this. Mohammed really let me off easy. I don't know why he didn't kill me. I can't remember a time he let someone live once he had them."

"Don't even think like that, you're alive for a reason and that's all that matters. Now let's get out of here, Boggy wants us all at the spot in an hour."

They made their way to Sam's car when Haffee said, "Here Sam, you dropped your keys." Sam unlocked the door to a black Buick Century and then pulled away from the curb.

"I hate police stations," Haffee said from the back seat. "Chris, are you sure you don't want to stop at Temple Hospital and get checked out? It's only a few blocks away."

"Nah, I'm cool. I'm just wondering why Sam has these hot-ass seat covers, it's like I got on a winter coat," Chris laughed.

"Boy you don't know nothing about class, I just got this whole car detailed and I'll be damned if I let you mess it up."

"Sam, make a right on this next corner," Haffee said.

"Are you crazy Haffee? This is in Roc's territory," Chris asked nervously.

"Calm down Chris, we're in between blocks two and four. He never does anything over here. His work would be too close together, you know that they were your blocks to run. Not only that, but we've got tinted windows so stop bugging. I'll be in and out real quick."

"Just make it quick."

Sam pulled over at Haffee's request. "Look Chris, whose house did that used to be?"

Chris looked up and smiled, "Crazy ass Rose, with that good head."

They both said the last part together. "You know it's funny that this is the same spot where all this shit started two years ago to this day. Now I understand the meaning behind the words, the beginning of the end." Haffee swiftly wrapped a barbed wire rope around Chris's neck. Chris tried to loosen the wire and cut several of his fingers. Slowly, Haffee began to tighten the wire as a blood chain formed around Chris's neck. "Mohammed didn't kill you so that I could, I needed to prove myself to Roc again because I've been with ya'll for the whole year just to see how things move on your side. And it seems as if the plan worked just right now. He wanted to make sure there was no desertion in my heart."

Sam pushed the power button to let down the driver side window. Chris's eyes widened, "What's going on…oh I get it, things are kind of tight for you right now. I know you wish you would have listened to me when I told you to read Robert Green's 33 Strategies of War and then you wouldn't have made the mistake of choosing the wrong side. But you can't get everything from a book right? If that were possible I wouldn't let you know about it." Roc laughed. "I did a lot for you Chris…I took you in when your people left you for dead and now it's my turn but I'm going to do it for real. Haffee, you know what to do."

Sam stepped out of the car and Roc passed him the keys to the black 600 Benz. Two cars slowly eased up the dark street. "Roc, thank you for the car and the money, I'm going to put this next to my white one."

"Don't mention it my old head, needed a new thing anyway, right?"

Mr. Holmes pulled to a stop in a brand new money-green Phantom EX100 and said, "Your mind is your apartment of peace and everything else around it is only furniture. So this is just a big sofa." Roc jumped into the back seat.

"Oh Roc, before you go, Earl Dash said that the check cleared for his re-election so the streets are yours for ninety days."

Roc replied, "I'm only going to need sixty."

Mr. Holmes drove off with Mohammed right behind them.

4

Deep inside the state of Delaware in a parking lot, NayNay's hair was a reddish brown with a few gold highlights and instead of her trademark baggy jeans, sweatshirt, and timbs, she was dressed in a Dior silver and black bustier with an Emilio Pucci black dress. She touched up her make-up in the rearview mirror and then checked to make sure the 9mm strapped around her left thigh was secure before exiting her cream Audi A8. She ran a hand over her 5'7" 130-pound frame to smooth out anything that may have been out of place from sitting during the long drive.

NayNay entered the two-story building and spoke to the security guard, "How are you doing Charles?"

"Fine and you Ms. Jones?" he replied.

"I can't complain, I'm still walking."

Charles couldn't respond; he just dropped his head and looked at the floor understanding her pain. She stepped through the metal detector. *Beep! Beep! Beep!* "Just go right ahead Ms. Jones; I know it's the scar."

NayNay never stopped walking. She passed the reception area and proceeded through the two double-doors that read *No visitors beyond this point without staff.* Cats and dogs could be heard barking as she used her key to access the elevator to get to the second floor. When it stopped, she looked around carefully before stepping out. As usual, the place was deserted except for a few paint cans, a power saw and a roll of dry wall that were all over the place. Yellow tape covered the doors and window stating that the floor was off limits due to remodeling. NayNay walked down a long hallway, making a right then a sharp left and stopped a few feet away from two men talking.

"Man I don't care what you say; Michael Jordan is the best player to ever touch a basketball. I didn't say black man, I said player. Don't get me wrong, Larry Bird was good but Michael was better and if he was a white man I would say the same thing," said Paul who was one of the men talking. He was 6'5" and 320 pounds.

Jason who was standing with him was 6'1", 260 lbs and replied, "I heard you but I still think Bird was the --," Jason stopped talking as he was caught off-guard by NayNay who was quietly turning the corner managing to come close enough to tap him on the shoulder without him knowing she was there. "Ms. Jones how long have you been standing there?"

"Long enough," NayNay replied.

They knew that they had just been caught slipping. "I'm sorry; I promise this won't happen again. We were just on point then you were right here. Please don't tell bossman," begged Jason.

"We've been doing this together for too long for that to happen," she responded.

"Thank you. We're going to give you time to do you but if you need me I'm going to be right down there," Jason pointed to a spot down the hall with two chairs in the corner and then walked away.

NayNay touched the door handle and a cold brisk feeling raced through her body. Her eyes closed and a lonely tear crept down her cheek as she thought back to the moment when she was hiding in the dark shadows of a corner with her 9mm cocked a hundred feet away from the E.R. entrance.

~ · ~ · ~ · ~ · ~

Top Dollar was on the opposite side in the cut, dressed in all black and right next to D's Denali acting as if he was on the phone in case someone pulled into the parking lot. The 45 automatic he had hidden behind his leg came with a silencer but Top Dollar left it in the truck because he wanted to wake up the night when he killed Roc.

NayNay heard instructions to be on point, "NayNay, the vic's in my vision and he should be at the door in 20, 19, 18." She grabbed her other gun from the center of her back. Top Dollar's voice came through the earpiece continuing to count down the seconds. 5, 4, 3 and then NayNay remembered saying "Die slow Roc," as her finger tightened on the trigger.

Manny had come out of the E.R. first and looked around feeling as if there were eyes on him but since he didn't see anything he went toward the Jeep. Raja stood outside the door on point. "I got him NayNay, I can get a good shot to the head and he's out of here."

"No Top Dollar, he has my baby in there with all kinds of IV's and tubes in his mouth. I need some of his body to feel the pain from my gun; all he has to do is move a little more to the left. Top Dollar I see him now." NayNay let off several shots and Top Dollar followed through with more shots. The sound of Lil Mac's panicked nurse calling for Dr. Woods' help, saved Roc's life as bullets flew through the glass missing his face by a hair. Raja retuned fire instantly, aiming in the direction that the shots were coming from, going from left to right as he ran for cover in between the cars.

Windows exploded as NayNay lead shots in the direction that Raja ran, hoping to cut him off. A bullet hit him in the back and another slammed into his shoulder. He was no longer able to keep his balance and dropped to the cement with his gun still in his hand. He listened to the footsteps that appeared to be getting closer.

"NayNay I see you; put him down…do you think you can finish him?"

"I don't know," she replied. "I'll aim for his head."

Top Dollar bent down and looked under the car when a bullet flew and just missed his face. "We got a live one here," Top Dollar said, rushing up to the sidewalk and opening fire. He was trying to hit the gas tank of the car that Raja was under but Raja had rolled down about seven cars and then popped out the rear. NayNay moved in closer.

Manny was talking on his phone when he heard the shots. He started the engine and pressed down on the gas leaving tire marks on the ground. His body was halfway out the window as he fired on Top Dollar, hitting him in the chest. Returning shots, Top Dollar hit Manny's windshield causing him to crash.

"Nooooo," NayNay yelled. She fired several shots at Raja who fell to the ground again. She then raced toward Top Dollar. "You're going to be all right Top Dollar. Let's get you out of here baby." She helped him into the car. "Can you drive?"

"Yes, it hurts but I don't think they both went through my vest."

NayNay picked her head up and made sure Raja was lying where she left him. Top Dollar started the car while yelling, "Let's get out of here before the cops are all over this place you dig."

"Give me one second, I have one getting on the bus to hell," NayNay answered.

Manny fought to free himself from being stuck in between the steering wheel and the car door, as he painfully watched NayNay walk up on Raja and slowly raise her gun to his chest. Two loud shots echoed through the parking lot. Top Dollar quickly threw the car in reverse and pushed the passenger side door open. NayNay jumped in with the blood from her mouth covering her mask making it hard for her to breathe. Roc's next shot from his 44 Mag blew the back window out as they disappeared into night.

~·~·~·~·~

"Ms. Jones, could I be of any help?" The sound of his voice brought NayNay back to reality as she rubbed her shoulder with the metal plate in it.

"No, I'm fine Dr. Woods. I just had to get myself together before I see him. NayNay entered Lil Mac's room that looked more like a small flower shop than a recovery room. "Hey baby," she said while walking to the closet to get some fresh sheets and another pillow. After removing the old ones, she retrieved a brown bucket, some Ambi soap, and a bottle of shampoo. She undid his braids that she'd done last week and gently massaged his scalp.

"Damn that feels good. I wondered what was taking you so long to get here, you're twenty minutes late. I thought you were going to stand your old boy up," Lil Mac said as if NayNay could actually hear him.

She removed his clothes and started to bathe him from head to toe as she filled him in on the activities of her past week. "Baby I can't wait for you to come out of this coma so we can walk out this door together and finish what we started. I pray for that day to come soon so that whoever did this to you will pay with their blood and it will flow as much as my tears do. I am going to make sure that the pain will come from my gun." NayNay's eyes started to water and tears began to stream down her face and dropped onto Lil Mac.

"*Please don't cry NayNay, we're family and real family doesn't bring pain to each other. I promise it won't be long now. I know it has taken me some time to figure this out but I made a map and I know which side the light is on so I don't even go that way anymore. I also learned a few new tricks and when the time is right, I'm going to show them to the world."*

"Solo, you don't know how many times I wanted to kill your brother. I had so many opportunities. He still doesn't know who I am and he put a metal plate in my shoulder and 150 stitches in my back. I wanted him dead so badly that I started to hate Top Dollar for ordering me to stand down. He told me that robbing a man of his revenge is like killing him yourself because his heart will never produce enough blood; it will always be thirsty for a taste of revenge that could never be fulfilled. Even after hearing that, I couldn't stop that feeling of hatred and wanting your brother gone until…"

Lil Mac's soul screamed inside, *"Until what? I know you're not getting soft on me because you're sitting here all pretty now."*

Meanwhile NayNay continued to tell him what she felt, "The night of your birthday when your Mother, Roc and I sung Happy Birthday to you and his tears put out the candles… he said the sweetest thing to you Solo. The man loves you and he even bought this animal hospital for you to be safe in. He is trying to protect you from Boggy until he gets him. Please don't get me wrong, I am with you until death but just think about it."

"Don't fall for that NayNay, that's the art of war and 48 laws of power shit he's been reading me. He wants you to believe he's one way, so that when he does something another way, you would never look at him as the one that did it. This is a war and he's in his bag pulling out all the tricks like a good strategist but I have a few myself. If this bed hasn't done anything else for me, it has given me a door to people's weaknesses."

NayNay picked up the remote control and turned to channel six. "Baby it's time for your daily news update. I can't have you not being up to speed on what's happening in the world."

The show had just started, "Hello I'm Molly Weiss and welcome to another episode of *In the Mean Streets*. That is exactly what it has been this week in the city of Philadelphia. Topping the news this evening is a man named Allen Davidson better known as Disco. Davidson was left dead from a gunshot to the neck in a row home in South Philadelphia three days ago. We brought you this story earlier in the week when we spoke with his sister Sarah Davidson and this is what she had to say as the pain showed on her face, "I don't know why anybody would want to kill my brother, he never hurt anyone."

"This here is the update. Police now confirm that Davidson was a cold-blooded killer in these streets of Philadelphia and is wanted for his part in the murders of five people. He is also believed to have participated in the planning of at least twenty others. This is what Captain Citric had to say about this, "Mr. Davidson was a part of a dangerous assault team who we believe worked for a man whose name I can not release at this time." The camera went back to Molly in the streets of North Philadelphia, "There was another man who was left at the scene handcuffed and has now been revealed as Chris Black. He had been released and then found dead at this very doorstep five hours later. Chris Black was stripped of all his clothing and laid here on this doorstep." The camera man zoomed in on Rose's old house.

"He had words written on him in blood. If we can get a close up on the ground here, you can still see the letters A and P, R. There are several other letters that make out the following statement, "A promise has been made on 7.15.07 now is the time to fulfill it." Viewers this date is actually a year to the day that this crime happened and the killing has not stopped. Yesterday a body was found outside the 39th Station so badly burned that the police say it will take at least a week to identify the person. Earlier today around 7:00 am, three masked men forced the two owners…"

"Oh my God, noooo not Leo and Riley," NayNay said listening to the news while putting her hand over her mouth.

Continuing to listen to the news report she heard, "Of the store Philly Raw located at the south end of 13th Street. The police don't believe the motive was robbery due to the fact that nothing was taken." NayNay couldn't believe her eyes. If she hadn't come to see Lil Mac today that would have been her lying on the ground with a white sheet covering her body in Lil Mac's store.

She quickly opened her cell phone and dialed Top Dollar's number but couldn't get an answer, then a second time but only reached his voicemail again. She picked Lil Mac's hand up then kissed it softly, "Sorry baby, I have to cut this visit short and I have to make sure Top Dollar is okay. Please get better soon. I need you; you're good for me and you saved my life." NayNay kissed his hand one last time and then tried to let it go but couldn't. Moments later she rushed out the door.

Lil Mac's mind continued to call out even though the words could not escape his mouth, *"Roc I knew you wouldn't let me down but I can be truthful with myself, you scared me. When Boggy raided your house and just missed you and Gizelle while she was holding your baby and then burned it to the ground, I was sure he would be dead before the next morning. That didn't happen so it appears that he has grown even stronger. Then he took blocks nine and ten on 5th and 6th on Brown and you just let him have it. After that he became cocky and you look like a man weakened. When you moved and sold Mom's brownstone I thought you tucked your tail and ran so that all I had to do was kill*

Boggy and the city would be mine but you wouldn't make it that easy. Now a year after I got shot you want to keep your promise, it's okay I got a few surprises for you."

NayNay and Dr. Woods were with two nurses as they came crashing through the door when he said, "Are you absolutely sure?"

"I swear doctor; he gripped my hand and held it tight for a moment before letting go."

"Then you must please step out," Dr. Woods ordered.

"I told you I had some tricks but ya'll haven't seen nothing."

5

Boggy paced back and forth with a mini 14 assault weapon held tight in his right hand in a basement located in West Philly. Thirty of his top soldiers looked on nervously. Gary laid face down on the ground in the corner with part of his brain dried up on the wall. The room was so quiet that a person could hear the power moving through the light fixture. Boggy broke the silence, "You see this? I didn't want to do this but Gary died for not doing his job in South Philly. That must not and will not transpire in this organization without the punishment of death."

Boggy stopped, raised his gun and fired four more shots into Gary's body. The powerful sound shot through the house. "And you Jack, how the hell did you let them take my block from me?" Boggy yelled as his body quivered from rage.

"They…they came from everywhere at just the right time and hit all the right spots like they knew the block before they got there."

"So I'll ask you this. Why didn't you die with the rest of your team?"

"Because Roc said…,"

"What, you mean someone said?" Boggy asked, cutting him off.

"No he said..."

"You're telling me Roc was there on the front line?" Boggy laughed at the thought.

"No, really it was him. He took his mask off so that I could see his face just before he killed Joe right in front of me. I swear if I could have put him down I would have, even if my life had to go with him. He doesn't care; he had this look in his eyes that I haven't seen in any man. Then he shot my best friend over eleven times and just laughed." Jack lowered his head and slowly shook it from side to side as he saw Joe's body hit the floor again for the hundredth time in his mind.

"What did he say?" Boggy asked impatiently. "He said he was playing a game that he doesn't want to win, but you forgot the first thing Mr. Holmes taught, so now he's going to give you a lesson in paying attention."

Boggy continued pacing around the room until he stopped behind Haffee and said, "At first I said this is the first time for a lot of you men to be at war where you'll see your friends actually die or it could be you. You just don't know enough and that's the reason why Roc just took four of my fucking blocks in a week." Boggy took his arm out of the plastic cast and rested it on Haffee's shoulder and continued, "But then I would be saying I did something wrong and didn't properly prepare you for this moment." Stopping and looking in the eyes of every person in the room, Boggy resumed his speech, "Then I said no; these are the same men that in this past year helped me take eight of Roc's most powerful money making blocks and turned around to give half of that back in one week. Suddenly it hit me, he knows too much. We have been infiltrated by someone in this brotherhood and today it must end."

Beads of sweat appeared on the corner of Haffee's face and trickled down the side. He yawned as he stretched with his left hand raised in the air forcing Boggy to back up a few steps. That was all Haffee needed to make it possible for him to slide his right hand into his waistline and grip his 16 shot Ruger. He gradually placed it into his lap when Boggy's hand had just made contact again, "So does anyone feel that they know who this person is?" Their eyes searched around the room looking at each other but no one said anything. "I guess I will take your silence as a no."

From the corner of his eye, Haffee saw Boggy slowly raise the mini 14 and tighten his finger around the trigger. He then closed his eyes and prayed, "Lord please help me." Haffee knew that after he killed Boggy, he wouldn't make it out of the house but he was damn sure going to try. *Boom! Boom!* The loud sound shot through Haffee's ears as he looked to see Jack's body flip backwards over the chair head first. Haffee held his ears as several other people did.

"Well I don't either, but I will find out," stated Boggy.

"Does that mean that Jack wasn't playing the fifty?" asked Boomer.

"I don't know what Jack was doing, but I do know Roc and he kills everybody he comes into contact with. Somehow he just let Jack go? That didn't look right. Now the game must change. If you had any doubt in these last 12 months about the person you heard so many of those damn street stories about…how Roc was being brave and courageous or how he lived by the saying kill or be killed; plays mind games so that you can't predict his next move; and will do anything to win…believe it! That person has just entered the building and this war has officially begun and I wouldn't have it any other way, so this is our last meeting together. I will have someone contact you three at a time, each team will have a direct order so don't speak a word to anyone outside of your circle, because you will pay with your life if anything gets leaked."

The vibration of Boggy's cell phone started again for the tenth time. He checked the caller ID to see who was being so persistent. The number was Deja's with the code 182 behind it. "I know this girl's not still mad about that threesome." He put the phone back on his hip and then finished talking. "And I mean…" he paused. Right then it hit him. "Oh shit, that was a seven not a two." Still vibrating he answered this time, "Boggy speaking."

"Why wouldn't you be? It's your phone I called," replied the voice.

"Who the hell is this and what are you doing at Deja's?" Boggy's mind was racing a hundred miles a minute. He just moved Deja to a quiet spot outside of Upper Darby a week ago. It was just as the bodies started falling; he wanted to protect her so this wouldn't happen.

Boggy covered the end of the phone with his hand and signaled for Bo, "Take your team and get to Deja now."

The voice on the other end spoke again, "You know who it is. It hasn't been that long. I think the reason why you don't recognize me is because my voice has much more ambition now. I know how you think Boggy; it's too late for that. Mohammed, you can leave now."

Mohammed's voice could be heard replying, "You sure?"

"Positive. If I know our old friend, his people will be here within ten minutes."

Hearing Mohammed, Boggy closed his eyes and pictured Deja for the last time. He knew he had to move on because she was gone.

Mohammed hung up the phone on his end and made his way out of Deja's place as Roc continued to talk to Boggy, "I know you called a meeting. Did you get my message?"

"Yeah I got it."

"How long did it take?"

"How long did what take?"

"For you to kill Jack," replied Roc.

Boggy answered, "As soon as the words left his mouth." They both laughed.

"I told him not to go back in but he wanted to warn Boomer."

"Roc, I know you don't think you're going to win this."

"Come on, we're not going to start wasting words. I just called to hear the voice of an old friend for the last time. Now it's about to get deep, starting with your two family members from New York that you sent to burn down my house in about…" Roc looked at his limited edition pink gold iced-out Bell & Ross watch. The time was 4:45pm. "Fifteen minutes."

Not waiting for a response, Roc hung up.

"Are you sure that you want him to know as much as you know?" asked Mr. Holmes, dealing the cards to the six men around the table getting ready to play poker.

"Yes, I need him to try to protect what is already too late to be protected so that when he does, I will punish the spots that are neglected," answered Roc.

"Now you're learning," Mr. Holmes remarked.

6

Three hours earlier, Raja and Manny sat on the roof of the old folks building with binoculars watching their block on 3rd and Chestnut St. in Coatesville Pa. Buff was a 100 yards away but close enough that if anything went wrong, Manny's 30-odd six-assault rifle would put an end to it. Buff was talking with two men from Reading, Pa who were trying to purchase two and a half keys of cocaine. He stood at a good 6'2" and 300 pounds. Buff looked up and down the street as Sammy, the taller of the two men, tried to convince him that he was a real hustler and not an undercover cop.

Buff knew the game so he hardly said anything. The traffic was packed in both directions as people crowded the sidewalks.

"I'm telling you family. I just got out the Feds. I was in Lewisburg then I went to Fort Dix with your brother and he's one of the realist people I know. Always talking that smooth laid back shit."

"So what does that have to do with me?"

"He said I could get a good price on two of them things if I got at you."

Buff pulled out his cell phone then looked at his watch, 12:45pm. "What did you say your name was?" Buff asked the other man.

"Why do you want my name?" he questioned.

"Because I'm going to call Butter and see if he knows you two nut-ass niggas."

"Man you're not the only one with work out this bitch. We don't have to take this, we're out," screamed Sammy as the two walked off.

"You two dumb-ass cops didn't know that real niggas that get money can get anything they want in jail." Buff laughed thinking of the thousand-dollar a month cell phone bill he paid for his brother.

"What do you want to do, let them fly?" Manny said into his mouthpiece as he cocked back the hack.

"No, let them go. They're just doing their job and our job is to not let them get to us."

"Okay Buff, enough about them suckers, let's go blow some money," suggested Manny.

They pulled up at Rick's Auto in Buff's black Lexus RX300. Ricky spotted them and pushed his worker off to the side. "Hey, go help that lovely lady over there, I got these three." Hollering to the guys, Ricky said, "Hey, how you said it baller big money player?" Ricky said in the best way he could to try to sound black. "What are you going to buy today fellas, the whole store?" They all laughed because they've known Ricky for years and he has always wanted to be down. "Manny, I have these two Jaguar XJ's that just came in and a brand new collector's edition Mercedes S550.

"What do you think Raja?" asked Manny.

"I feel like biking it."

"Then we're stunting like my Daddy."

"Whatever you say boy, walk back here. Manny should I get the lady to get the fake paper work ready because it's nothing but cash with ya'll?"

"You already know," Manny answered.

"I need the fastest motorcycles you have in here," stated Raja. "That would be this monster, the Suzuki GS1200 Bandit. It flies pass 250 mph and with the power kick, that's damn near impossible to get caught on. You got three of them?"

"No I got two, but I got something just as good plus it can hold the weight of Buff here as well." Rick raced back and came out with a brand new BMW R1100 S.

"We'll take them and put racing tires all the way around on each one. Tint the head gear too." Buff went to the truck and came back with a green duffle bag. He counted out eighty thousand and gave it to Ricky. "And have my truck towed to the top of Ash Park."

"Whatever you want Big Buff and next time you come by I'm going to give you a car on me."

They hit the turnpike doing 110 mph. Raja tested the power from the jump flowing in and out of traffic, hitting a top speed of 160. Their earpieces were in place for communication. "Manny, check out the girls in the red Range Rover about three cars back, they're on you kid."

"Fuck it, I'm going to give them something to really jock for." Manny slowed down to 35 mph to let the Range Rover pass him. They waved as they beeped the horn. He waited until they were a quarter mile ahead when he hit the gas hard while popping the clutch then dropping the gear down making his front wheel pop straight up into the air. He picked up his speed by the second, 45, 50, 80, 90. Manny flew by the Range Rover on one wheel and no hands, and went straight through the easy pass without stopping. They were moving so fast that the toll lady didn't know what passed her. Manny looked at his watch, it was 4:30 when they exited the west side HW on 119. They made a left at the Kentucky Fried Chicken at the bottom of 125th. They dropped the shields over their eyes as they eased up 131st and Broadway.

"Triangle offense," Manny ordered. Buff made the right, pushing the bike pass 60 up hill while Raja went left. Manny stayed in the same direction moving at 30 mph going through the Broadway streets: 133, 134, 139, on 145th and Broadway, right in front of the hip-hop store where hustlers were on their top game. Everything was being sold from leather jackets, Louis Vuitton bags, watches, Coogi sweaters, coke, weed, cars, food, to even girls. Whatever the make and model, it was there.

As out-of-towners walked pass, hustlers grabbed their attention. “What you need peoples?” asked one man.

“Nothing, I’m looking for my man.”

“What you need homes? Hard or soft? Look at this, this is all butter, no cut,” said Dante while flashing the out-of-towner a freezer bag full of powder cocaine.”

“Nah, I’m cool man, I don’t get down like that.”

“You don’t have to lie to kick it homey, what the fuck you doing up here then? This ain’t no damn tourist attraction and if you shopping, take that shit on 125th to Dr. J Nigga.”

“Hey popi, what you got right there?” asked another man who saw the product.

“Whatever you need homes, we got it. Soft, fried, blunted, you name it, I’ll get it.”

“I need that soft white, how much a gram?”

“$25”

“A quarter, damn popi, you’re killing me,” the man stated.

“Hey, hey it’s post 9/11, homes. Everything is up now. We need Reagan back, just say no!”

“You right, let me get a whole one.” The man flashed Dante a zip-lock bag filled with money when another hustler saw the move and stepped up.

“Hey what’s up big man, what you need?”

“What you think he needs, nothing. You see me standing here so don’t even play yourself son.”

“Come on Dante, I got to eat too, he might want what I got cause it’s better.” The second hustler said.

“I don’t give a fuck, get out of here.”

The other hustler yelled out, “And it’s cheaper big man, it’s that china white.”

Hilton saw the situation going on with his brother and approached the scene. "What's going on over here?" No sooner than he finished his last word, his eyes rolled back in his head. Raja's Mack 11 shot through the block while he made the bike hop the curb onto the sidewalk as two shots barely missed him. People dashed in all directions. Buff entered from the top of the block seeing that his timing was seconds off from all the action. He gripped the front brake tightly putting all his weight on the front, doing a suicide on the bike as the back wheel sprung freely to his left. It gave him enough room to drop the kick stand and he was off running down the hill in one motion.

Boom! Boom! Boc! Boc! Boc! Buff fired on the four men beside the van shooting at Raja, catching them by surprise. They didn't have a chance; Buff was back in his element. Manny took his eye off of Dante for a second and he was halfway up the steps sprinting for the building door. Manny then dashed after him, skipping steps as Dante moved quickly through the hallway. He stopped by the elevator and pushed seven when Manny came through the door. "Go ahead, homes. I'm not selling nothing no more they just killed my brother and they're going to pay, watch."

"Yeah, I know," Manny raised his gun, Dante's eyes widened. *Boom! Boom! Boom!* The elevator door opened just in time to save Dante's life. Manny rushed the elevator, getting three fingers from each hand in between the door. He forced the door back open when Dante drop kicked him in the face.

"Get the fuck out of here, homes." Manny fell and hit his head against the back wall. He looked at the number that was lighting up as the elevator was moving and then took off down the hall to the stairwell and kicked the basement door in. "Raja, I got a live one in here."

"He's still on?" Raja asked puzzled, for he knew Manny never missed a target once he had it in his sight.

"Yeah, I tried to out him but he did some Bruce Lee shit."

"I got you. As soon as I make it out of this I'll back you up."

"He's on the seventh floor."

"I got you." Manny could hear massive gun fire through his ear piece as Raja talked. He knew that he had to hurry before the cops hit the scene. Manny popped the lock on the fuse box.

Inside the elevator Dante sweat profusely. "This shit has to hurry the hell up," he screamed just before his cell phone rang. He was hoping it was help as he answered, "Hello?"

"Cousin, watch your back, they're coming for you."

"Who?" Dante asked

"Roc."

"Well, he just killed Hilton in front of my face. I told you, Boggy, not to get me into your bullshit. You said that he wouldn't find out it was us. I swear if I make it out of here you're going to pay," yelled Dante.

Boggy laughed, "I'm not worried about that. If they're there it's a done deal. You're out of here, ha-ha-ha."

Right then all the power went out and Dante started to panic. He was pushing each button in a fritz but nothing would work. He grabbed the elevator phone that had not worked in about a year, "What the hell?" It still didn't work either. Climbing up on the safety rail he released the emergency hatch. He pulled his body up and was halfway through when the elevator doors opened up. *Boom! Boom!*

"Turn the power back on," Raja said, looking at Dante's lifeless body. Hearing a noise he looked around for its origin, spotting it he picked Dante's phone up and placed it to his ear. "Ha, ha, ha," laughter filled the other end. "You're next," said Raja before hanging up the phone.

7

A week later Detective Michael threw several punches and kicked at his locker in the police locker room at the 39th Station.

Undercover Officer Dell grabbed him by the arm, "Calm down Michael, it's going to be all right. We'll get them."

"Get off of me," Michael pushed Dell roughly in the chest and made Dell fall against the locker on the opposite side. "That's easy for you to say, you're not he one that failed. So unless you can tell me who did this to my partner…get the hell out of here now."

Dell wanted to protest but didn't, he just shook his head and said, "The Captain wants everyone in the conference room in five minutes." Before walking out through the double doors, Michael checked to make sure he was now alone. Satisfied, he retrieved the 38 special with the serial number scratched off out of his brown bookbag. He placed it in his ankle holster, straightened out his pants and thought to himself, *I will not fail this time*, and left the locker room.

Michael went into the conference room just as Captain Citric walked onto the podium. There were over 20 television crew members present and most of the 39th Station officers sat at attention. Detective Michael moved within the crowded room and took a seat next to DEA Phil Giles. The two officers didn't say a word to each other. They just nodded their heads on eye contact, knowing already what had to be done.

"Ladies and gentlemen, today our flag flies at half staff for a fallen, but never forgotten officer that has served this country for well over 20 years. Sadly this officer happened to be Detective Josh Rayfield who was a respectable man and husband that was left outside this very station burned to death. He had to be identified by the injury to the bone in his right leg. This cannot be allowed to happen again. I have expanded our intelligence, increasing our manpower and today will mark the start of Operation Take Back the City. Let me make this clear to all of the murderers, drug kingpins, robbers, and whoever is doing something against the law…you will be met by aggressive law enforcement that is concentrating on putting you behind bars. Detective Rayfield's burial ceremony will take place at the private site the day after tomorrow. If you have any questions, Sergeant Baker will answer them, thank you."

Sergeant Baker stepped up and took a question from a blond-haired woman first. "Hi I'm Nicole Stanton from Download T.V., is it true that both of Mr. Rayfield's hands were cut off?"

"I believe so. Next question?" he responded.

"Kristina Bell from Real Rap T.V., did Detective Rayfield have any enemies that you know of at this point in the investigation?"

"No, he was a great officer and an outstanding person in every way. Any person that wanted to hurt him is a sick person, next question."

"Molly Weiss from C.V.T.V., it was said over the year from the many complaints, that Detective Rayfield was a violent officer that would not hesitate to use force if a person didn't do what he asked, something would happen to them like being punched in the face or having a rope around the neck. Could it be one of those people who sought revenge?"

An angry Detective Michael quickly replied by yelling at the top of his lungs, "This is bullshit. I don't have to hear this. Detective Rayfield was the best officer I ever met." He knocked over a few chairs and stormed out of the room. DEA Giles rushed after him. "Get a close up on that. See that ladies and gentlemen? They say the truth shall set you free and I think they may have something there. This is Molly Weiss for C.V.T.V."

Outside, Detective Michael jumped in his undercover Dodge Intrepid and roughly turned the key to start the engine. He began to pull off as agent Giles banged on the passenger side window, "Open the door, I'm in."

Letting agent Giles in, he then hit the gas hard. "Agent Giles you don't want to get into this because someone is going to pay and they're going to pay tonight." Detective Michael's hands gripped the steering wheel tightly while he pictured Rayfield's body.

"I said I'm in," replied agent Giles unhooking the 380 automatic off of his ankle and cocking it. They rode through several of Roc and Boggy's blocks, shaking down anybody they could find.

"Detective Michael all of these guys are nobodies, they're just block runners."

"Yeah you're right." Ready to give up, Detective Michael drove down 5th and Brown, one last time. "Look at what we've got here. Run him through." Agent Giles pushed the suspects name log with several aliases into the car computer. "What does it say?"

"Here it comes now. Suspect is a known Muslim named Mohammed Shabazz. He's an ex-war soldier who was dishonorably discharged for over aggressive force, needs mental therapy, known to be armed and dangerous. Proceed with a hundred percent caution. He's also wanted in question for several murders…I guess we've found our man."

"I guess so." Detective Michael turned the corner to circle the block. Shamone stepped out of the house as they passed.

"Mohammed did you see those two D.T.'s?"

"Yeah I see them. Al-Hum Du'allah," Mohammed answered in Arabic, which means 'All praise to God'.

"Well come on, you know they're going to come back around on some bullshit," Shamone said, walking down the steps.

Mohammed grabbed his arm, "Soldier I have never retreated a day in my life and I don't plan to start now."

"That's why I ride with you Mohammed, but this isn't our war. It's just me and you going into the house, that's all. So come on, here they come," Shamone insisted.

"That's where you're wrong youngin'. Whenever a man puts on a uniform that stands for righteousness, decency and integrity, then turns it into the face of the oppressor until it is changed back into the original form, it is always our war." Mohammed rose up to his feet.

"I told you they were going to try to run," stated Detective Michael.

"No he is just standing there like he's waiting on us."

"Well, here I come damn it." Detective Michael looked at the picture of Detective Rayfield on the dashboard before he sped up.

"Do you think they're close enough Mohammed?" Shamone asked.

"Yeah," he replied.

"Well, what are you waiting for?" stated Shamone when quickly, Mohammed pulled out a chrome 9mm from behind his back. *Boom! Boom! Boom!*

"Go, go! They're shooting, hurry up," screamed agent Giles as bullets slammed into the hood of the car. "Reverse damn it, reverse…oh shit…watch out."

Pieces of glass flew off the windshield. Detective Michael raced back up the block in reverse when the block reacted following Mohammed's lead, shooting from their respective porches. Another person dropped his blunt while pushing his car door ajar and opened fire. *Boc! Boc! Boc!* He blew the front windshield out. The Intrepid darted into traffic crashing into Jo-Jo's white BMW. Detective Michael sprung the steering wheel 360 degrees then back 90 and took off down the block.

Seeing that they were gone, Mohammed said, "Now we can go into the house."

8

For the past six months, Roc had barely gotten any sleep for many reasons. First, Captain Citric kept true to his promise as the DEA, FBI, and the local task forces raided every known drug, number, prostitution, gambling, and stash spot throughout the city; which ended with many of Roc's lower level corner men being picked up, forcing him to put three lawyers on call just for the purpose of bail. The next reason was his beautiful wife Gizelle. They'd been fighting for the last three months – every night that Roc came home – and that was becoming only two nights out of the week. Gizelle wanted and needed him to spend more time with her and their newborn. Roc, on the other hand, wouldn't open up to her and instead he closed them out. Gizelle could see the pain that was taking the life out of the man that she loved whole heartedly and she didn't know why it was happening. Though she tried to help him, Roc would refuse to speak about it. From there they would always end up fighting.

Then there was his younger brother Lil Mac who was blessed to come out of his coma about five months ago. Roc was so happy he cried. "Okay Robin, we're back baby boy," he said after he had the car dealership put a red bow around the black Maybach he ordered last year for Lil Mac. It was delivered to the hospital right outside his window. Just three hours after receiving the news from Dr. Woods, Roc and his mother entered the hospital with their arms full of presents to find the two security guards tied up with their mouths duct taped shut. Roc dropped his bags, "Stay here

Mom." And then he took off through the double doors pass the elevator and up the stairway. Turning the corner, he could see the body of the two bodyguards that he brought in from New York laying face down on the ground with their hands cuffed. When Roc approached the door he released his gun, hoping but knowing the answers already.

Roc kicked the door open to see the room empty except for Dr. Woods who was knocked out on Lil Mac's bed. He brought Dr. Woods back to consciousness, "Dr. what happened?"

"I don't know. It took place so fast; they just came and took him." Ever since that day there wasn't a second that passed that an all out manhunt wasn't in search for Lil Mac. Today Roc sat behind the red walnut wood desk in his upper office in Club Soldi reading over the statement that Sam Clinton gave him on the workers from block number five that was busted last week. Once finished, he sat the whole pile to the side but a few papers and activated the intercom by hitting the button. "Alexis."

"Yes."

"Please contact M. Easy and notify him that his vacation is now over and that you'll be faxing him some chapters on loyalty. Tell him to see to it that the students that failed are finished completely."

"No problem Sir and Gizelle is on line four, would you like me to put her on hold?"

"No let her through." Alexis was 5'7" tall, 130 pounds, and thick in all the right places. Her eyes were gray and she had dark beautiful skin that had a glow to it and would usually have men doing a double take when she walked by.

As the phone line light flashed, Roc took a deep breath before he answered, "Hello baby."

"Roc where are you at?" Gizelle said with an attitude.

"What? Where did you call?"

"Oh you have jokes, well let's put it this way. Where the hell are you supposed to be?" As Roc's thoughts searched his mind for the answer Alexis entered his office. He held a finger up for her to wait.

"I don't know, where am I supposed to be?"

"You don't know or you don't care? Roc what the hell is wrong, can you please tell me what I did for you to start treating me like this so that I can change for our family. I don't know how long I can deal with this."

"Deal with what? What is it that you have to deal with because any want that you ever had I made it a need for me to get it for you," Roc replied.

"I never asked for anything but you Roc and for you to be there for me like I am there for you but it seems that you've forgotten that."

"How the hell can I forget anything when you're always on my damn back?"

"On your back, so now I've gone from being your wife to being one of your problems?" Gizelle's crying could be heard through her voice.

"It's not that, it's just…"

"Save it Roc. Just save it please, whatever you have lost inside of you that kept you balanced you need to find it because we need that Roc back. There is something ripping you apart, and by the way…that place that you forgot to be is here with me and your child at Deux Photography Studio taking our first family picture."

Roc heard the phone go dead in his ear before he threw it up against the wall. The phone crashed into a 20 x 24 gold and glass framed picture of Roc and Boggy in the Hamptons with 24 bottles of Perrier Jouet Belle Epoque on the table for Boggy's 24th birthday. Roc saw the picture and thought his life was becoming like that glass, breaking apart. He closed his eyes and laid his head on the desk top.

Alexis heard enough of the conversation and saw the look of pain on Roc's face. She could tell he was hurting deeply and moved behind the desk and softly patted Roc on the back. "Are you okay, do you need anything?" He didn't respond, just sat there deep in thought because of the issues with his family. "You can talk to me Roc, I'm here for you." She smoothly started to move her hand up and down to caress his shoulders and lower back. "You hear me?" When Roc didn't protest, she kissed the back of his neck on the right side, the middle and then the left. She moved her tongue in circles along the side of his neck while sucking until she found his ear lobe. Her tongue slid in and out of his ear as she wrapped her arm around his neck then moved in front to face him.

Alexis eased Roc's head back into the chair with him still not opening his eyes as she kissed down his chest after undoing each button. She unfastened his pants and with her right hand jerked his manhood until it hardened.

"That feels good Gizelle," Roc whispered.

"I'm not her baby but when I'm done, you will not remember her name," replied Alexis. Her tongue touched the top of his manhood, lightly teasing him.

At the sound of her voice Roc opened his eyes, "Oh shit…what the hell are you doing?" Roc jumped to his feet and back peddled a few steps trying to quickly re-button his pants. *Go down big man! Go down*, he thought to himself before he spoke.

"Alexis what is this?" Roc looked down at all the lipstick marks on his chest. Alexis stood up and said, "I'm sorry Roc. It's just that I've been seeing how Gizelle's been treating you when she comes by the club and instead of you going home to her you stay here in your private room. Then the pain I just saw on your face...I don't know what to say…I couldn't take it anymore. A good man like you deserves and needs to be loved correctly."

"And you're that woman"

"Yes I am," Alexis approached Roc.

"Alexis wait," Roc put his arms out to put some distance between them. "I don't know who you think I am but I'm going to tell you. I'm a boss who was brought into this world by a true soldier and coached by a Don. We don't cheat on our wives; that's for suckers. If I'm man enough to call her my wife, I will be man enough to let her go first before I disrespect her in that manner. This is the woman that took a part of me inside her and helped bring it to life and that is where my heart lies, with my family. But I do thank you." Roc wrapped his arm around Alexis and softly kissed her on the forehead. On contact she closed her eyes as her panties became wet.

"So does this mean that I'm not fired?" she asked. "Why would I fire you for caring about my feelings in a time of need? I'm thankful for that, plus if I get a divorce I'll know where to find you." Roc laughed while he hit a six-digit code into the pad under the edge of the desk. The bottom portion of the wall opened up, showing over fifty stacks of money. He grabbed two $10,000 stacks and sat them on top of the statements before handing it all to Alexis.

"Roc no, I couldn't take that," Alexis said when she saw the money.

"Alexis let me ask you a question."

"What is it?"

"Since when did you start telling me no?"

"Never," she answered.

"So we're not going to start now. And please tell the boys we'll be moving in a half an hour."

"Okay boss."

"Now you're starting to understand," Roc replied as he stepped through the two doors at the back of his office into his private room to take a shower.

9

Roc walked out the back door of Club Soldi with four sets of eyes watching him from a distance as his Cadillac Escalade pulled to a stop with the driver leaving his door ajar. "Top Dollar I can hit him right now while he's alone," stated Fox while he tightened his finger around the trigger. The scope of his M 16 was locked on Roc's head who was sitting in the driver's seat dialing on his phone.

"No, you can't and tell him why Solo."

"First of all, he's not alone at all, if you just look passed his truck three cars up on the opposite side of the street by the green dumpster."

"I don't see anything. There's nothing there but a dumpster," replied Fox as his eyes researched the area.

"That's why he's standing there for you to think that. Look at the ground a few feet up from it by the tree," directed Lil Mac.

"Oh stuff…I would have never seen that," Fox answered, as he saw part of Manny's shadow with the end of an assault riffle sticking out.

"That's one," said Top Dollar.

"Now back up on the right side of the truck, at a ninety degree angle in the second parking lot at that black Lexus truck."

"That's two."

"Then there is the man on the bike who is on the left side. He's been there for over twenty, talking on that phone."

"So?" interrupted Fox.

"Look at his eyes, they're everywhere. He's not paying attention to anything but his surroundings. Then his bike is on ready for movement and his jackets open for quick access to a 45 or 9mm but whatever it is, it's not going to be pretty, explained Lil Mac.

"So, they're in like a triangle?"

"Indeed."

"But what's that got to do with me blowing his head off while he's sitting there?"

"Because the truck's bullet proof," Top Dollar and Solo said together. Top Dollar looked at Solo and smiled as he said, "I taught you well Solo."

"That you did. But I got that right there from Roc."

"You know Roc?" asked Fox.

"What? Where the hell ya'll get this guy from?" questioned Lil Mac.

"He's my cousin," answered NayNay.

Roc pulled up to the corner and Manny jumped in before he pulled into traffic. "He's on the move everybody. Get in position to follow. For hell's gates will open tonight for Roc even if we have to steal the key," stated Lil Mac.

Roc cruised through the streets of North Philly while talking with Manny. "I hear you had a run for your money up in New York, are you okay?"

"Are you serious? We were in and out within twenty," said Manny.

"I'm serious as that bump on your head."

"Oh! Now you're Anthony Johnson?" they both laughed.

"So what's good with you Roc?"

"You know ever since we took most of Boggy's blocks and forced him to go underground, the streets have been kicking back money like the ATM machine but I will not be satisfied until I pay for his burial."

"That's understandable and I know you mean every word of it but that's not what I asked you. I asked what's going on with you."

"You can tell too?" Roc asked shocked at how the feeling he was taught so well to hide was now being shown.

"I wouldn't be your friend if I didn't."

"On the real Manny, losing Lil Mac hurt but the look on my Mom's face after she found out he made it through the coma then to just lose him like that," Roc snapped two fingers together, "Again crushed her heart and she gave me this look that I will never forget. Like she knew it had something to do with me. 'Bring my baby back to me Odell,' is all she said to me since that day. I have turned over every rock and stone in this city and we still don't have a lead on him."

"What about Boggy? Has Haffee's report come in yet?" Manny asked with concern on his face.

"Yeah he hasn't heard anything about Lil Mac on their side and he runs mostly all their spots but by him not knowing where Boggy's at, Lil Mac could still be with him. So that is a possibility. This shit has just got me so mad I'm ready to explode."

"Do you think there could be any truth to what Boggy said about him being Solo?"

"What? Solo tried to kill me and why would Lil Mac want me dead?"

Manny knew the thought alone pained Roc but he had to push farther for his own clarity.

"I know Roc, but it's just funny how the Get Money Clique has been moving on the D.L. for the past eight months and then Lil Mac goes missing. Only two months after that their names start to ring again in some places stronger than before. They took 13th Street back and didn't stop there. They have the next five all the way down to 18th and you know it's only a matter of time before Top Dollar and Solo will come for you."

"And I'll be ready to put in work or die, whatever it may be but until then it's all about Lil Mac."

"Roc don't worry, we'll find him," Manny said sure of it, but just not which side Lil Mac would be on when they did.

"That's what I told my mother and I'm a man of my word so he will make it home."

Roc continued to drive through his territory for an hour, clearing his mind when he spotted several people on the corner of 6th and Brown. He pulled to the curb, parked and jumped out.

"Roc what are you doing? Hold up this isn't safe," Manny called out as he exited also. As Roc approached the group, his body became hot as though his soul was being recharged. Everywhere he looked the vision of what took place there when he was an up and coming hustler entered his thoughts.

~ · ~ · ~ · ~ · ~

He looked to the left and he could clearly hear Mr. Holmes scream, "Roc get him up off of you. He wants to wrestle; but he's too big for you to let him grip you."

"If you want to get money out here you have to show them you belong," screamed Stevie Blue. Roc pushed the big man off of him and threw three hard punches connecting to the man's face.

"Now kill his body." On Mr. Holmes' command Roc attacked with several punches to the man's mid-section. The man fell to one knee as Roc sent an overhand right with a short left hook to his chin that knocked him out cold.

Roc took a few more steps and looked to his right, with another voice entering his mind, "Roc, don't be running up on my sales when I'm doing business," demanded Doe-Doe.

"*Your sales*? Then how the hell did I get the money," Roc laughed.

"You're laughing but I'm for real."

"You hear this nigga Boggy?"

"He heard me, you just make sure you listened," Doe-Doe said.

"Fuck it we're going to see how real you are out this bitch. I'm shutting this shit down." Roc said before attacking the block with a passion, rushing to each and every sale, "Yo, yo right here. He got garage. You know who it is with it that raw." Roc yelled to junkies walking up the block, stopping them as he took care of over twenty-something people standing in line in front of him. For thirty minutes as Roc put the block on freeze, denying any hustler the ability to touch a dollar, Doe-Doe having enough; made his way through the crowd.

"Roc you're not going to let anybody get money?" asked Doe-Doe.

"You asking me or are you telling me something again?" Roc replied as he slid his hand on his new 9 mm.

"All right young hustler you made your point, now let me get some of this paper."

~ · ~ · ~ · ~

Roc laughed at all the memories before he asked, "Men what's the price for the dice to hit the wall?" The group turned and saw Roc in a pair of Ermenegildo Zegna cream dress pants, a yellow buttoned-up tailor, handmade shirt by Ascot Chang with a black gator belt and matching shoes and laughed.

"I don't think this is your type of party old head," said Tu Quan who stood at the edge of the crowd.

"Let me be the judge of that," Roc stepped into the crowd with Manny at his side.

"Solo do you see this? I would never have thought it would be this easy, you dig?"

"I see it; this is what we're going to do. Me and NayNay will position ourselves on the other street on Fifth and Brown. Directly up from the truck and just as he gets there, say good-bye and hello to the new bad guy of the city. Fox, you stay there in case you can get a clear shot beforehand and just in case they go the other way for some reason. I need you Top Dollar, posted up on that cut off block."

"Okay let's make it happen."

Roc was in the center now with the dice in his hand as Manny kept all the bets in order. Roc had hit four points and missed one, now his point was four.

"Bet five hundred," yelled Slim.

"Bet, drop it," called Roc as Manny put both bets by his feet.

"Bet a grand," hollered Ruff.

"Listen I'm taking all bets, just hand it to Manny and if I don't got it on me, it'll be here in ten minutes," stated Roc.

"Man who the hell is this guy acting like we don't see paper down here? He's got this fucked up. He bet three grand on that four straight and three on the ten four." Said Jo-Jo while dropping the money and kicking it at Manny.

"Yo Buff," Manny called.

"What's real?"

"You can see me from your position?"

"Damn right. I'm not letting you out of my sight down here."

"Me either," Raja added. "I'm just making sure because Roc just took it back to eighty-eight out here on these cats."

After throwing the dice five times, Roc hit the four the hard way, two deuces.

"Oh shit this nigga is on fire."

"Yo Ace let me fade him," yelled Jo-Jo.

"Come on Jo because he's killing me."

Jo-Jo walked to his new baby blue BMW and popped the trunk. He grabbed two bookbags filled with money and returned next to Roc letting it fall at his legs. "Bet this."

Roc picked the bag up in one hand and moved it up and down, then said, "Bet."

"You can't tell if you can cover it by doing that, it could be all thousand dollar bills."

"Yeah, so I was making sure it wasn't gold bars," said Roc.

The crowd broke out in laughter that put Jo-Jo in his feelings.

"Anymore bets?" Roc asked.

"You asking for more but I don't see nothing to cover that," stated Jo-Jo.

"I respect that player," Roc replied and then pulled up his sleeve revealing his iced-out rose-gold, one-of-a-kind Gauthier watch. He took it off and handed it to Jo-Jo.

Feeling the weight of it, Jo-Jo smiled as Roc said, "That's worth two and a quarter but I paid a hundred and eighty thousand because the store owed me a favor. So if I miss just give me the change."

"On which..."

Before Jo-Jo could finish Roc said, "Don't worry about it, if I miss this we're even."

Whispers moved through the crowd as people said, "Who is this nigga?"

"You hear that, this cat is major?"

"This boy's not playing any games out here."

"That shit's fake."

People got on their phones and called more people, now there it was over fifty deep. Roc was ready to release the dice when someone screamed, "Hold up big betters coming through, coming through big better." Roc turned to see the crowd parting like the Red Sea with two men stepping up like Moses and Aaron, the older one asked, "What's the betting limitation?" The crowd started to talk about how Roc was now out of his league.

"He's not ready for old head, his money's too long," stated one man.

"Watch old head fuck him around," commented another person from the back.

"There's no limit, what you say out your mouth…have it because it's a bet," replied Roc.

"You're right son, bet a million. Yeah I know who you are and your worth and you know who I am, correct?" questioned the old man.

"Correct…bet."

"Oooohh this shit is crazy."

"I told you old head was the real deal." The crowd went into frenzy.

Roc let the dice fly, the first one was a four and the other one showed a three then it sprung off to a six. "I'm going to show you niggas how I used to eat on these streets before I turned them white in the summer. Jo-Jo, touch the dice because I don't want you to say shit."

Jo-Jo picked them up and sat them on five and a two. Roc shook them until he heard his rhythm then let them roll. A five laid flat and the same deuce showed and slowly came to a stop. In the last second the two sprung off and stopped on another five.

People in the crowd jumped up and down as Manny grasped all the money. The old head walked up and gave Roc a big hug. "Roc I'll get that to you as soon as I can." Then they both started laughing.

"Mr. Holmes what the hell are you doing down here in this part of town?" Roc questioned.

"What are you talking about? This part as you call it is what defines the man who I am today. I'm always going to be around here even if I become a billionaire. I was five doors down in Mrs. Lisa's house eating the best soul food on this side of the city when I heard it was a square out here throwing money around."

"Yeah?" said Roc.

"The question is what made you finally answer your soul?"

"How did you know?"

"It's your eyes. I see nothing but ambition in them and I haven't seen that look in months, but it's nice to have you back."

Roc turned around and with both hands full of money he said, "Ya'll done?"

"Done? Bet that shit you young maggot," screamed Ayzo.

"Bet." Just like that the game was back in full swing.

"I like the shooter," hollered Mr. Holmes who won about thirty thousand off of Dame.

"What's the bet?" asked Dame.

"The same two thousand."

"Come on O.G. with this jerkin' my dick shit, bet this six grand I got here or no bet."

Mr. Holmes shook his head from side to side before speaking, "Young man you got life seriously fucked up." People were shocked hearing the old man who owned several stores on the block use profanity. So as it happened everyone got quiet while he continued. "What can I get from you that I don't already have? What's a hundred or two hundred thousand? That's no money; my young soldiers put that on their pinky. I've been around the world three times and should have been dead nine times so there's nothing else for me to do but give this corporate game I have trapped in this brain to my next in line before I pass. So don't ever come at me with a disrespectful mouth until your money can uplift the black people as a whole."

A black Altima pulled to a stop with the driver ready to exit like the passenger when he paused and dropped back into his seat. "What's the hold up, let's get this money Boomer. They said it's sweet," yelled T.C.

"Do you see who that is?"

"Man…that's Roc." T.C. jumped back into the car and put his seat all the way back. "I hope he didn't see me, I told you to get darker tint," complained T.C. "Shit I'm going to get him out the way for Joe right now." Boomer picked up his phone and dialed as he slowly pulled off taking in everything about Roc's appearance.

"Take it easy on him old head, he don't know any better. Isn't that right?" Roc asked Dame.

"Raja, you got the target?" questioned Manny into his earpiece.

"Got him."

"If it goes left, put him down," said Manny.

"Yeah that's my bad, I was just trying to get where you're at old timer," Dame apologized.

"Well this is a start." Mr. Holmes went into his pocket and gave Dame the six thousand out of his suit jacket along with his money back.

"Thanks."

A kid in an old Rocawear hoody, jeans and timbs approached the crowd screaming, "Store run, store run. Anybody store run?" He then pulled out his pen and pad and worked the crowd writing down order after order. Then he came to Roc and Mr. Holmes who were just staring at him. "You need anything from the store sir?"

Roc bent down to face the kid. "Yeah shorty, I need something but you have to tell me your name and then I'll give you this." Roc pulled out a hundred dollar bill.

"Aaron Williams."

Roc looked at Mr. Holmes and shook his head. "Who's your dad, Lethal Aaron?"

"Yes, you know my dad?"

"Yes, where is he at?"

"In jail."

"Where do you live kid?"

"Right there." Little Aaron pointed to a row house three doors down that had seen better days.

"All right. Here," Roc gave him six hundred dollars and asked, "How many brothers and sisters do you have?"

"Two little brothers," he answered.

"Listen, take this money and make sure you take care of them. That's your job for the rest of your life and tomorrow morning I want you to go around the corner to Miller Sneakers and tell Ms. Fisher that Roc sent you and to give you a summer job okay?"

"Yes sir." The kid smiled showing every tooth in his mouth.

"Now I don't want to see you out here anymore, you understand? If I do then you're fired. Now get out of here."

The kid took off running when someone screamed, "Five-O watch out one time!" Police cars came up the one way street. The helicopter spotlights lit up the night that was just beginning to fall. People ran in every direction dashing right pass the six cop cars. Roc however, never paid them any attention while he walked Mr. Holmes to Mrs. Lisa's house.

Confident that he was safe, Roc along with Manny headed back to their truck just as cops pulled their guns on them, "Freeze or I'll shoot!"

"Buff you on this," asked Raja with his gun ready to fire.

"Yeah I'm going to take the ones on the right and you get the left side. That will give Manny enough time to do him," answered Buff.

"All right we move on four."

"You with the yellow shirt, get on the ground! The other guy, you can go. Now get moving!" demanded the police officer with the bullhorn. Manny didn't move but slowly sat the brown bag of money on the ground. He could hear Raja start the count: 4, 3. Smoothly he moved his hand to the rim of his waistline where his gun rested in the middle of his back.

Roc looked at Manny go into action and realized what was about to take place then remembered that he didn't have his gun to join the party and yelled, "Stand down!"

Manny turned his head in Roc's direction. "Stand down Manny, maybe next time," Roc smiled before being pushed to the ground and handcuffed. Manny shook his head as Roc was thrown into the back of the car that took off down the alley.

"This can't be happening, you dig."

"Don't worry Top Dollar, everything happens for a reason," replied Solo as he smiled. "I want you to listen carefully NayNay make sure you get that house address, this is what we're going to do…"

10

Detective Michael had been at his desk for hours at a time going through several of Detective Rayfield's files that he didn't know existed until four days after the funeral. It was Wednesday and Mrs. Betty Rayfield came to retrieve her husband's belongings. To ease the pain that was so easy to see she was dealing with, Detective Michael held back his own tears and cleaned out his partner's desk and locker. While doing this he spotted a box with a few worn out letters on it. All that he could make out were the letters: my b o ke per. *"My book keeper?"* Detective Michael thought as he asked, "Betty can I hold on to this box for a while? I promise to return it soon."

"Take what you need Michael, you're family but please bring the person that did this to justice," she replied with tears filling her eyes.

"I will, I promise."

As he read over many folders he realized most of the photos and notes came from the ten officers that Detective Rayfield had doing eighteen-hour surveillances on Roc and Boggy. They did this daily until the funding was cut. There were recordings of every 911 call that was connected with the two. Detective Rayfield also obtained any traffic light, telephone pole and ATM machine that contained a camera within a three-mile radius from any attack from Roc's team and the Get Money Clique. Detective Michael put each photo with the notes to match in chronological order, but was still coming up with nothing.

Next he placed them in order by rank, which ended with the same results. As the days rolled by, he hit the streets hard shaking down informants of his and Detective Rayfield's and still came up empty-handed feeling like he was in over his head. He slammed his fist on his desk hard, "Damn it I know I can put this together, it's all right here but I can't put my finger on it."

Putting both hands on his head, he pulled at his hair.

"Hey, Michael be easy. Using force like that will break your wrist," said Officer Dell while he poured a cup of coffee approaching Detective Michael's desk.

"I know Dell…it's just this case. I'm sure it has something to do with Rayfield's death and the person who did it."

Dell stepped closer putting his hand on Detective Michael's shoulder and said sincerely said, "I know he was like a brother-from-another-mother to you and now, you have become "my brother's keeper". Just know I'm willing to help you, all you have to do..."

"Hold up," Michael interrupted. "What did you just say?"

"I said that I would help."

"No before that, about the keeper."

"My brother's keeper...it's a biblical term."

"I know what it means but you just don't know what it means to me." Detective Michael hugged Officer Dell and said, "Thanks," as he raced off into the officers locker room. He pulled the box free and grabbed a black marker and filled in the worn out letters to spell My Brothers Keeper. *"I know you said it was all connected; now I think I got it."*

He removed everything off of his desk by pushing it to the floor and placed the photo from the two main files in the middle. He separated them in three rows. In the first was the scene of every bloody attack starting with the takeover of 13th Street. Picking up the picture of a dismantled Troy he stated, "You started to run; you just should not have stopped."

~ · ~ · ~ · ~

Michael remembered the day Troy walked into their office and said to him, "I'm telling you man...these guys are young killers. They're the Get Money Clique or team, whatever they call themselves. They can't be any older than 16 or 17 and they came in there just busting their guns killing people."

"Slow down Troy, can you tell us who they work for?" Rayfield had asked him.

"Solo."

"Are you sure?" Detective Michael had questioned.

"Without a doubt, I will never forget that name Solo because he said it like he was sure that he was the only one."

~ · ~ · ~ · ~

After remembering that conversation, Detective Michael put the picture back into place as he read over the notes from the West Chester police department that stated that witnesses reported there were four individuals: one older male and three younger ones. One of which is believed to be a female. The second row had the picture of the undercover block surveillance that showed the flow of the drug trade and the head Lieutenant that ran them. The last row was all the information that Detective Rayfield had when he went missing.

He moved each picture from row to row trying to find some kind of pattern when it hit him. "I'll be damned," he said gripping up his coat and dashing for the door.

When Captain Citric saw him he called out, "Michael get back here and clean this damn mess up."

"Not right now Captain, I'm busy," Detective Michael continued out the door and to his car.

Driving up to a beautiful row home on a quiet street in West Philadelphia, Detective Michael quickly removed his tie, then wet his fingers with his tongue and ran them through his hair. Satisfied with his reflection, he got out the car and rang the door bell.

"Yes, can I help you?" said a fair-skinned woman about 160 pounds with a questionable look on her face.

"Yes I'm Charles Hart from Columbian Life Insurance. I assume you're Draeh Rich, mother of the late…" Detective Michael paused and opened the file with D's picture in the top right corner. Sure that she saw it, he quickly closed it like it was top secret and continued. "Daryl Rich, I'm so sorry for the loss of your son Ms. Rich but when you didn't come down to the office about the claim you filed…"

"Claim…I filed? Sir you must be mistaken, the only claim I had covered my family because of my job."

"No, it says right here. I'm sorry do we have to do this out here?"

"Excuse my manners, please come in," Ms. Rich said, welcoming him into her home.

Detective Michael's eyes were everywhere as he scanned each picture on the wall while being lead into the living room. "Have a seat."

"Thank you. As I was saying about the claim number 081022, your name is listed as the beneficiary of a $100,000 policy that was paid in full until he sadly passed. So if you can prove that he is your son and that you're Draeh Rich, I will have the check in the mail within a week." Detective Michael put on the best fake smile his heart would allow, praying that she bought it.

"Well let me see, I have his birth certificate upstairs," Ms. Rich said as she started toward the stairs with Detective Michael right behind her.

"I must say, this is a lovely house for a person that is a correction officer."

"Oh baby, I could never afford a house like this. A friend of my son's brought this for me," she explained.

"He must be a really good friend."

"He's an angel and he pays every bill on the first of the month even when I ask him not to because he does so much for me all ready. Excuse me it has to be downstairs in the china closet," Ms. Rich stated once she finished her search.

"Go ahead, please take your time."

Detective Michael sat in a chair patiently but as soon as she hit the last step he was on the move. He rushed to the first room on the right and slowly turned the knob. Looking inside, *this has to be her room*, he thought before going off down the hall to the next room. While entering, he could tell that this was D's room from all the pictures of him and other people on the dresser and walls. "Bingo." Detective Michael walked over to the nightstand and picked up a picture of D and Lil Mac in their 745 IL BMW. They both had 24 inch rims and the doors open on each vehicle to show off the six DVD televisions that they had. Going through drawers, Detective Michael didn't find anything so he moved through the closet and saw a box on the top shelf with "D's" written on it. He tried to stand on his tippy toes but it was still too high for him to reach.

Clothes started to fall as he jumped up into the air to retrieve the box.

"What the hell was that?" Ms. Rich said about the loud noise that echoed in the distance while closing the closet door in the room that she was in before walking up the steps. Detective Michael got up off the ground and looked at half of the items that were in the box that now lay out on the floor. He gathered a few items when he thought that he heard a noise down the hall.

"Oh shit," he looked around at the big mess he made. Ms. Rich had just reached the top step and picked up speed, rushing to the back. She went into the first room on the right and saw that nothing was out of place then headed to where she left the Detective at. Detective Michael quickly tried to kick the clothes back into the closet as the sound of Ms. Rich walking down the hall got closer. He went to the door and saw her entering the hallway. "Damn…this can't be happening; the Captain will have my badge for this for sure."

Ms. Rich made it to the back to the room and pushed the door wide open. She looked around twice.

"Did you find it Ms. Rich?" asked Detective Michael from the chair she left him in.

Ms. Rich didn't respond right away, feeling that something was out of place. She continued to look around and then asked, "Why are you sweating like that?"

"Oh I…I always sweat hard when it's hot."

"Oh hell no, this house has central air. I'm from North Philly not North and Philly." She stepped out into the hallway and saw D's door ajar. "What the fuck?" Ms. Rich opened the door and saw that D's clothes were all over. As tears flowed down her face she quickly moved to the closet to get D's black 45 automatic and cocked it. "Not my baby, you bastard," she raced back to the room and raised the gun, leveling it off while closing her eyes before pulling the trigger twice. *Boom! Boom!*

Detective Michael fell when he heard the shot as he made it to his car door. The car started moments after the front door of the house opened. Again she raised the gun letting off four shots that blew out the back window as Detective Michael pulled off down the street. "Damn, this is the fourth car in six months," he screamed to himself and then brushing the glass from of his clothes and hair.

"64.com Detective Michael, are you out there? Please respond."

"Copy, this is Detective Michael. What seems to be the problem?"

"Detective this is dispatch, Officer Dell and Agent Giles have been trying to contact you for the last half an hour. I will put you through to Officer Dell because he's on the cell with us."

"Okay thanks."

"Michael."

"Yes Dell."

"You wouldn't guess who they just brought into the station in handcuffs."

"Should I?"

"You couldn't ever get this one so I'm going to tell you…the one and only Odell Miller."

"Roc…you've got to be joking?"

"Well I'm not."

"I'm on my way."

"Hurry because I don't know how long they can keep him."

"I'm there, over and out." Detective Michael thought to himself, *"I guess you are looking over me partner,"* as he pulled out a picture of Lil Mac, Top Dollar and a person with braids, baggy jeans and timbs that he couldn't identify. What caught his eyes was the fact that they all were iced-out in G.M.C. chains. "I will not fail you this time," he pushed the Chevy Caprice pass ninety miles per hour and headed to the station.

11

With Roc's head down and his hands cuffed behind his back, Detective Brian paraded him through the 39th Station to the sound of applause as officers stood to their feet. Halfway down the hall, Roc raised his head to look into the faces of his enemies. When more than half of the clapping stopped, Roc just smiled. Captain Citric stepped out of his office and yelled, "Brian put his ass up on the fourth floor."

"Will do Captain. See, you have done it now. Your high-priced lawyer can't get you out of this shit. You'll be lucky just to make it out of this room," said Detective Brian through his tightening teeth.

"Are you serious?" asked Roc.

"Damn right I'm serious."

"You can't be talking to me like that," Roc replied.

"Let me tell you this Mr. Miller or Roc, whatever you prefer, I'm not scared of you. You're just another thug with a little bit of money and the first time I catch you crossing that line I'm going to bust your ass…literally." Detective Brian flashed his 380 on his ankle, "now get in there." He pushed Roc hard in the back and sent him face first into the interrogation room.

Roc turned sideways as he crashed his shoulder into the concrete wall. Detective Brian was about to close the door when Roc called out, "Hey Brian."

"What asshole?"

"Can I get a light?"

"No, there isn't any smoking in here."

"I don't smoke; I start fires…ha-ha-ha," Roc laughed.

"You son of a bitch," Detective Brian reopened the door with the force of a lion as he dashed in, wrapping his large hands around Roc's neck and cocked back his right fist.

Roc looked him dead in the eyes, "I swear…if you put your dirty hands on me you'll never use them again and I mean that."

"To hell with you," Detective Brian let his right hand fly as it landed an inch away from Roc's face.

Special Agent Branson release Detective Brian's hands and said, "At ease officer, this case is way bigger than your emotions. So if you don't mind leaving, I need to speak with Mr. Miller alone thank you."

With a puzzled look on his face, Detective Brian asked, "And who the hell are you?"

While walking Detective Brian to the door, he responded, "I'm the person who will have your job in a minute if you're still standing there once I take my coat off. And tell your Captain to hurry up with my damn coffee."

Leaving, Detective Brian said, "Roc you...," before he could finish Special Agent Branson slammed the metal door in his face.

"I know you don't know me and I barely know you but give it six years at the rate you're going and I will know everything about you," said Special Agent Branson in a mellow voice that sounded more like a philosopher than an officer. He walked over and took the handcuffs off of Roc. "Nice watch, that's a one-of-a-kind. I stand corrected, I give it two years. No more than three."

Roc's brain raced as he tried to figure out what edge Special Agent Branson was working. Roc had run through over a hundred of these interrogators but this one was different. He had a level of confidence that Roc had never seen.

"I'm going to help you out because I know you're asking yourself who is this guy. I'm DEA Branson, better known as Satan to the big bosses of the underworld. That is what brings me here in this hell hole to see you."

Roc took a seat in the hard wooden chair and said, "Okay Satan, all that you said is fine and dandy but I don't have any rap for you. My 5th amendment rights will start now and I would like to see my lawyer."

"I completely understand that Mr. Miller and as soon as he gets here I will notify them to send him right up. Until then I would like to show you something." He retrieved his briefcase and sat a photo of a Mexican man, 210 pounds, 5'7", with black hair and a thick beard stepping off of a jet standing in a suit in front of Roc.

"Do you know this man?" Roc didn't respond.

"I know you don't know him but this man is your co-defendant, Diego El Sovida. He made almost a half billion dollars in marijuana last year. Then there is this man, Sunan Kudari." The photo showed an Asian man with dark sunglasses, brown hair that was slicked to the back standing at 5'10" and 185 pounds. He was sitting in a chair, with two beautiful women standing on each side of him while he talked with another man whose face could not be seen, all that was visible was the back of his head. "Mr. Kudari here is the king of heroin. When I say king, I mean that when his drugs which kill millions of people each day are in route to the U.S., many countries in the Middle East like Yemen, Jordan and Iraq are forced to stop fighting, fearing that they will interfere with his shipments. They try to avoid any repercussions that would occur to continue to receive the millions of dollars that he pumps into their economy."

Special Agent Branson walked around the table as he said to Roc, "Here, look at this one. That is Adrian

Cortez. He is the head of the larger Columbian cartel and he's smooth I must give him that. We're not sure if that is his real name so when we tailed him to Asia, I was shocked we were able to obtain a picture of him. See, Pablo was rich and didn't care how much of his poison he sent over here which made him a prime target. Now Cortez has all the same trade but he's more into controlling his empire by the showing of pain to anyone he can. Not even caring who it affects, that's what makes him a threat." There was a knock at the door that interrupted Special Agent Branson. "Who is it?"

"Detective Brian," a voice replied.

~ · ~ · ~ · ~

Moments earlier, Sam Clinton and Mr. Holmes pulled up in front of the station along with Mohammed and Manny who were parked down the street.

"Manny do you see this shit?"

"Yeah, this shit is crazy. They have the boss like he's the mayor out this bitch," Manny answered.

"That's because he is," replied Mohammed as Sam exited the car. Reporters were all over him screaming out questions. Mr. Holmes waited until all the attention was on Sam before getting out of the car, walking outside the circle of reporters and then up the steps.

"Mr. Clinton is it true that Mr. Miller is being held for first degree murder?" asked one reporter.

"The word going around is that a 36 count indictment has been passed down listing everything from money laundering to wide-scale distribution of narcotics."

Sam Clinton replied, "Now, how many times have we been through this ladies and gentlemen? I'm sure this is just another one of their misunderstandings that I'm about to straighten out. So if you will please excuse me, I have to get an innocent man out of jail."

Sam joined Mr. Holmes at the front desk as Captain Citric approached, "Mr. Clinton what is it that I can do for you?"

"You can start by letting me see my client."

"Listen, I'm going to do just that but you need to know this is bigger than me, I'm not even allowed in the room."

"What do you mean? You're the Captain here aren't you? Or is someone else running this taxi station," asked Sam with a touch of anger in his voice as he pulled out his cell phone and started dialing.

"Be easy Mr. Clinton, I don't even know where this man came from. Five minutes after it went over the scanner that we had Mr. Miller in custody; he walked through the door with two men. He showed his gold shield from Washington and took over."

"What's his name?" asked Mr. Clinton.

"He's DEA Special Agent Branson."

Mr. Holmes eased Sam's phone shut and said, "You really don't want to do that."

Sam looked at Mr. Holmes questionably then demanded, "Well tell him I want to see my client now."

~ · ~ · ~ · ~ · ~

Back upstairs Special Agent Branson opened the door, "Detective Brian who told you to interrupt me while I'm talking?"

"The Captain told me to let you know that Mr. Miller's lawyer is demanding to see him."

"Well tell Sam Clinton, if he wants to keep that pretty house he thinks no one knows about in Jersey, he will give me ten more minutes." Special Agent Branson then slammed the door in his face again.

"Now where were we? Oh, Mr. Cortez the cocaine monster. All these people are a part of the corporation team. Have you ever heard of them? What does that term mean, corporate money?"

Roc remained silent but after hearing the questions, his eyes lowered and his forehead tighten as he remembered what Mr. Holmes said, 'Don't you think it's time to hang your shoes from the ropes and get this corporate money?'

Special Agent Branson thought to himself as he watched Roc, "Now we're talking," and said, "Mr. Miller this is where you fit into all of this, so pay close attention." Grabbing a stack of pictures of Diego El Sovida, he dropped them one right after the other. Roc watched it like a movie, playing in slow motion as Diego walked down the steps of a Jet to be met at the bottom by Mr. Holmes. Roc's eyes widened at the sight of his mentor. Special Agent Branson repeated the act with the pictures of Sunan Kudari sitting in the chair. As they dropped, Roc saw the snap shots move from zero to a 360 degree angel and stopping at the picture where the back of Sunny's head and the face of Mr. Holmes could be seen.

Roc rubbed his forehead nervously. "Now listen to me good because I don't give many deals to trash like you. If you cooperate and become a government witness along with telling me everything you know about Mr. Holmes and Adrian Cortez, I promise to let you see little Larry Odell Miller Jr. reach the age of ten before I come for you. By then you'll be moving at this level because you will not stop, it's in your blood."

At the mention of his son's name, Roc was on his feet with veins popping out all over. He looked Special Agent Branson dead in the eyes and said, "Hold up man…first off, just for the record I'm not a cop. I'm not your witness. I'm not a rat and I'm not a coward. Don't do me any favors. I'm a man and I stand by what I do so if you feel you can stop me from living this good life then go ahead and try. Second, Mr. Holmes doesn't sell drugs, I can't explain why he's with those people and I'm not going to try. I don't know Cortez or whatever his name is so if that's all, I would like to go home to my family now."

"Have you ever met him?" Special Agent Branson asked.

"What?"

"Tough guy…I said, have you ever met him?"

"No."

"That's a damn lie and I hate liars," Special Agent Branson threw several photos at Roc hitting him in the chest as the rest lay flat on the table. Roc couldn't believe his eyes.

"Isn't that you and Mr. Holmes in the Peninsula Hotel in Hong Kong at the front desk? Oh my God who could the other man be, is that Mr. Cortez? Yes it is!" Agent Branson questioned.

Roc dropped his head and let out a deep breath as he thought about that day they were on vacation and Mr. Holmes asked the man in the picture something. 'Hey excuse me sir could you tell me what time Casa Lapostolle wine tasting begins?' Cortez had answered, 'Six o'clock, second row.' Mr. Holmes thanked him and they shook hands. That was the photo that was on the table.

Special Agent Branson got Roc's attention as he stood there thinking about the photo. "Now for lying to me, you just bought yourself six months in jail. You better pray that Mr. Holmes doesn't fuck up because if he does you're going down with him and that's the good news. The bad news is that you just made it on my list. Special Agent Branson put his coat back on and then opened the door to see Sam Clinton standing there. “Sam, nice to see you again”

“Excuse me, do we know each other?”

“I know you and that’s all that matters,” Special Agent Branson said and kept walking.

“What the hell is going on Sam?” Roc asked. “Don’t worry I have it all taken care of. An anonymous call was placed by of all things a cell phone. Mohammed sent a text and said he’s working on getting the number as we speak. The complainant stated that you had drugs and weapons, which wasn’t found.”

Roc laughed at the thought of the last time he had to be present in the room with drugs was when he first got his new Columbian connection to make sure the two hundred keys had the $50 bill in the middle of each of them which proves the seal had not been broken, proving that the work was pure grade A material and that was over ten years ago.

“You will be out of here within the next hour.”

“Have you spoken with Mr. Holmes?”

“I’m glad you asked that, he was downstairs with me waiting on you and then he started acting kind of strange and then went back to the car.”

“Good, tell him to jump on the D.L. until we can talk because…” Roc stopped in the middle of the sentence as two cops rushed into the room.

“Mr. Miller you have the right to remain silent.”

“Hold on, what the hell is happening here?” asked Sam.

“He’s being placed under arrest.”

“On what charge?”

“For assaulting a D.E.A agent” the officer responded.

12

Lil Mac opened his eyes to check the digital clock on the nightstand which read 2:45am and then rolled out of bed. After his shower he placed a Nike Zoom Kobe II hoody sweatsuit on with matching running shoes. He went into the kitchen and grabbed six raw eggs, a bag of wheat germ with three cans of vanilla Ensure from the refrigerator. After mixing them all together, he drank it straight down. This has been his every day regimen since he left the hospital at the weight of 155 pounds, which were mostly bones. At first Top Dollar would have to wake him up several times, "Boy if you don't get your ass out of that bed…The moment you have been dreaming about for so long is near and you will be prepared you dig? Now get up."

Together they would run two miles before doing a hundred sit ups, ten sets of ten pull-ups, and two hundred push-ups. Then it was on to the gym where Top Dollar put him through an hour of hard mass weight-increase training. "Push it! Come on Solo, it's only 225 pounds, you can do better than this."

Lil Mac replied, "Damn Top, you're trying to kill me."

"No…not me but I know someone who is."

In the first two months Lil Mac gained 20 pounds of muscle as his set numbers increased by ten percent. While his body frame grew over months, so did his mind. He read over every book that Roc read to him again until he had them memorized word-for-word. Then he read about the German Empire Hsiang Yu and how he put fear into people for centuries. To relax, again and again he would watch the movie, *The Lion of the Desert*, which was about a man named Umar Mukhtar who fought a war against Rome for 20 years on religious faith, for his people and land. He put their horses against tanks and farmers against generals. Once he was caught on the battlefield at the age of 73, all he asked for was that they didn't lie and say he begged for his life at the hands of his enemy. With all this in mind, Lil Mac prepared for the worst and planned to become the best. Now, after six months he stood at 6'2", 215 pounds of solid muscle.

Shaking the bed roughly, "Get up old man, the moment has arrived and I'm ready now. We'll see if they're prepared for me." Lil Mac pulled the covers off of Top Dollar.

"Okay, okay I'm up player. Damn, I'm up…that's not smooth to do player, you dig?"

"I'm not trying to hear that, get up."

In the surveillance room, Lil Mac looked at the ten TV Monitors that oversaw the three-story, five bedroom, two bath home that rested on two acres in Valley Forge, Pa. Top Dollar bought it after NayNay got shot, feeling that with his two Top Warriors down, it would be a good time to step aside and move their man from a distance to rebuild. He prayed for the moment when Lil Mac would say that he was ready to be back at the head of the table and only then would the roof be placed on the house for it to be finished.

Top Dollar walked into the video room wearing a Todd One sweatsuit, an IPod with all Earth, Wind & Fire on it and black gator dress shoes. "I hope you're ready soldier because I'm about to show you who the old man really is," Top Dollar commented while stretching his legs. The electronic sensor gate eased open as they jogged threw it at a nice pace and then it closed. "What do you think about the information that Fox came back with?" asked Top Dollar while speeding up the pace at the quarter-mile mark.

"I don't know... something's not right; I can feel it Top. He's got to be missing something. From the photo, everything looks like it's a go, but it can't be that easy."

"That thought has crossed my mind. So what are you going to do, call it off until we can get a better look ourselves?" Top Dollar questioned, turning his Ipod onto phone.

"No! Whether the outcome is good or bad, our fate must change tonight. Plus Fox is a part of our team and if we can't trust his judgment on a stakeout, what do we need him for?"

"You're right."

"We must believe in his eyes like they're ours."

"Yeah I know," said Top Dollar.

"You better, plus I sent NayNay to look over it again in case the clown is wrong," Solo laughed.

"You no good..." Top Dollar just stopped talking as Solo disappeared down the road, quickly moving at top speed. Trying to keep up, Top Dollar stopped knowing that Lil Mac's legs had become too powerful. They met up at a private park where they did their push-ups, sit-ups and pull-ups on the monkey bar.

"Come on Top, we're only on the eighteenth set and that's only six." Top Dollar released the bar and dropped down to the ground.

"I don't care what you say, that's ten to me and I'm done you dig? Now let's go hit these weights before you kill a player out here."

"Well I'm going to give you a head start on the way back because I don't want you on these dark roads by yourself old man."

"Oh now you're talking slick son...I mean Solo."

"It's okay Top Dollar, call me what you want. You deserve it."

The words warmed Top Dollar's heart as he smiled. They entered into a state-of-the-art fitness center. Top Dollar had it built in the back of the house next to the firing range. The layout was a one-floor, three-room station that looked to be a four-car garage from the outside. In the first room, Top Dollar had dumb bells from five to a 150 pounds lined up along the mirror covered wall. The free weights went from 10 to 100-pound plates and there were two of everything from flat incline and decline benches to shoulder racks and preacher curl machines. The next room to the left possessed three treadmills and two Stairmasters with 13 inch plasma TV's connected to each one. The eight piece bowfinger weight center filled the rest of the room. The back room occupied three glass showers and a steam room with a surround-sound stereo system.

"Now you're in my house and I'm about to show you where Run got it from." They did four sets of back exercises with Top Dollar coming out on top, he out-pulled Solo by over 20 pounds. "I know and you know, ya'll young cats don't have nothing on the fresh to def Top Dollar!" Top stepped back and popped the collar of his sweatshirt like it was a new price tag. On the curl bar, for Top Dollar's second set he rep'd 65 five pounds ten at a time.

"Your steel young buck."

"I know. I just hoped you were warming up." Lil Mac added 15 more pounds to each side of the bar and then started to rep it. "What number am I on?"

"Ten."

"You see this old head, it looks like my shit is about to bust out of my arm." He curled some more and then said, "That's twenty. Now, get your money."

"Oh you haven't said nothing slick to a can of oil. Champ, watch out I'm going to double that." Top Dollar gripped the weights tightly curling it five times and halfway up on the sixth he said, "Don't touch it... I got it," before he let it crash to the ground.

"You all right Top Dollar? What's wrong is it too heavy?" Lil Mac asked while he laughed.

"Don't do that; don't try to play a player. You saw it slip out of my hand. That's from all that damn sweat you got on the bar. Something must be wrong with you. You're over there sweating like running water."

Lil Mac just continued to laugh.

"Oh what I'm the new Steve Harvey in this joint? Let's go to the flat bench, I'm going to give you something to laugh about," stated Top Dollar. They went back and forth adding on 10 pounds to both sides of the bar for each set. Lil Mac strained to get the 295 pounds off his chest and back in the rack Top Dollar smiled while upping the weights to 315 pounds. "Now you're about to enter the big leagues and you haven't hit this yet." Top Dollar smacked the bar before he slowly brought the weights down to his chest. Steadily it moved forward until mid-point where it eased to a stop. Lil Mac stepped closer to grasp the bar fearing that the weight would fall on Top's neck.

"Don't you dare, this bitch is mine," Top Dollar said as the movement of the bar continued upward until it found its base back on the rack. Top Dollar jumped off the bench and smacked his chest four times, "Your turn He-man and watch it, she's throwing it back tonight."

"No Top Dollar, you got it. I think I'm going to hit the shower and get ready for the mission."

"Damn right I got it, this is my house and you can't get the keys until I give them to you."

Lil Mac was headed to the shower when Top Dollar's words stopped him. Turning around, he said, "Top…a wise man once said or maybe twice that you never show a man your total strength until you're powerful enough to surpass him forever." Lil Mac walked over and slid two 25-pound plates on each side.

"That's 365 pounds kid, have you lost your damn mind? You don't have to prove nothing to me."

"I know. That's why I never showed you that I could hit the 315." Taking a deep breath, Lil Mac lifted the weight into the air. The muscles in his neck and arms flexed as he bounced the weight off his chest. Top Dollar looked on wide-eyed as Lil Mac pushed with a force he hadn't witnessed before. The weights moved rapidly back up, ending with Lil Mac smoothly sitting it back into its cradle.

Lil Mac remained silent until he opened the door to the shower room, "Top Dollar?" When no answer came, he turned to see Top Dollar struggling to get the weight off the rack.

"What player?"

"If you're not man enough to keep it, you're not supposed to have it. Now run them keys."

"My partner never lied about that," Top Dollar said as he threw the keys to the gym to Lil Mac.

"And Top, I hope you like it back there."

"Don't believe that jive. That wasn't no wise man that was a sucker in a suit."

13

Lil Mac sat in the steam room for twenty minutes to open his pores and to relax his tightened muscles before entering into the shower. While soaping up his body, he thought he heard a sound in the distance. Wanting to think that it was nothing he continued to wash but his military mind state stopped him. He turned the water off just as the noise reoccurred this time sounding as if it was getting closer.

Sliding the glass door back, Lil Mac looked around to see nothing out of place. He hit the intercom button on the wall, "Top Dollar, you there? Somebody pick up." Getting no answer, he gripped a towel and quickly wrapped it around his waist while rushing to get his gun. "Damn…I left it," he whispered to himself.

He turned his head toward the direction of the door to the left, hearing yet another sound. Lil Mac's thoughts ran rapid as if he were trying to put together puzzle pieces all at once. First he associated the sound with one or more people searching for something. No matter what it was, he wasn't going to stick around to find out especially since he was empty-handed. His mind quickly pinpointed where he could access the closest weapon. In each corner of the drop ceilings within the two other rooms, Top Dollar placed a gun in all except the shower room. "He's going to have to change this shit," Lil Mac thought as he killed the light while heading for the side door.

The door to the shower room quickly opened forcing him to dive under a small wooden bench that barely covered his body. Through the darkness he could see the body outline of the intruder as the person cocked back their gun. Stepping into the room, he searched along the wall on his left for the light switch. Pinned in with the enemy only six feet away and heading in his direction, Lil Mac thought as the footsteps got closer, "If it's my turn at death then he must look me in the eyes so that I can return the favor in hell."

Lil Mac eased out from under the bench onto his feet when he saw the intruder raise his arm. He braced himself to meet his maker but the intruder turned in front of him going for the right side of the wall. "I guess we'll talk another time big man." Lil Mac said to himself as he dashed to the door.

Feeling movement, the intruder let off three wild shots into the darkness. From the flash of the gun, he witnessed part of Lil Mac's face and called out, "Solo stop, it's me."

While Lil Mac raced through the door. His wet feet made contact with the rubber mats and he slid across the floor. Fighting to keep his balance, the towel dropped just before he slammed into a flat bench. Now nude, he hastily got to his feet and rushed for a weapon when a Timberland boot swiftly took his feet out from under him. Lil Mac flipped over onto his back hard, with blood running down his chin from a busted lip. He was breathing heavily as stars filled his sight. A warm liquid covered his bottom lip and then his neck. *"Why haven't they shot me yet?"* he was thinking when he suddenly felt something lay upon his arm. Shaking his head to regain his clear vision, he spotted a pair of black, ice cream jeans, a black parish hoody, and black chucker Timberlands. On his left there was a red bra and matching thong with a naked NayNay resting in his arm.

When they made eye contact she asked, "Please be gentle, you know what he did." NayNay was speaking of her father who started to molest her at the age of ten. Lil

Mac thought back to that sad torment that ended three years after it had begun.

~ · ~ · ~ · ~

Her father entered her room drunk like so many other nights after working a 12-hour shift. NayNay's mother had just left for work, leaving her alone again and there he would be…unbuckling his pants. "Is daddy's little girl ready for daddy?"

"Like no other time," she answered.

"That's my girl." When his pants hit the floor, so did his body. *Boom! Boom!* NayNay pulled the trigger of Roc's 9 mm until it cocked back empty. She held it tightly as if it was her savior and refused to let it go. Lil Mac came out of the closet and wrapped his arms around her from behind.

"Let it go, I have to get it back before the cops get here."

"No," she replied. "With this he'll never touch me again."

"I'll get you another one, I promise," Lil Mac assured her.

"You promise?"

"I promise!" At that point, Lil Mac eased the gun free and then messed up the room to make it look like someone tried to rob their home with it ending in her father being shot. The police bought the story, who couldn't really care less.

~ · ~ · ~ · ~

That scared little girl was gone. Lil Mac now looked over at a beautiful woman. He rolled on top of her and looked into her lovely gray eyes and said, "I promise. But you didn't have to kick me." Then he slowly kissed her softly and passionately. As their tongues danced, NayNay wrapped her arms around Lil Mac's neck. He lifted her off the ground with their lips still connected and smoothly laid her onto her back on the flat bench.

"Oooohh," she let out a lot moan as her insides became on fire from the way that Lil Mac sucked and caressed her breasts. His moist lips sucked on the tip of her nipples until they were hardened.

Lil Mac then began to move his hands down her abs as his lips and tongue followed every motion. NayNay couldn't contain her moans as they got louder when Lil Mac eased his second finger into her soaking wet tunnel of love. The screams of, "Oooohh….it feels so goooood," echoed off the walls as her pain began to turn into pleasure as Lil Mac's lips wrapped around her clit while his tongue moved rapidly up and down on it. Her taste became like honey to a bee as he smoothly ran his tongue alongside her inner walls. He parted her legs even more. Feeling that she was ready to climax, he gently moved the tip of his manhood in and out of the rim of her core. The warm heat of his manhood sliding deeper inside of NayNay forced her to put both hands on his massive chest, "You know you're really my first?" she questioned.

Sliding her hands around to his back, she pulled him closer to her. "Yes and thank you," Lil Mac whispered as he slowly worked himself deeper inside of her with every stroke. She dug her nails into his back, breaking skin. As each inch of his manhood stretched her love box, it made the satisfaction too overwhelming for her to control. Lil Mac smoothly switched positions, wrapping one of her legs around his waist and the other over his shoulder while working his hips at a medium speed with a rhythm that hit the sides of her love box walls. NayNay covered her eyes with her hands as they, along with the rest of her body shook uncontrollably.

"Stop…hold up please, stop!"

"What's wrong NayNay? Are you okay?"

Taking a deep breath, NayNay tried to respond as her orgasm declined, "I… I really don't know. I never experienced a feeling like that before. At first there was just a small trembling vibration but it kept building until I couldn't hold it inside of me anymore. So please tell me I didn't just…you know what on you?"

Lil Mac smiled while answering, "No you didn't girl. That was something else."

"Then can we do it again?" NayNay asked.

Lil Mac wiped away the tears from the corner of NayNay's eyes and then picked her up into his arms. As he carried her off, NayNay sucked on his ear and neck as they entered into the shower. Looking into her eyes, Lil Mac asked, "Do you trust me?"

"With my life," she replied without blinking.

"Who taught you how to shoot your first gun?"

"You did," NayNay answered.

"Now let me teach you this," Lil Mac said. "Put your hand right here and hold onto this." With her back up against the wall, her legs wrapped around Lil Mac's waist, she gripped onto the shower handle like he asked. Their lips connected as he felt the tightness of her pussy walls wrap around his bulging dick. The intensity of the kisses between the two built as their bodies rubbed together. Lil Mac rotated the tip of his dick up and down on her clit, making her nice and wet before easing back inside of her. He hit the stereo, to hear the sound of Guy's 'Let's Chill' through the speakers. Knowing that she was hot and ready, he began to push harder and faster for several minutes. "Oooohh," then he went slow and deep ending every push on his tippy toes. NayNay's feet curled to the way he squeezed her ass while he pulled her closer to him, making them one.

Lil Mac swiftly moved his hand to the right and bit down on her bottom lip as the water race over their bodies.

"It's cold Solo!"

"I know…I need it to be that way so that I can heat it up." Flipping her over onto all fours, he entered her from the back. With each stroke he massaged her clit with his right hand while caressing her breast with the other. Bending down to her ear he whispered, "There is no other after me."

"I know."

"And there will be no me without you." The stereo now playing 'Sweet Lady' by Tyrese, NayNay started to cum. Her shuddering pussy muscles pulled Lil Mac deeper into her and forced him to follow as he came inside his queen. His mind state was now prepared to go get his crown.

A short while later, in a warehouse deep in the heart of West Philly, twenty or so men dressed in all black stood around two pool tables that had been pushed together. They were looking over a blueprint of a large compound. Top Dollar was in the center with a laser stick pointing out the weaknesses in its structure.

"Khaled, I want you here," Top Dollar identified a spot 200 yards away from the house's rear exit. For Khaled, that was more like two feet. He was a sniper by trade in the army but now a hustler in the streets by choice.

"Daz I need you here at the front of the house on the right and Nelly you'll be on the opposite side. Your jobs are important, I need you both to make sure our entry is smooth and our exit is even smoother. Calvin, Ayzo, and Fatel…you will cover the perimeter while the rest of us split up into teams. My team will enter from the back; NayNay your team will gain access from the second floor balcony."

"So I guess I'm going in the front door?" asked the man who slowly removed his hoody. The room went crazy as people jumped up and down hi-fiving each other. Some pulled the trigger on their guns letting bullets fly into the air…*Boom! Boom! Boc! Boc! Boc!*

"Oh shit it's on now."

"Yo is that really him?"

"The one and only!"

"Man I'm getting on his team."

"I bet he got that gold 45 automatic on him"

"What?"

"Yeah they say he keeps three guns on him at all times and one of them is an 18 karat gold 45 with a pearl handle."

Whispers went through the crowd as many saw their boss, that they'd heard so many stories about for the very first time.

While being patted on the back and praised, Lil Mac stepped out from the circle that formed around him and up onto the pool table. "I see a lot of new faces in here tonight and that's only right, being that I have been missing in action for damn near two years," he laughed. Continuing, "But that is the past. Tonight I ride for the Get Money Clique, we ride together with no life more important than another. I will protect your life as if it were my own. I just ask for you to do the same. No one must see us coming and the world can't hear us leave. If everything is done correctly…tonight the city of Philadelphia will become our Rome. After that, what are we going to do?"

"Get Money!"

"What?"

"Get Money!" the crowd screamed, hyped up.

"Then let's get it!"

Six vans parked in the shadows while each team moved into place. 'Solo's team 3 is ready…Team 4 is ready to move…Two also…We move on 'Go' in ten, nine…"

~·~·~·~

Mr. Holmes placed Roc's jewelry into the wall safe while thoughts of why and what Special Agent Branson wanted to see Roc for, crossed his mind. He didn't think for a moment that Roc would say anything more than his name, if that. For Mr. Holmes knew Roc was schooled by the best…him. While thinking, out of nowhere a red flashing light with the words 'Intruder Alert' appeared on his 64 inch plasma and 20 inch computer screen, bringing him back to reality. The screens quickly switched to a ten square split picture frame showing him what each camera saw at that moment. Mr. Holmes witnessed several men rushing his house from the back and sliding down ropes from the roof onto the second floor. "It's a shame that people are in such a rush to meet their maker these days," he said and smiled.

14

An old man with gray hair and a cane walked slowly through the Italian section of South Philly on Mable St. As he passed by, the kids teased him, "Hey moolie, take your black ass back across town."

He just nodded his head lightly and kept it moving. Halfway up the block, he passed a window that read Joey's Pizza. "Come to think of it I am kind of hungry."

When he approached the entrance, two big 300 pound men named Pauly and Bruce blocked it. "And where is it that you think you're going?"

"To get something to eat if you don't mind."

"Not here old man," said Bruce.

"Why not son?"

"Because I said."

"We're closed so go ahead on up the block. There's another store on the corner and get yourself a big plate of pasta," stated Pauly.

"Boy, I marched with Dr. King, been jailed with Rosa and I stop letting a white man tell me what to do when I was ten. I would drink anywhere I wanted and use the bathroom the same way…to hell with what a damn sign said. It always said what I wanted it to say, me only. Now get the hell out of my way!"

The old man started up the steps when Bruce tried to grip his arm but instead caught the end of his cane. "Don't you touch me; I'll call the damn cops on you…you slick haired bastard."

Inside Joey's, four people sat in a booth when the word 'cops' caught the attention of two of the visitors. "Joey what the hell is going on?" One of the men questioned, going for his 45 automatic which rested in his waistline as did his partners'.

"Hold on fella's, be gentle. All this is uncalled for. I'll handle it," said Joey as he excused himself.

"What the hell is going on out here?"

"Nothing boss, I told the man to go eat somewhere else but he won't listen," answered Pauly ducking another blow from the cane.

"I can eat where I damn well please."

"Pauly get your hands off that old man."

"But boss you said don't let nobody in until you're done."

"I know but you're bringing on too much unwanted attention," Joey whispered into his ear before speaking out loud. "Come in sir, sorry for the inconvenience."

"Don't worry about it, I was in World War II, did you know that?"

"No I didn't. Please order whatever you want, it's on the house," replied Joey, helping the man up the steps.

"Oh I see why you didn't want me in here now."

"And that is?" asked Joey as his hand slid onto the gun in the center of his back.

"Because it's two of us in here already, one more and we'll be running the joint like back in 68."

Joey took his seat back in the booth, "I'm sorry about that but as I was saying…when you were with Roc we had an understanding. You know we stayed out of your part of the city and you stayed out of ours."

"That's true."

"Then what happened Boggy?" Joey slammed his fist on the table. Boggy and Bo looked at each other then stood to their feet. Joey stopped them saying, "I'm sorry Boggy this whole ordeal is just so upsetting." Joey used his left hand to massage his temple before continuing, "I got the family on my back about you owning two blocks in my part of town. That's why we had to have this meeting to see if we could come to an understanding before things get out of hand."

Boggy's face reddened as he blocked Joey out with his own thoughts, *"I know this pasta eating coward didn't just come at me on the low. I swear if I didn't have this war plus them Get Money clowns on my ass I would slap half this nigga's face off. Then I would shut his whole shit down. That Nabisco delivery truck outside would be full of my men. The mailman would have a mini 14 in his bag and the workers fixing that stop sign would cut off any movement from the outside until I'm done killing his ass."* All this went through Boggy's head before he sat back down.

"Thank you, I know your kind could be reasonable."

"Listen, cut the fucking jokes Joey. I'm only here because I don't have the time to be killing all you fake ass godfathers."

Bo quickly kicked Boggy in the leg, cutting him off. "Joey, excuse my friend, as you said…it's this whole ordeal that has everybody on edge. What we need to know is what has to be done to reach an agreement and avoid war."

"That's easy, give back the two."

'Three," Boggy interrupted.

"What?" said Joey.

"I said three, we now own three blocks on this side of town."

Joey's face turned red as if steam was coming from his head and he screamed, "When did this take place?"

"Last week and it's doing twice the numbers already."

"This shit has to stop."

"And who is going to stop it?" asked Boggy as Bo tapped his arm telling him to chill.

Joey leaned back and crossed his legs while resting his head on the top of the booth. Spotting the signal, several men rushed from out of the bathroom with their guns pointed at Bo and Boggy. "You can cut the act now Boggy; I know your men are only at 65 percent if that. That means you can't survive without Roc anymore."

"So you know a lot of shit but you say that to say what?"

"That you can die right now and who woul…"

"Excuse me gentleman I couldn't help but to overhear you arguing and ya'll need to stop. Move over son, are you using that salt?" The old man with the cane eased into the booth next to Joey.

"Not right now Mister this is a life and death situation." Joey smiled and tried to ease the old man out of the booth. "So if you don't mind, please take your plate back to your table."

"On any other day son, I wouldn't care what you did with this black man." The old man's voice changed to a deeper, stronger tone as he swiftly cocked back the side of the cane then the bottom popped open to reveal the tip of a barrel to a twenty two rifle. Sticking it firmly into Joey's ribs, he continued, "But I got a message on good faith from my boss that Boggy must receive today." The three men turned their guns on him. "If I were you Joey, I would look around at my surroundings before they get you killed."

Joey's eyes quickly examined everything, looking in all directions trying to watch the people surrounding him. He looked to the left as the mailman was marching Pauly and Bruce into the store at gun point. The old man pointed out the front window to the third row home on the right. Joey's eyes widened as he saw the white drape of his aunt Lisa's home slid back with two men in fake Nabisco uniforms standing on each side of her, one holding her by the throat. "You don't have too long Joey because when the boy…" Just then, the sound of the back door being kicked in followed by six men dressed in construction gear rushed into the room.

Joey gave another signal and they all placed their guns on the table. They rushed Joey's men ordering them to get face down to the ground and cuffed their hands tightly around their backs. One man covered the table with a Mack 10 as the other dropped the blinds and flipped over the sign to show that the store was 'Closed'. The old man stood up and hollered, "Now you motherfuckers are closed!" He then looked Boggy in the eyes and said, "Are you hard of hearing nigga? Off with the two 45's you got on your waist…now! You too Bo, let that 9mm rest on the table. And this is the last time I'm going to say it. Even if I don't want to, I will push your shape up back with a permanent part."

"Looks like it's ride or die," said Boggy with his 45 in his hand pointed to the ground.

Wondering how many he could kill, the old man said, "I know but now is not your time. I just have a message for you but if you're dying to die…I'll take you there." The old man then removed the old hat, gray wig and fake teeth.

"M. Easy…you're back? What up nigga?" On sight, a smile appeared on Bo and Boggy's face for their friend and go hard soldier. M. Easy came home from the penitentiary around the time the Get Money Clique name started to ring. He was only home two months when he asked a few of them to move away from his mother's house selling drugs, once they refused he killed them both. After that, Roc sent he and his family on an all expense paid vacation to Mexico.

"Yeah, and we need to talk about this bullshit going on with you and Roc," M. Easy replied.

"Aaawww….isn't this nice, a family reunion," said Joey before M. Easy's left hook knocked him out.

"NY, clean all this to a tee and put these clowns in the freezer. I'll meet ya'll back at the spot."

Boggy jumped up and raced over and kicked Joey in the face, waking him up.

M. Easy grabbed Boggy's arm. "Let me go M. Easy, this coward came at me with a move."

Boggy fought to break free but couldn't. He looked down into the eyes of Joey's bloody face and said, "Tell whoever made you to make another one because you're done. I will be back for you and that's a promise." Boggy landed another hard kick to his face while M. Easy pulled him away.

"Not now, you have bigger problems to deal with."

The three rode in the car for hours, talking like brothers while they passed blunt after blunt back and forth. Boggy told his half of the story that went from him willing to die for a person to how he wanted that person dead.

"I hear all that Boggy and any person that puts a hole in your body, you have a right to be mad at but this is bullshit. This is you and Roc. Listen, I'm going to let you in on a secret because hearing that ya'll are going at it is one thing, but seeing it is killing me. But you have to swear in blood that you won't say anything."

Bo passed the blunt to Boggy just like Roc did back in the day when they made their pact. 'We're going to own these streets together for life,' Roc said. Boggy smiled at the memory as he took the blunt, hitting it several times until the tip became cherry red. He removed his iced-out watch and placed the hot blunt next to the other mark. On contact you could hear the skin sizzle while blood bubbled down his arm.

"That's enough…damn!" M. Easy yelled.

Boggy just smiled and said, "Now tell me."

"First you have to understand that Roc is now playing at a whole other level."

"What? I'm not going for that. Whatever level he's on, I'm there!" Boggy stated furiously.

"Maybe physically but if you would just hear me out, you would understand it's his words that now have a meaning within a meaning. He always picks the right person for the right job."

"Why wouldn't he? You get a sniper for a killer, a boxer for a fighter…everybody knows that," replied Boggy.

"That's what I would do also but Roc has become deeper, he chooses them emotionally…just like this situation. He could have anybody watching you but no, he sent for me all the way in Mexico, while I'm lying on a ranch smoking the best weed in the world by the pound. I had them Mexican women doing everything and anything…you feel me?"

"Do I?"

They laughed and smacked hands as M. Easy resumed the conversation, "I guess he wants me to see how easily he could have taken your life being that we were all really close friends. And he didn't. He thinks that when he does, it will go down easier with the men in his ranks that still have love for you."

"That's bullshit, if that nigga had me dead he would have gotten me out of here. Fuck what he's telling you."

M. Easy slammed down on the brakes and pulled over to the side. With a reddening face, he looked Boggy dead in the eyes and said, "You still don't get him. Why would he have to say anything when I was there?"

"What?"

"I was there with a six-man team the night Mohammed made you think you could fly. I know you didn't really think that after everything you did to him that he would only send three people for Boggy, the killer of Philly…did you? Mohammed's good, but damn! When ya'll raced around the corner on the front of the block there were several guns locked on your head and the van that blocked your exit…"

"Oh shit…that was you?" Bo said, remembering the man in the navy blue Yankees hat with dread locks. He'd locked eyes with him as he passed their car to get into the van that had been parked there for a minute too long.

M. Easy pulled back into the flow of traffic, "Yeah it was me and Roc that had ya'll boxed-in dead."

"So what happened, because I didn't ask anybody for a damn favor? This is war. If you get me, crush me."

"To be real, he just smiled and said 'let him go, this is his warning'," M. Easy replied.

Still confused and shocked Bo asked, "He was there?"

"Yeah ass! He was the seventh gun," answered Boggy, outraged at himself for thinking he had outsmarted Mohammed when really he was the fool.

M. Easy parked in the back of a white end house in South Philly. "Boggy, think about your next move please…one O.G. to another. Today that whole team was from New York for a reason."

"Emotionally…I feel you," Boggy said, cutting him off. "So how is he handling this new situation?"

"You know better than me that Roc is going to be Roc no matter where he's at."

"So he took it over?"

"You know it. Now he's talking about the Roman Empire, the Trojan horse and some David Copperfield shit…whatever that means but here…" M. Easy handed Boggy a brown folder.

"What's this?"

"The message…he said you'll have more fun with it than we ever will."

M. Easy hit the button to pop the trunk while Boggy read over the file. Boggy couldn't believe the words he saw.

"Where's he at?"

M. Easy pointed to the back. Boggy opened the trunk to see Boomer lying there unconscious. Boggy gave a special call and Haffee with three other men came running. "Take this rat ass nigga into the basement."

M. Easy began to pull off as Boggy stopped him. Lowering the window he asked, "What up…you all right?"

"Yo, how the hell you know where I live?" Boggy asked.

"I told you he was on some next level shit. I wouldn't be surprised if he knew I was going to tell you all of this." M. Easy smiled before pulling off.

After everyone went into the house, Boggy stood alone hitting the last of the blunt while taking in everything he had just heard when a car slowly moved down the alley. Recognizing it as Mr. Johnson from down the street, Boggy relaxed and waved not knowing that waving back at him was Mohammed. Caught off guard he dropped the blunt and reached for his gun but Mohammed was already down the road. Boggy just shook his head, letting out a deep breath, "This nigga is on some new shit."

15

Roc rested in cell block C-24 on a double mattress bed in his Gucci silk pajamas talking on his iPhone to Sam Clinton while reading the Wall Street Journal. The cell looked more like a room in the Comfort Inn with the handmade wall to wall carpet and matching toilet seat cover from towels. A fresh color of peach paint coated the walls instead of the institution's regular yellow. The desk was lined with a handheld DVD player and a PSP with over fifty disks for each. In front of the cell stood two 300-pound men, Danny and Bones, who were paid a thousand dollars a week to make sure Roc wasn't disturbed. The way he lived and ate couldn't have been achieved by many people. To some, money is a way to a better life but behind these walls and barbed wire fences, it only made you a target.

When Roc first stepped into the paddy wagon over two months ago, twenty pair of eyes observed him. He remained silent and took the open seat on the left side. His handcuffs rested at the bridge of his watch which lit up the darkness on each passing street light. B-Slife who was 250 pounds and just arrested on an armed robbery and gun charges, was the first to make his move. He waited until the van stopped at the light and then told the kid who couldn't have been any older than 19, "Move the fuck out my seat now!" Without a word the kid went to the back and sat on the dirty floor.

The van went silent, for people knew what was about to take place. "What's good main man? I'm talking to you watch man." When Roc still didn't respond, B-Slife became furious, "Listen pussy, you don't got to talk but I know you can hear. I'm take-a-life B-Slife and when we get to the roundhouse I'm going to knock you the fuck out and get that pretty sweater, watch, and shoes up off you. Matter of fact, I'm going to get them pants, too. I can wear that shit to court." Roc looked the man in the face and smiled.

The crowded bullpen at the roundhouse was a standing room only. There were junkies, bums, hustlers, killers and robbers packed into holding tank after holding tank. Several people were pushed through the door along with B-Slife, and then a few more followed by Roc. Roc didn't keep moving with the momentum of the rest of the crowd to the back though; he stepped to the side and remained at the door.

After everybody was in and counted, the guard started to remove the handcuffs. Roc was the second person in line. Once his hands were free he took his watch off, placed it in his pocket and dipped back into the crowd. B-Slife tried to keep his eyes on his next vic. "Where did this clown go?" B-Slife scanned the left side of the room as a powerful right hook connected to the side of his face followed by a left. Still handcuffed, B-Slife couldn't do much to stop Roc's aggressive assault. He threw blow after blow, knocking B-Slife out only to wake him up with another punch.

The correctional officers rushed in after five minutes and pulled a bloody-fisted Roc off of B-Slife. Roc broke loose, yelling "Get off of me" and threw his sweater at the man, hitting him in the face and said, "Here, it cost fifteen hundred sucker, you paid for it."

"Come on buddy, that's enough," the correctional officer said pulling Roc away.

They moved Roc to another holding cell. When Roc went up for bail three hours later, the judge stated, "There isn't anything here for him to make bail on… it says here that he was sentenced to six months by Judge Branson in D.C. and the paperwork was sent here for him to serve it in his district."

"Sam what the hell is she talking about?" Roc asked angrily.

"Calm down Roc, don't worry I will have you out of here in no time. There has to be a mistake, as soon as you can touch a phone, call me."

"Come on Mr. Miller, that's your time. Let's go." When Roc hit R.N.D in C.F.C.F the word had already spread that the untouchable has been touched. Inmates stood in the hallway to get a look at the cities most dangerous individual. As Roc passed, some people put plans together to make him pay for protection. Others just wanted to be put on his unseen team that was eating on the streets.

"Mr. Miller, I'm Mr. Rice the Captain here at this institution and for your safety I believe that you would be better off in protective custody."

"Excuse me Mr. Rice, do we know each other?" Roc kindly responded. Mr. Rice smiled, feeling important in front of so many of his staff because a man on Roc's level believed that he could know him.

"No, I don't think so but I do go…"

"Then how the hell do you know what's best for me?" Roc rudely interrupted.

"I advise you to let me stay in population like everyone else," continued Roc.

"Mr. Miller you're not everyone else and I don't want to hear anymore about it. Take this man to P.C.," Two C.O.'s grabbed hold of each of Roc's arms, taking him away.

Roc turned around and said, "Mr. Rice I don't think I caught your first name. You know just in case we have the same friend."

Mr. Rice looked over the room and smiled before answering, "Jermaine."

Roc sat in P.C. for 21 hours, then his cell door popped open. A man with his right eye slightly closed, hair messed up hiding mostly under his officer cap and mud covering half of his pants and boots said, "Assalam Alaikum."

Roc couldn't tell who it was until he got closer. "Damn Jermaine, I didn't know you were Muslim."

"I'm not, that's what he told me to say."

"Oh my bad, I forgot …our friend," Roc smiled.

In population Roc felt like Mandela, receiving love and praise from almost everyone around him but the reality of their sad situation hurt his heart. There were homeless men losing priceless days of their lives in a 6 x 9 box because they couldn't afford $150 for bail for trying to find somewhere to sleep which resulted in them getting charged for trespassing and sent to prison. Roc saw kids that were 18 and 19 locked up for drugs and murder and he couldn't understand why. When he was coming up, the only job a black man could get was mopping floors and waiting tables. So to get ahead in life many took on some type of hustle.

Today, life is so much different. A black man can become anything and these kids were too young to say they were even denied for trying. Roc understood the game so he would never judge a person by his own strength. Wanting to help, he called Sam Clinton asking for the names of every person whose bail was under three thousand and that wasn't a rapist, had not assaulted a woman and had not done anything to children. In a jail that held about two thousand people, that number was 15 %. "Now get them out of here," Roc demanded.

"What?" replied Sam Clinton.

"Bail them all out now and tell Kim and Brittany to find a job for anyone that is willing to work."

Special Agent Branson visited Roc three times, each ending with him not getting a word out of him. As Roc walked the tier, he made sure there wasn't a man shoeless or that went to bed hungry. One day the warden called Roc down to his office. "You asked to see me?"

"Yes Mr. Miller, please have a seat. The reason I have you down here is because I've received requests from damn near every inmate in this jail to move to your block. I heard all about you paying people to teach other inmates to read and how they move like soldiers together instead of taking from one another. But now it's disturbing my daily operation here, so if you can't help everyone…you need to stop it."

"Okay," Roc answered as he removed himself from the seat and left. The next day, Miller's Sneakers donated 3000 pairs of Nike Captivates. From the reputation that Roc had, many were afraid to approach him but those who did, he never turned away.

"I'm telling you Roc, I personally have been down to Washington four times in the last two weeks complaining about Branson's actions and you know what happened this last time?" Sam asked as his face began to turn red.

"No, what?"

"I got an email telling me that my New Jersey home was up for sale in a Sheriff's auction and they asked me if I would like to purchase it back. I'm telling you, this man has some power but he just messed with the wrong person. I'll have you out in a week if not sooner, I promise."

"I thought you said he has power," Roc asked finishing off the end of his morning newspaper.

"Yes, the power to block case law but to hell with the law… it's time to put the people to work that we have put in those pretty skyline offices over the years."

"All right, what about Mr. Holmes, have you heard from him yet?"

"No but I spoke with his secretary and she said he must have gone on vacation a week early because the yacht left the dock over two weeks ago."

"So no one has seen or heard from him in several weeks?"

"Yes but you know him, he's probably halfway around the world having a good time. He'll pop up with a gift for everybody."

"You're right, just get me out of here," Roc disconnected the call with the feeling that something wasn't right.

Roc stepped into the shower and ten minutes later, "Lock down, all inmates report to your cell. Lock down!" the C.O.'s yelled.

"Boss you hear that? What we going to do, you locking up or are we making them wait until you're done like last time?" asked Bones.

"That won't be necessary. The lock down is for Mr. Miller, he has a visit," interrupted the C.O.

"Boss you have a VI."

"Whose lovely voice is that? Ms. Rich?" asked Roc.

"You know it's me baby, so go ahead and take your time while I lock these inmates in, starting with your two secret service men and then I'll be by your cell to get you."

16

Roc entered the visiting room after receiving a razor sharp hair cut along with a freshly pressed uniform. He was settled two seats down from a lawyer and his client where he couldn't help but to overhear their conversation as he waited. "Listen to me son, I just read over your case and they've got you."

"How do they have me? I didn't have any drugs on me?" the client asked with a puzzled look on his face. He looked to be only about 20 years old.

"It doesn't matter, they have several witnesses willing to testify to the fact that you threw several grams…hold on I have it right here…it says 126 grams of crack cocaine and with the feds now picking your case up and you being a second time offender, you're facing a twenty-year sentence." The lawyer stated with conviction.

"I hear that but did you contact Mrs. Clark and the people she was with because they saw everything. I was going onto my porch when the cops ran by chasing someone. Then a second cop car came flashing their lights into my face, ordering me to get down on the ground. That's when the first cops walked back around the corner with the zip lock bag and said something about 'we all look alike' and then they locked me up. Mrs. Clark and them saw all of this so when we go to trial we'll need them to get on the stand."

"Trial? You must not have understood me Mr. Hill, this is the feds… you can't fight them. They have an 85% conviction rate, look at what they did to Mike Vick and he's a millionaire. I don't want to see you do 20 years kid so I talked with the prosecution and he's willing to give you a deal…if you cooperate."

"Cooperate for what? I didn't do anything so how can I know something?"

"It doesn't matter, you're here and it's my job to do my best to get you out so make something up if you have to. I'll be back to see you on Monday for your answer."

Mr. Hill remained seated, looking as if he was in a daze.

Roc shook his head realizing that the dawn has been broken and a sad new day had begun.

"Mr. Miller, right this way please. Your visitor will be here any moment now."

"Okay, I'll be right there. Roc stood up and tapped the kid on the arm, "What's your name?"

"Sean," he replied. "What block are you on?"

"B block."

"Okay, Ms. Johnson is your caseworker right?"

"Yeah"

"When you go back upstairs, tell her that Roc said to let you call your new lawyer Sam Clinton and tell him that you're now a part of the family."

"All right…thanks Roc," said Sean as he shook Roc's hand.

Roc was placed into a quiet room off to the side. "Thanks Ms. Rich."

"You know I got you baby." When the door opened, Roc was on his feet in a second to embrace one of the two people that owned his heart.

"I'm sorry baby; I should have never taken it out on you."

"It's okay, I understand."

"I know you did baby but I didn't. You were hurting as well it's just that I'm so used to you taking care of everything and when it didn't happen it was you I blamed." Tears rolled down her cheek as Roc softly brushed them away.

"Don't start crying on me Mom. Everything is going to be okay."

"I know, look." Mrs. Miller stepped to the side, leaving Roc and Lil Mac standing face to face.

"Boy get over here!" As they hugged, Roc thought he felt a little resistance but dismissed it. As they talked for hours about why and how Lil Mac was kidnapped, Roc began to recognize the strategy Lil Mac used to answer…but not answer his questions. "So what about the phone call that was made from your room an hour and twenty minutes before the masked men rushed in and took you."

"Phone call?" Lil Mac's eyelids tightened, while looking up into the air as if he was thinking hard.

"Yeah, to a 215 number," Roc said.

"Oh that was Dr. Woods, he called you didn't…" Lil Mac paused, scratched his head and then continued, "Or was it…"

"Do you remember where they took you?"

"Yeah it was somewhere with a lot of trees like deep in New Jersey or upstate New York." Roc cracked a smile as he thought to himself, *"After all these years he still thinks he's hiding something from me."*

Ms. Rich approached their table, "Fifteen minutes left Mr. Miller."

"Oh baby, you better give me some sugar," Roc looked from Lil Mac to Ms. Rich as they hugged and kissed each other on the cheek.

Tears flowed heavily down Ms. Rich's face as she tried to speak through her crying, she asked, "Boy please don't you ever scare me like that again. When we buried D, I told myself that I wouldn't have anymore kids so I would never have to feel that type of pain ever again. That pain came back when you got shot."

"I was just at the right place at the wrong time," Lil Mac said, then stopped to look at Roc who dropped his head. Then he proceeded, "But I'm a soldier and we always bounce back to keep our dreams moving like nothing happened."

"That's a great outlook on life; you've gotten so big and handsome." Ms. Rich said to Lil Mac.

"Stop it, his head is already too big," said Mrs. Miller.

"I know that's right," she replied as they both laughed.

"Did your friend tell you about the fake insurance man that came by?"

"Yeah he told me."

"I think he was a co…"

"I know, I know," Lil Mac quickly interrupted. "Ms. Rich I'm going to call you tonight because we have a lot to catch up on and being that our time is short…" Lil Mac checked the time on his bright new watch. "There are still a few more things that I need to say to my big brother."

"All right go ahead and take your time baby. I got you."

When she stepped away, Roc said, "Mom can you do me a favor?"

"Anything Odell…you know that."

"Please go and get me some chicken wings."

"Boy stop playing, you haven't eaten meat in over ten years."

Roc looked into Lil Mac's eyes while answering, "I know but at times you have to go back to how you were to remain who you are today and please don't cook them all the way… I need to taste the blood." Roc watched her until he was sure she was too far away to hear him and then he grabbed Lil Mac's wrist with a force unknown to Lil Mac. "Where the hell did you get that?"

"What?" Lil Mac tried to meet Roc's power to release his arm but it didn't move.

"Mac, don't play with me where did you get this?"

Roc popped the cuff button on Lil Mac's Bathing Ape button up shirt and pulled the sleeve back roughly as he pointed to the watch.

"Oh this?" Lil Mac freed his hand and rotated his wrist looking at his new watch, still amazed at all the high VVS diamonds in it. "I got it from an old friend as a gift. He has a few of them."

Roc fell back into his seat and closed his eyes as the realization actually hit that what he tried so hard to accomplish had ended in failure. He reopened his eyes as his blood boiled and he spoke through tightened teeth, "There's not another one of them in the world so stop the bullshit and tell me where Mr. Holmes is at!" Roc demanded.

"Do you really want to know or do you want to stay in that fun, dreamland you live in when it comes to me?"

The tension built instantaneously as the two brothers looked each other in the eyes for the first time, as bosses. "Enlighten me," said Roc.

~ · ~ · ~ · ~

"See…it went like this, intruder alert flashed on the screen as Mr. Holmes rushed to a picture of George Jackson with red eyes. The words 'blood in my eyes' was written under it. He pushed in the eyes and every light in the house turned infrared. Then suddenly a flat sheet of metal eased down on every exit.

Four members of NayNay's six-men team crashed through the second floor window just before it closed. The other two hung from the safety rope on the side of the house. "NayNay we can't get in what's our next move?" they screamed into the earpiece.

"Drop to the ground and back Top Dollar up."

"Copy."

Solo's team approached the front main entrance. "Drop your glasses and let's move…go!" screamed Solo. *Boom! Boom!* He let off several shots from his 12 gauge into the pearl white glass and wood door frame when white lights popped on from nowhere, turning the darkness into day. The door was now covered by two thirds of steel as it blew off the hinge. "Everybody the door's open let's go. Khaled, Daz, take out this light. NayNay, you're in right?"

"Yes"

"Okay find the power line and cut it now." Solo dashed for the door, as it inched closed he slid into the open space just before it locked shut. He stayed low while he passed the shotgun to Fatel and retrieved two new glock 357's out of his waistline. "Melo, you and AP go upstairs on the right and ya'll three come with me."

Solo's team moved through the living room with Fatel at the front, Ayzo and Lance in the middle giving Solo the rear to protect.

"You want me to give the word now?" asked Jasmine as she and Mr. Holmes watched the surveillance screen in his secret back office.

"No, let him get all the way in first," Mr. Holmes answered, pushing a button to slow down the steel gate and then he released it just as Top Dollar slide through the crack. Now you can give the word,"

"Attack Ladies…Attack."

With their guns cocked, NayNay and Rob went from room to room looking through everything, checking to make sure that there was nothing left behind. They exited the fourth room and hurried to the third. NayNay put her back up against the wall. She looked in each direction as Rob kicked the door in and she covered his back. Rob rushed into the room to the closet with double doors and let off five shots into the frame before opening it. There were clothes flying everywhere as he tossed them out of the way. "All clear in here." Rob turned around to cover NayNay who was now out of sight, moving the shoes out from under the bed and making sure that no one was there.

The closet's back wall slid to the side and Melyssa and Susie stepped out dressed in all black. Susie put her chrome 380 to the back of Rob's head and said, "Bye sexy." She then blew him a kiss before pulling the trigger. Rob's body slammed into the hardwood floor. NayNay crawled deeper under the bed, her eyes searching for any movement and suddenly she spotted two pairs of legs. There was a person on each side of the bed. As they circled the bed, Melyssa spotted the shoes out of place and pointed to alert Susie while cocking a pink 9 mm. Instantly a slug cracked the middle of Melyssa's knee cap. She fell onto her chest, busting her chin on contact.

NayNay was now face to face with her, "Bye bitch!" *Boom! Boom! Boom!*

"Nooooo!" screamed Susie as she jumped into the window sill just before three bullets slammed into the wall where she was just standing. Susie let her gun loose causing feathers and cotton from the pillows to fill the air.

A bullet caught NayNay in the upper back. "Aaaaahhhhh!"

Lil Mac heard the cry through his earpiece, "NayNay…NayNay are you okay?" When he heard no response he screamed, "Lance, fall behind in position and take the rear. Make sure this lower level is clear first before proceeding." He dashed into the kitchen looking for the back stairwell that he remembered from the blueprint. "Melo, AP…where ya'll at?"

"I'm on the left moving toward the master bedroom," responded AP.

"I'm on the right side approaching the second floor entrance," said Melo.

"What's taking you so long," Lil Mac yelled.

"I got lost from all these damn rooms, he has floors in between floors."

"Fuck that! NayNay is down on your floor so find her now!"

"I'm on it," Melo confirmed.

"AP…and you watch it"

"I know, something's not right." Lil Mac scanned the kitchen and then stopped. "There you go," he raced up the steps, skipping a few with each stride.

Kim's eyes watched Solo's every move. She waited until he made it halfway up the stairs before moving the three brooms and two dust pans she hid behind in the mop closet. With her gun cocked, she headed up the steps cautiously on Solo's tail following Mr. Holmes' command.

Solo made it to the top of the stairs that lead into a hallway but not sure if the area had been secured, he walked with extreme vigilance and checked every room that he passed.

Kim entered an empty hallway, "I've lost the target," she whispered.

"He's in the fourth room on your right."

"I've got him." Kim put her ear to the door to listen for any movement. "I got you!" She screamed while kicking the door open and letting off five rounds which connected to Solo's shoulder and upper back. The impact knocked Solo up against the steel bars as he squeezed his trigger to return fire, missing wildly. Kim slowly raised her gun and fired two shots. There was nothing but silence as Solo blinked rapidly, thinking he was dead until he heard a voice. "They were just warning shots and I ran fresh out of them. Now drop your weapon!" she demanded.

Several pictures flashed in his mind of the men he respected the most and thought of what they would do in his situation. "If it's my time to die so be it," he said and then quickly tightened his grip around his gun before kicking off the wall while jumping to the side in the same motion. Solo tried to level his gun off and three shots pierced through the air. On contact, Solo's gun flew from his hand, "Aaaaaaahhhhhh!" The pain in his forearm shot through his body. He landed face down between the bed and the dresser. He could feel a presence over his body and thought, "I've got to see it coming."

With that, his muscles tightened, he swiftly rolled over onto his back. His heart pounded while he tried to make eye contact with the shadow that stood over him. "I guess it's not your time to make your exit, you dig?" Top Dollar helped Solo off the floor.

Seeing the blood dripping from him, he asked, "Where are you hit at?"

"To hell with me, we have to get NayNay," Solo replied.

Top Dollar raised his gun and shot out the dresser mirror, the crystal diamond cut dove into the center of the headboard and the two lights in each corner of the room.

"What the hell did you do that for?" Solo asked.

"I'll tell you later…let's secure NayNay."

"Melo, what's your position?"

"I'm now on the second floor and I just killed two pretty pieces of ass but there's still no sign of NayNay….we'll find her."

NayNay returned fire from the left corner of the bed, keeping Susie from charging her.

"What's her location now?" asked Khaled.

"She's five feet to the left from the second window and twenty feet deep with her back to you, behind a chair." NayNay responded while still firing,

"Move her back at least ten feet," replied Khaled from his position in a tree. Moving along the side of the bed, NayNay let off a series of shots.

Susie could feel the large chair was ready to give way from the impact of each bullet cracking its frame. Not wanting to be left uncovered, Susie faked her body right and then as NayNay locked and fired, she went to the left and fired.

NayNay saw that she was fooled and quickly swung her gun in Susie's direction when two bullets slammed into her chest. Another one stuck her in the neck as she screamed, "Noooowww" before plunging to the floor on her face and losing consciousness.

"Did you hear that?" asked Top Dollar.

"Yeah, it came from down there, everybody move out," Solo ordered. Top Dollar's team finished the search while he and Solo followed the sound. Inside the room, dust particles, dry wall, and stones filled the room from twenty rounds of Khaled's powerful M-16 assault machine gun. Solo dashed straight to who lay still on the ground. Rolling her over, he spoke softly, "You can't go out on me like this…please open your eyes." He watched blood come from her neck. "Top Dollar, find this man in ten minutes or we burn this house down, with him in it!"

Top Dollar put his finger to his lips, "Shhhhhh." Then he raised his gun and fired, hitting the same spots as before.

NayNay's eyes reopened blinking repeatedly. "How long have I been out?"

"Too long," Solo answered, helping her to her feet as she looked around the room.

She stopped at Susie's lifeless body, "That's what you get bitch. Rob…give her hell when she gets there. Thanks Khaled."

"Always," he responded through his earpiece.

NayNay removed the bullet proof vest with the chest plate now cracked in three places.

Solo cleared the blood from her neck to see that it was only a flesh wound. He removed his vest and handed it to her. "Now let's go take what belongs to us."

"Solo?"

"Yeah Top Dollar?"

"Watch what you say," he answered.

"Top, fill me in while I'm on the move," Solo interrupted, racing for the door.

"No…this way!"

He turned to see NayNay slide back into a wall in the closet and disappear.

With only three cameras remaining, thanks to Top Dollar and all of Mr. Holmes' guards down, it was to that point that Mr. Holmes decided to make his departure. He grabbed several important files and a black 9 mm off of a dresser. "We must leave now," he rushed from computer to computer eliminating each program. "Business and Corporate, delete."

~ · ~ · ~ · ~

"Once finished, he opened the secret exit wall and I was standing right there." Lil Mac put his two fingers together to make a gun shape.

Roc couldn't believe what he'd just heard. "Please tell me that you haven't harmed him," Roc questioned sincerely.

"Not yet but if you don't let go of your blocks in North Philly along with a hundred and fifty of them pretty white squares…in 30 days he'll be dead."

Roc leaned forward infuriated, "Boy, who the fuck do you think you're talking to?"

"Odell, if you don't watch your mouth in front of me. You know I raised you better than that," said Mrs. Miller as she brought in the plates of food and placed them in front of her sons. "What are you fussing about anyway Odell?"

"Nothing Mom, he was just trying to tell me how the old Jordan that played in D.C. can't compete with the next generation's best, Kobe. And as you were saying," responded Lil Mac while keeping eye contact with Roc the whole time.

"I'm stating that Kobe's nice now, but if it was do or die for him his rookie year, he would be laying in a Nike casket."

"Excuse me," said a fair looking C.O. who was so scared to come and interrupt Roc's visit that it took her twenty minutes to get up enough heart to approach. She continued, "I swear, I hate to interrupt your beautiful family Mr. Miller but your visiting hours have been over for a half hour and we can't let the inmates out until your family is no longer in this prison by Captain's orders but in no way am I rushing you sir."

"Okay, thanks," Roc said as he stood up giving his mother a big hug and several kisses.

"You take it easy in there son and know that God protects the innocent, so you'll be just fine. But please don't let these people in here make you into something that you're not baby, like they did your father."

"And what was that Mom?"

Mrs. Miller lowered her head looking down at the floor and replied, "An animal."

Roc raised her head back up with a finger under her chin, "Don't worry beautiful, I'm going to be just fine…you hear me."

"Yes baby."

"Now show me that pretty smile that could only have been made for your face."

"Boy you're silly," Mrs. Miller laughed giving Roc the smile that always melted his heart. Lil Mac put his arm out for a handshake that Roc looked past and then gripped him in a tight hug.

Roc's right hand locked into Lil Mac's left arm at the elbow while his left pinned Lil Mac's neck against chest as it wrapped around his shoulder. Roc whispered into Lil Mac's ear, "Please don't do this. If it's about the money, I'll give you a million, two million. I promise anything, but don't go out like this. Dad was a slave to these streets until he died. Then I became one so that you wouldn't have to."

"See," interrupted Lil Mac. "That's where you always went wrong Roc, by trying to think for me instead of asking if I wanted to be a slave. This is my life and I will make my own choices. In the end…I will face my destiny but don't worry, by the time you finish your six months I'll have the whole city on lock like Wilson Good was back in office."

"Lil Mac if you do this I can't save you, there is no turning back after this point…you know that."

"Don't worry about that, I'm in it until the death of me just like Mr. Holmes unless you do what I asked. Oh and before I forget, tell your men to fall back and stop protecting Boggy…that's what they're really doing, not watching him. So a promise can truly be fulfilled, something you couldn't do."

Roc squeezed him tighter, again speaking through tightened teeth, "You're playing a game that you can't win."

Lil Mac responded, “You know I have watched you my whole life, taking in everything that I could and you watched me my whole life and never knew who was right in front of your eyes, so we’ll see. I know your eyes are open now.” Pausing, Lil Mac then kissed Roc on the cheek, “Thanks for the watch.” He then walked off but before reaching the door, Roc called out, “Solo!”

Lil Mac turned around and answered, “What?”

“Do you know the reason Jordan came back wearing the number 45?”

“No, why?” questioned Lil Mac. Roc smiled and walked away.

17

Detective Michael sat on yet another sleepless stakeout sipping his tenth cup of black coffee. He was parked in the middle of 15th Street with a pair of high-tech binoculars stuck to his face. He watched the continuous flow of traffic moving along 16th Street. There were cars packed, bumper to bumper while crowds of people covered the sidewalks. To Detective Michael they didn't mean anything, he was waiting on what he believed to be the key connection to putting the Get Money Clique, along with Roc and his team behind bars forever.

"Dell, can you get anymore Intel on that guy in the red Philly's cap with the white state property jacket. He's on your left side." Det. Michael adjusted the binoculars to get a closer view as he witnessed the man passing off three large stacks of money to receive a big package. "Try to see if you can make out the contents of that bag before he makes it to the safe house."

"Copy, in motion," responded undercover Officer Dell who was dressed in a black and gray Mohammed gear hoody sweatsuit. A hidden microphone was stitched into his top drawstring. The black Kufi he wore was pulled down lower over his right ear to conceal the earpiece receiver.

For this assignment Officer Dell wore his beard grown out fully instead of his usual clean shaven appearance. He stepped away from the U-Haul truck where he sold everything from cell phones, new Jordans, Timbs, Red Monkey Jeans, Bathing Apes, to Muslim oils and bean pies.

"Issuallah good brother. You'll watch the truck while I send the money our way." Officer Dell looked down the block and spotted his target 20 yards off to the left heading his way. Noticing that the safe house was closer, Dell decided to cut him off halfway. "Yeah good brother Khaled, Assalamu Alaikum"

"No disrespect Mr. Husain, I'm off my deen right now, trying to get this money so I'm not trying to hear that," stated Khaled as he attempted to walk by when Dell placed a soft hand on his shoulder.

"Issuallah, you'll come back soon but if you can give me a minute of your important time, I have these new IPhones so cheap you can get one for your whole team. They come with everything, 30 second video, music, internet, you name it!" Officer Dell took a phone from his hoody pocket and continued, "You want to take a picture of a loved one, you hit this" the phone flashed twice.

"What the fuck did you take a picture for?" Khaled yelled, moving his face out of the way of the camera's aim.

"I'm sorry, we don't need that," Officer Dell said while he removed the flash and then turned the screen light down. "Just give me three hundred and put it into your bag." Officer Dell began to drop it halfway into the bag when Khaled pushed him back hard in the face. The force sent Officer Dell flying up against a parked car.

"What the hell are you doing? Don't you ever put your hands on something that belongs to me!"

"My bad good brother, I thought you wanted it. Issuallah, it will never happen again."

Khaled quickly balled up his fist. "I said miss me with that shit the next time Husain. I'm going to leave my fingerprints on your Kufi."

"Khaled, what's happening out here, you alright?" Top Dollar questioned, smoothly laying his hand on his 9 mm as he and Lil Mac stopped next to him.

"No, there's no problem. I was just a little out of pocket and brother Khaled was kind enough to remind me of that. I'm sorry, Assalamu Alaikum." Officer Dell walked off back down the block at a quick pace, until Lil Mac stopped him.

"Husain!"

"Yes, good brother?" said Officer Dell with sweat running down his forehead as he stood in front of a kid that looked friendly and self-confident but possessed the coldest eyes he'd ever seen.

"You know, the next time I hear your name it will be one time too many," Lil Mac said.

"Dell I'm coming out there," yelled Detective Michael, having a bad feeling on what was about to take place. If his thoughts were accurate, one of these two men was Solo and the only thing that came with that name since the first time he'd heard it, was death. He started the engine of his unmarked Ford Mustang.

"No" Officer Dell said out loud responding to Detective Michael.

Lil Mac asked "What?" while making eye contact with Daz who stood on the roof that was on the opposite side. He then ran his three fingers over his mustache. On cue, Daz cocked back his 30 odd six rifle locking it on the back of Officer Dell's head.

Officer Dell shook his head no to signal Detective Michael not to blow his cover when Lil Mac caught him. "Yes…no, but not to you good brother. I said no to Satan, this can only be an act of his work. To take something so innocent and then turn it into this," Officer Dell tried to explain.

"It's on you Top, you call it." Top Dollar looked back and forth from Daz to Husain.

Detective Michael dashed out the end of 15th Street into the intersection, speeding through a red light and just missing a black Acura. He fishtailed wildly before regaining control of the vehicle and straightening out. Detective Michael crossed onto 16th Street while Officer Dell's eyes searched for the best escape route. He found none and thought to himself, *"Michael's not going to make it but I'm not going to die alone. I hope they give me a twenty one gun salute."* Slowly, he eased his hand onto the pistol located in his leather holster that was hooked on the inside of his sweatpants.

Suddenly, Top Dollar said, "Husain, for your mistake…instead of paying a thousand a week to sell out of your mall on wheels, for the next month make it two. Now pack it up for the day."

Detective Michael eased up on the gas peddle and dropped low behind the tinted window. He watched Officer Dell closing the back of the U-Haul truck.

"That was too close for comfort Dell."

"You're telling me, remind me the next time I offer to help you to keep my mouth shut."

Back parked in his same spot, Detective Michael waved to Officer Dell as he drove by.

"Be safe Michael, you're on your own now."

"Damn it."

"What?"

"My target is about to be on the move and he just put the package into the trunk."

'That's good," stated Dell.

"How is that good? We don't know what it contains and the Captain is already on my ass. I'm not even supposed to be within a hundred feet of these guys."

"Stop your bitching and get your computer ready to receive."

"Please tell me you got me something on these bastards."

"You know me, I'm the best. I don't know how good they are, I was only in the bag for five seconds."

Detective Michael had a big smile on his face as soon as several pictures appeared on the screen. He whispered, "I got their asses now partner."

Lil Mac finished giving Khaled his instructions on how to run his shift smoother. "I'm telling you Khaled, you got to keep your crazy-ass young bulls in check for now and tell them to stop shooting people." Khaled grinned, prideful of his team of assassins. "No I'm serious!" said Lil Mac.

"I know Solo, they're just all restless ever since you stepped out and let these niggas know you're the man. There's nobody getting out of line so there's no more work to be put in."

Lil Mac shook his head, "Tell them that their wait won't be long because if I know Roc, the way I think I do…during these past three weeks of silence he's been planning and re-planning. When he is done, they will need every bullet they ever bought."

Top Dollar and Lil Mac started heading to their cars. Pulling into traffic they made a right onto 15th and King Ave. Lil Mac pushed the gas peddle lightly putting the twin Benz pass 80 mph onto the expressway. Detective Michael tailed his suspect for 20 minutes from at least four cars back, waiting for the right moment. Knowing the bust he needed was only moments away he thought to himself, *"You wanted me off this case...said that I made it too personal and that it's leading no where. Well now I'm going to show you Captain."*

"Dispatch, over."

"This is dispatch one, copy."

"Detective Michael here and I'm in pursuit of a new 2009 pearl white Mercedes Benz, license plate number G, as in gray, E – T – M – O – N – E – Y, I repeat that's GETMONEY."

"Copy, I'm running it now…that plate comes back as a dealer tag registered to a Draeh Rich, owner of D's auto located at 21st and Vine in North Philly."

"Are you sure?"

"I'm positive, it says it right here."

"I'll be damned," Detective Michael said speaking out loud, now faced with the realization that the Get Money Clique was smarter than he thought. By the vehicle being owned by a place of business and the owner of that business being dead, Detective Michael knew that if his suspect's fingerprints weren't on the package, it would be hard to make the case stick. "It's too late to stop now!"

Lil Mac parked and stepped out into the divine weather of 85 degrees. He could hear the music playing off in a distance from the beautiful 100-foot yacht that rested in the water. Lil Mac dropped his gold YS glasses over his eyes and said to himself, "I told you Mr. Holmes that you could bet I would make it to this lifestyle one day. I just didn't know it would be yours…haahaahaa."

On the yacht people crowded the indoor and outdoor dance floor while DJ E Red spun the latest Jay Z track. Others filled the swimming pool and bar area. Lil Mac moved through the crowd shaking hands with many of the major players in the city.

"Damn young player, I see you brought it back to money. You made it do what it does. For a minute I thought all you young cats forgot how to see a real dollar since ya'll been too busy killing people over nothing. Talking about keeping it real…this shit here is real," stated Poppin Tags Shorty as he popped his collar to his Gucci double-breasted suit before flashing his iced-out blue face Rolex with the matching chain. He continued, "It can't get no realer than real estate you feel me baby?"

"I feel you shorty."

"You better, because if not…in the end you'll have nothing." They hugged and as they parted, Shorty said "This next jewel I drop is not free, new breed, but I'll charge it to the game. People are just like real estate and I invested in you, that's why I'm here and you're getting my business. But I didn't double down, yes you're on Top but you have yet to be tested by someone worthy of the crown. There are also a lot of doubters in the shadows, many wanting that spot so bad that you can feel them coming…so watch yourself because everybody else is." With that said, Shorty nodded his head that he was finished.

"Ain't you too old for them Shorty?" Lil Mac replied. Poppin Tags Shorty held his arms open as two beautiful women took hold of each one.

"There is nothing old about me but my money player!" he answered, leading his girls onto the dance floor and leaving Lil Mac lost in his thoughts.

"Solo…Solo"

"Why wouldn't they be?"

"Solo what was that, I couldn't hear you," asked Fox once again interrupting Lil Mac's victory vision.

"Nothing but a true story, in time I will share it with you but what is it that you want?" Lil Mac asked getting straight to the point since he didn't like Fox because of his carelessness. Fox never thought about his actions before he did things and Lil Mac knew at some point in time one of his teammates would pay dearly because of it. If it happened, NayNay's family or not…Lil Mac would make sure that Fox left the earth.

"Where the boxes at? Everybody on the upper deck is waiting."

Looking at his watch Lil Mac said, "Tell them to be patient, we'll get money in a few minutes. What about our other situation?"

"Oh they asked for you," replied Fox.

"Then I must not keep them waiting." Lil Mac moved through the lower section of the yacht until he reached the back master bedroom. As he entered, he usually would take time out to admire the room's beauty. From the classic paintings lining the walls to the handcrafted wood cabinets and bed frame. Then there was the gold and marble faucet that he would slowly run his hands over. However, today his mind was on one thing only, the person lying in bed.

Lil Mac lightly tapped on the person's legs to bring them out of their nap. Confident that they were now fully awake he questioned, "You were asking for me?"

"Yes, seeing that I haven't been released by now lets me know that you're serious."

"More than any man you ever met, old head."

"Then it's only right that I give you a warning, I have a meeting in three days with very important people. If I don't make it, they will come looking for me and they'll find me at any cost…and that means you shall pay the price that no man I have ever met has," said Mr. Holmes.

Lil Mac sat in the three thousand dollar Marcus chair with his feet resting on the bed and replied laughing, "And you're telling me this why…because you care about my well being?"

"No, for Roc."

"What? Roc don't give a damn what happens to me!"

"No, those are your feelings, don't you ever put your thoughts in Roc's soul because you'll never be the same. Even after everything you did to him, if a hair was to be touched on your head he would feel it. But this is the big leagues where people don't move off of feelings, they react off of principles. So, they won't only kill you…they'll come for you're next five closest kin, starting with your mother," explained Mr. Holmes.

"What? My Mom?" without warning, Lil Mac punched Mr. Holmes in the face and screamed, "Look at me! What do my eyes say now old man?" The impact from the blow had knocked Mr. Holmes off the side of the bed. He regained his composure and rose to his feet using his handcuffed hand to wipe blood away from his busted lip. He smiled as he took a seat much closer to Lil Mac, refusing to lose eye contact.

"That you're willing to die for your mindlessness; no matter if the world said that they would follow you…you would let them die with you?" Mr. Holmes answered.

"That's where you're wrong old man, we're not the ones dying, or bleeding for that matter. So tell that shit to the niggas we ran through."

"Now you're starting to see."

"To see what? I'm not Roc, so stop with that philosophical shit. Say what you mean."

Mr. Holmes thought to himself, *"I always do…if you would have just paid attention."* He then spoke to Lil Mac, "The key words are 'ran through.' All of your life Roc has made it easy for you, even when you didn't know it." Mr. Holmes' voice became louder, "You ran through those blocks because Roc made them weak for you."

"That's a damn lie!" Lil Mac screamed, jumping to his feet.

"Is it? Just think about it. When Roc thought that Solo was just another hungry hustler foolish enough to come for his spot, he followed the first rule without error and crushed your team completely on Rose's block. If you were there, you too would have perished."

Lil Mac started to walk back and forth across the floor as he thought about the many men he lost that very day. "That wasn't me that was D's mistake."

"Are you not the General?"

"Yes…without question."

"Then their blood is on your hands."

"That's why my next move was severe…to avenge the death of them."

"Negative!"

"What?"

"Your next move was severe yes, but only to you."

"And how is that?" Lil Mac sat back in the chair eager to hear his response.

"First, you couldn't finish a top enemy from two feet away."

"Oh you're talking about Boggy? Fuck him, I can kill hi…" Mr. Holmes held up a finger that stopped Mac from continuing. "If you did, it would never have had the same effect as the damage you caused when you didn't. That was your second mistake, you showed emotion in front of your team…leaving doubt of your leadership in their hearts. That error gave up your most productive defense."

"Which was?" Lil Mac questioned, seeing that Mr. Holmes had the power over him to have him hanging on his every word.

"Your identity, so once Roc started to figure things out who you really could be, he would change his block workers and put in everybody that he thought would tell or that he knew had already told. The people that were so envious that once they became powerful would try to come for his spot from the inside. They all were on the block you ran through. So, in all actuality, you were working for him." Mr. Holmes laughed, "Ha Ha Ha."

"That was a good story but there's nobody in my team that has enough heart to cross me and leak information." The sound of the door slamming against the wall stopped Lil Mac from continuing his conversation, he had his gun cocked instantly and aimed at Fox's head as he rushed into the room.

"Solo, come quick…the cops got Top Dollar." Lil Mac dashed out the door behind Fox.

"Solo," Mr. Holmes called out, stopping Lil Mac before he'd gotten too far.

"What old man? Roc knew about this too?"

"Maybe but I'm going to give you this wisdom on the show of good faith and so you don't make the mistake of calling a man a liar again. My name alone is worth more than your weight in gold. You never did find out how Roc got to Black and his un-bosses without them knowing each other did you? Or how when you came back from a trip that you didn't know you were leaving early for and they were waiting on Top Dollar…missing his life by a hair. It was Sun."

Lil Mac repeated the name, "Sun?" Running his hands over his braids, it hit him, "Oh shit. Sun works for Roc now but he was KB's cellmate for months before he was killed. So it would have been easy for him to read his mail or listen to his phone calls. My bad old head…it will not happen again!" Lil Mac disappeared and alone Mr. Holmes stated, "I'm not your old head and in time you'll see why."

18

Lil Mac made it to the yacht's upper deck where he could see Top Dollar's Benz stopped by an unmarked car out in the distance of about a hundred yards. The sun had just begun to set and as the night crawled in, the red and blue flashing lights looked as if they were glowing in the darkness.

"You want me to handle it Solo?" asked a hyper Fox.

"Just chill, Top Dollar can out talk any cop so let's just see which way this thing is headed first." NayNay approached, giving Lil Mac a kiss and a pair of binoculars as she wrapped her arms around his waist hugging him from behind. "Happy birthday beautiful, how do you like your party so far?" asked Lil Mac as he watched the cop exit his car and tell Top Dollar to lower his window.

"You know I don't like parties, I would have been just fine with you and my gun," NayNay replied laughing and then said, "But now that you've asked…where are my presents?"

"Don't worry, they're close."

Over where Top Dollar was being stopped by the cops, as soon as his window was down Detective Michael asked, "License and registration please."

"No problem officer. I have them right here, never know when you will be around, ass."

"Excuse me? What did you say sir?"

"I said it's your world, I'm just here to get them quickly for you officer." Top Dollar said, handing over his license and registration.

"The reason I'm stopping you, sir, is because there is reason to believe that this vehicle is transporting a large amount of an illegal substance. So would you please step out of the car?" Stepping back, Detective Michael smoothly unsnapped his hip holster.

"Officer I don't usually come into contact with law men so if you would be kind enough to enlighten me to the fact that when stepping out, the car becomes a warrant?"

"It hasn't sir."

Top Dollar could see through his rearview mirror that another cop car had just pulled up behind him. "So that means you don't have a right to search and I'm not giving it to you. Now give me my ticket," stated Top Dollar.

Detective Brian walked up and asked, "Detective Michael is there a problem here?"

"Not at all, sir." Top Dollar answered.

"Excuse us," Detective Brian pulled Michael off to the side to speak in private. Top Dollar's eyes were glued to his rearview mirror as he eased his 9 mm into his lap.

"What's going on here, isn't that Maurice a.k.a. Top Dollar, the person you've been so obsessed with lately?"

"Yes, but…"

"No 'buts' Michael, if the Captain finds out you're still on this case after your last stunt, he will have your badge."

"I know but I have him this time, from the Intel that Dell…"

"Oh no, tell me you didn't bring him into this too," interrupted Detective Brian.

"Never mind that, damn it! There are three keys of cocaine in the trunk of that car right now."

"Are you sure, because if you're wrong…I wasn't here and I'm not going down for this."

"I'm positive."

"Here these pussies come now and I'm not going out like no sucker," Top Dollar muttered to himself, gripping his weapon tightly.

Detective Brian turned around with his firearm aimed at Top Dollar and demanded, "Sir, please step out of the vehicle with your hands in the air where I can see them." Top Dollar slowly exited the car and Detective Michael quickly handcuffed him and patted him down. Detective Brian began to search the trunk, removing several tailor made suits, London fall hats, and twenty pairs of new gator shoes. He then noticed a large bag. "Hey Michael, is this it?"

Nodding his head, Detective Michael whispered into Top Dollar's ear as he detained him, "I got you now Solo."

"Solo? I know I'm here by myself lame," Top Dollar responded.

"Cut the crap, you know what I am talking about, your gang the Get Money Thugs."

"Never heard of them, ass."

"You will."

"Michael, get back here," yelled Detective Brian.

"I'll be back to take your ass to jail!" Detective Michael assured Top Dollar. At the trunk, next to Detective Brian, Michael watched as he pulled stacks of money out of the bags. He smiled from ear to ear as four white wrapped packages lay at his feet. "What did I tell you, the Captain was all wrong."

Detective Brian retrieved the drug field test from his car. He opened the first one. It revealed a card on top of a white box that read 'Happy Birthday NayNay.' Inside there was a pair of car keys with the letter B on it. As Brian ripped open the second package, Detective Michael asked,

"What's the B stand for, Bunker? Is that where you store your drugs?"

"No, Bentley," Top Dollar answered smiling. The next package was then opened and contained the same thing, a card but this time with D's name signed on it and a box that held a Cartier watch.

"I don't know how…"

"Save it Michael, you're just lucky I answered the call. I'm sorry sir for any trouble we may have caused you, you're free to go," said Detective Brian, as he took off Top Dollar's handcuffs.

"I have to be honest; I'm a little upset, men. Nothing is supposed to touch this wrist but diamonds and gold so the next time a mistake like this is made, I will be forced to file a complaint." Top Dollar put his car in drive and pulled off. Just then, a shot discharged, blowing out Detective Michael's driver's side window.

"What the hell? Shot's fired, Officer…"

"No Brian, the Captain can't know about this!"

Back on the yacht, Lil Mac was furious as he removed his hands from his ringing ears. Looking in the direction of the sound, Lil Mac gripped the 40 odd six rifle out the arms of Fox. "What the fuck do you think you're doing?"

"That was harassment Solo, they can't do that to Top Dollar," Fox answered.

"Yeah, you're right. NayNay…thank your family for just ending your party. Now go get Mr. Holmes, we're moving and tell AP to get that bag out of my car and make it quick before the cops come back," Lil Mac instructed.

"Okay, I got it."

Once NayNay was out of sight, Lil Mac landed a hard right to the side of Fox's face. Fox fell to the ground on all fours. Lil Mac then firmly grabbed Fox by the chin, making him look at him in the face. "The next time I tell you to chill and you don't listen…I will put your body on ice."

"Solo!" NayNay called out, running and out of breath.

"What?" said Lil Mac, nicely helping Fox to his feet.

"Mr. Holmes is gone."

19

Roc chased Gizelle as she dashed around their king-size bed, leaving him on the left side while she stood on the right. "Roc will you go ahead please and leave me alone."

"And why would I do that, sexy?" asked Roc, inching closer to her.

"Because I asked you to nicely."

"You know that has never done it for me, I need it rough!" He moved in a little bit more.

"I don't care what you need."

"I need you," Roc responded as he jumped across the bed, landing face first onto the soft mattress. His arms were stretched out and wrapped around Gizelle's waist as she tried to run.

"Roc let me go."

"I will, as soon as you clam down and tell me what's hurting your heart. You used to always talk to me." Roc sat up and pulled Gizelle closer to him as he took in her lovely scent. "You smell so good."

"Roc no, I can't tell you my feelings."

"Why not baby?"

"Because I don't know what you'll do to them" Those words leaving her mouth cut a deeper hole through Roc's heart as he listened to her cry.

He turned Gizelle around to look into a face of pain that he'd caused. Roc gently wiped away her tears with the tip of his finger, while staring into her beautiful eyes. He began to sing with a smooth mellow tone, *"Hey girl, what's been going on in your life, talk to me baby."* Roc moved her hair to the side and kissed her neck softly while continuing to sing his Freddy Jackson remix, *"Your hair, the pretty clothes that you wear, bring back memories talk to me baby."*

"Roc…you haven't sung to me in years."

"And I'm sorry for not doing a lot of things lately baby. But those tears will be the last ones that you drop because of me." Roc carefully took in every part of Gizelle's body as he undressed her.

"Roc wait…promise me that we'll just leave this city behind us and start over today."

"And where would you like to go?"

"Anywhere… as long as I am with my family"

"I promise," Roc answered then lowered the lights as he pushed play to let Mr. Jackson finish the words to his own song.

Disappearing into the hallway for a few moments, he quickly returned with a tray of delightful toys. Roc rubbed hot honey coconut oil, just out of the microwave over Gizelle's body. "Ooooohh baby, that's hot." He started with her upper body, moving his hand in a circular motion, massaging her neck and shoulders. Roc worked both hands to relax her muscles. A shocking chill raced up her spine that was hot and then cold, causing her to let out an even louder moan feeling the ice cubes that Roc had placed into his mouth. He then wrapped his lips around her nipples and breasts.

Roc began to kiss Gizelle hard and passionately, while bringing her legs up into the air, spreading them apart. He sucked on her toes, knowing his woman's body as if it was his own, he smoothly went into motion. Without warning, as Gizelle lay their submissive to every touch from her husband, Roc slid his manhood deep inside of her. "Aaaahhhhh," Gizelle arched her back, accepting the forced pleasure from his long, thick dick that sent waves of sensation through her body. Roc pumped into her core. With each stroke, her pussy walls gave way, making room for Roc's satisfaction. He pulled Gizelle to the edge of the bed with his feet planted for better balance. Holding her in the air by her ass cheeks, Roc pulled his manhood out to the rim of her drenched outer lips then pushed it right back in again, hitting the bottom with each powerful thrust.

"This is what you want right? For me to give that pussy a black eye? Yeah, I'm going to give it to you…this is what I do, take that, take that!" Gizelle worked her hips, trying to catch a rhythm to Roc's ruff neck poetry love. As the sweat rolled off Roc's body onto Gizelle, he flipped her over onto her stomach as his manhood rested in the center of her ass crack, covered in wetness. Suddenly he pulled her from the bed, Gizelle held on to the end of the mattress as Roc continued to work every want and need. Her breasts bounced rapidly as Roc's manhood felt like it was coming through her stomach lining.

As her body became on fire, Gizelle started to vibrate….she could feel that she was about to cum when the phone rang, "Nooooo!" She opened her eyes and looked around the empty room. Gizelle pulled the pillow out from between her legs then threw it across the room. The phone rang again for the third time. "Hello?"

"What took you so long to answer the phone?"

"You!"

"What?"

"Never mind Roc, what do you want? Larry Jr. is asleep."

"Gizelle, what did I tell you about talking to me like that?"

"I don't want to hear that right now Roc, you also said you would never leave me again and look where you are."

"Please don't do this now."

"If not now, then when Roc?"

"Real soon, I promise but I need you to do me a favor."

"You want a favor, unbelievable." Gizelle let out a deep breath as she switched the phone to the other ear.

"Yeah I am," Roc replied, sadly understanding his wife's pain.

"Okay, what is it?"

"An old friend of mine named Mr. Jones' plane lands at 7 am."

"Roc it's pass seven. It's quarter to eight."

"I know but his taxi is in route to see me; I need you to pick him up once he leaves here at 10am and drive him around so that he can handle some business. Gizelle, the man is very wise and important so respect that."

"I hear you Roc, but I don't like it. I don't know him and you've never talked about him"

"That's how important he is and bring Larry Jr. because he's been wanting to see him."

"If you want me to bring our son around him, I trust that he's a great person."

"Would I let you down?"

"I'm not going to answer that, how will I know him?"

"Don't worry; he'll know you because when you're not around, I always paint a pretty picture of you."

"Bye Roc."

"What…wait a minute…" before Roc could finish, Gizelle disconnected the phone. Thinking to himself, Roc stated, "Now the games will begin."

At 10:15am Gizelle cruised down State Road in her black Volvo v40 wagon with Larry Jr. strapped in his car seat. She noticed a man with a beard and cane, who looked to be in his late fifties. Mr. Jones was dressed to impress in his Isaiah navy-blue three-piece suit. His blue and white tie matched the Laura hat that sat tilted to the side on the top of his head. Gizelle pulled to the side and said, "Excuse me."

"Yes Gizelle, I'm Mr. Jones."

Looking at him up and down, Gizelle was thinking, *"Well he does look kind of friendly with that warm smile but if he tries anything I will bust his ass."*

She moved her purse that held her 380 automatic in it, closer to her before she unlocked the door.

"Hi, I'm Mr. Jones."

"Gizelle."

"I know, it's nice to finally meet you after all the beautiful stories that I've heard from Roc."

"Is that so?"

"Yes, it is but do I sense a touch of uncertainty in your voice."

"It's a long story. Where would you like for me to take you?"

"If you don't mind, I need to go to Chestnut St. in South Philly."

"That's not a problem," Gizelle replied.

All the way there, Mr. Jones played with Larry Jr. making him laugh non-stop. "Pull over right here please." Gizelle pulled into a parking space in front of a lovely white house with two kids playing football in the front yard. Mr. Jones closed his IPhone and moments later M. Easy came down the steps.

"Mr. Jones, you're back."

"You know how it goes."

"Yeah, if you're back it can't be good for somebody at all."

Mr. Jones smiled, liking the fire he saw in M. Easy after he realized what was about to come before asking, "Have you heard from your friend?"

"Not yet but if Mr. Holmes doesn't contact him within 24 hours before the meeting and let him know that everything is still a go, he will send a search team. Then, even if Mr. Holmes makes it, Lil Mac will still be marked for death."

"We can't have that happen but I only have 42 hours left, that's not enough. You used to live with the man…you must use your friendship to our advantage. I don't know how but you have to buy me more time."

M. Easy replied, "Okay I will try."

"M. Easy, for this to happen with us coming out on top, we have to reconnect the dots to bring our whole picture back together. Have someone make the phone call, about the meeting at 800 tonight."

"Now you're talking, I'm on it now."

M. Easy started to walk off when Mr. Jones called him back, "M. Easy!"

"Yeah"

"Call the kids"

"Mike, Billy…Mr. Jones is here."

"Yeeaaahh," the kids yelled, dropping the ball and racing to see who would make it to him first.

"Hi Mr. Jones."

"How are my two favorite football players doing?"

"Fine," they answered together.

"You two are staying out of trouble, right?"

"Yeah."

"Okay, that's good enough for me." Mr. Jones went into his pocket and counted out ten 20-dollar bills, "Five for you Billy and five for you Mike."

They jumped into the window and gave him a big hug around his neck. "Thanks Mr. Jones."

"Let me go, I can't breathe," he replied.

They quickly released him, scared…until they saw him smile. "You tricked us."

"You always have to keep a trick in your pocket, remember that."

Gizelle pulled back into traffic after she received her next set of directions and then asked Mr. Jones who was once again playing with Larry Jr.

"Do you have any kids Mr. Jones?"

"Yes one, why do you ask?"

"Because you fit so well with them. I haven't seen Jr.'s face light up like that since before Roc left." Mr. Jones could see that Gizelle's soul was in pain from Roc not being there.

He rubbed her shoulder lightly as he spoke, "A child's life is nothing more than a mirror reflection of what they see in who they respect. Being mindful of that, no matter where I'm at in my life…in their presence, I'm Mr. Positive."

"That's so sweet."

"Thank you," Mr. Jones' voice went into a whisper, "I just caught onto that lately."

"Excuse me; did you say something Mr. Jones?" Gizelle asked.

"You can park right here." Mr. Jones hit the horn twice, then paused and did it two more times followed by one. Out of nowhere Mohammed appeared at the passenger side window.

"Oh shit…where did you come from?" Shamone came shortly behind him.

"Al hum du'Allah. It's nice to see you once again Mr. Jones."

"Likewise Mohammed, it's just sad that I need to put you back in the battlefield as soon as we meet."

"We're soldiers and that's where we belong. So what's the mission?" asked Mohammed, knowing that the battle was now over and the war had just begun.

"You must go retrieve our mutual friend in this matter so that everybody can be at eye level."

"It's done."

"And Mohammed…without a mark please. Shamone what I need from you is to have one-third of the product ready by tomorrow because I'm moving the meeting up a few days. It's time to push them to see just how strong their stance is."

"But Roc said to give them a hundred and fifty of our best which is nothing so why chance them hurting Mr. Holmes?" Shamone questioned.

"Well…for one, I'm not Roc, secondly this is the last time I'm going to explain myself, and last…Mr. Holmes was in danger when he touched his first pack in this game. And the difference between a hundred and fifty keys and fifty keys is an 848 charge and an 841, the 848 being the Rico act where we all go to jail for life and the other is the 841 where a man like myself can step up and take the case then have my lawyer beat it if it is a set up."

"A hundred and fifty keys with two-thirds of flour coming right up."

"Oh and make sure you have it Mohammed at the meeting at 8."

"Will do!"

On point, Gizelle pulled off and asked, "Where to now?"

"If my memory is correct, you love seafood…is that right?"

"Yes, you are correct."

"Well, Buoy One it is."

"I love that place."

"So do I," said Mr. Jones. On the way there after calling several more people, Mr. Jones continued to keep Larry Jr.'s attention when all of a sudden Jr. called him, "Daddy, Daddy" as he pulled at Mr. Jones' beard.

"No Jr., he's not your Daddy, that's Mr. Jones. I'm so sorry about that Mr. Jones it has been some time since a male has been around him. He just misses his father." A single tear flowed out the corner of Gizelle's eye.

"Don't worry, Roc will be with him soon enough."

Inside the restaurant they ordered and while they waited, Mr. Jones tried to find the reason for Gizelle's pain. He saw deep into her eyes. "If you don't mind me saying so, you look lovely from head to toe today."

"Thank you! You're so very kind," she replied.

"But it's your insides that are in need of healing. For many people, a big house, several cars, and never ending access to money is a dream come true. However that's not the case with you, your heart is different. A simple kiss from your husband throughout the day can replace many of those things and you would be just as happy."

"Yes," Gizelle said, closing her eyes as she thought of Roc kissing her. As upset as she was with him for not being there, she would give anything to have that right now. "How can you tell?" she asked Mr. Jones.

"I too have been married, to two women at one time and you can never forget that look of the one while you're with the other."

"Excuse me, I don't understand…I'm Roc's only wife."

"Yes, you are and he loves you wholeheartedly but he is also married to the game as well…and like I, he too realizes that he loves his family more than the game. However the game fought back and it's pulling him in deeper. Now the edge he once had to win is gone because he doesn't love it anymore. At this point he knows your pain, believe me because he feels it also. That leaves him no choice but to second guess his decision. He wants to make sure you won't be hurt too much if at all, but for him to win and make it home to you safely he will need to become his former self one last time…with your support."

"Roc knows that he will always have my support, in anything that he does," said Gizelle.

"Does he?"

"Yes Mr. Jones, but why couldn't he talk to me like this instead of blocking me out?"

"Maybe he did and you didn't know it at the time." Their food arrived at the table with Mr. Jones feeding Larry Jr. most of his lobster dipped in garlic sauce. He promised Gizelle he would drive before ordering her a glass of red wine to calm her nerves. She felt badly that she didn't see that Roc needed her more now than ever; and for the first time she was afraid to hold him down because of her fears. She wanted Roc to be safe and she now knew that in order for him to do that, she was going to have to trust his judgment and stand behind him.

Mr. Jones buckled Jr. into his car seat.

"Daddy, Daddy."

"Stop it Jr. That's enough, Mr. Jones is not your Dad! I don't know what's come over him today."

"It's fine, you know kids, they see what they want to see, not what's in front of them," replied Mr. Jones. Pushing the Volvo at the speed of sixty-five, Mr. Jones drove out onto a country road about 45 minutes outside of the city. He stopped at a gate and typed in a ten-digit code and the gate eased open.

Recognizing the place, Gizelle asked, "Who do you know here?"

"A dear old friend," he answered. The Volvo moved slowly through the cemetery and then stopped alongside of a clear clean road. "If you would excuse me, I will not be long."

Mr. Jones walked through the graveyard until he stopped at a black and white marble sculpture of an angel headstone. He bent down and pushed the leaves aside. Gizelle looked on, waiting to see who Mr. Jones could know here also. When he stopped, her eyes grew large as tears filled them. "You bastard!" Gizelle quickly opened the door and called out, "Mr. Jones," while holding Larry Jr. in her arms. She waited until they made eye contact and then said, "Larry go and be with your Daddy."

Larry Jr. pushed his little legs to the max as he raced into the arms of Roc. Roc picked his son up into the air as Jr. grabbed his beard. "You knew who I was the whole time didn't you champ? See Dad, this game must not reach him," Roc placed Jr. higher into the air as if to give his father a better look before he released him to go play.

Roc continued talking to his father, "And there's not a power at my disposal that I'm not willing to use to make sure he's protected from it. But he's not the reason why I'm here. I'm here because I let you down. I did make sure that they never needed or wanted for anything but somewhere along the way, I turned David into Goliath. Believe me, I know I have to fix it but how do I fix something when the person thinks there is nothing broken? Yeah…you're right, I know I must break it but it's going to be hard because people must die. Sure, if that's what I have to do to save my family, it's done. I promise you again Dad, if it does go bad and I have a choice…get a bed ready for me."

20

In the back row of the Magic Movie Theater, Boggy sat nearly alone except for Trina and his four bodyguards posted at every exit. Trina was a sexy, 5'8" tall, 130-pound, dark-skinned beauty with her face in his lap. "Yeaahhh," Trina ran her wet hot lips down the length of his dick before taking it deep into her mouth when a side door opened, letting the hallway light invade their darkness. Boggy looked down as she licked the tip of his head and said, "Damn, I love my dick size."

A man was stopped at the entrance as Bo's Mack 10 rested in his rib cage. "Sorry man, this section is closed."

"Bo, if you don't get that gun…"

"My bad!"

"Now where is he at?"

"In the last row, all the way up top." The man slid into the open seat next to Boggy."

"My main man Haffee, what brings you down here? My bad, you want some?" Boggy said referring to Trina.

"No, I'll pass," Haffee answered.

"Well…pardon my thugness, Trina, Haffee, Haffee, Trina."

Trina came up for air and said, "Hi Haffee, you're cute."

"That's enough bitch, and put some of that hot butter in your mouth and do what you do…yeah that's it. Now what were you saying?"

"M. Easy has called a meeting and said it's important and he needs to speak with us," said Haffee.

"That's our friend right?" Boggy asked.

"Yes, he is cool, he has never crossed us."

"But he still works for Roc?"

"That's true."

"Then there's nothing else to talk about, fuck him. We're going to go through with our plan. We wait until Roc's people hand over all that good 'caine to Solo and as soon as he stops to drop it off we take everything, the product, the money, and his life! After we bleed the block with their work, we will give Roc a welcome home party he'll never forget. Just make sure our men don't lose that tail on Manny and his crew. Now that I'm gone, they're Roc's most trustworthy soldiers and they'll lead us right to the meeting place."

"Will do," Haffee eased out of his seat.

"I'll holla at you later and you, too, Trina."

"Mmmhhhhmmm," she responded.

Haffee walked 10 feet away and turned to say, "Boggy, I almost forgot…he said that if you refused the invite, to tell you that it was something about your level of understanding."

"What?" Boggy jumped out of his seat, pushing Trina off to the side as he fastened his pants. Moving toward Haffee, Boggy stayed low using the rim of the seat for cover. He pulled Haffee down to the ground next to him while calling out, "Bo, have the men check the entire surroundings now!"

Boggy looked at Haffee as if he could see his soul, "What did you just say?" Haffee was moving his lips but Boggy was hearing the voice of Mr. Holmes as everything came back to him, 'Loyalty and if ever separate, give a way of warning. Next, show good faith for the love. Then if that doesn't work, give him a level of understand before you look him in the eyes and you kill him.' Boggy then remembered the words of M. Easy, 'Roc just smiled and said let him go, this is his warning.' Boggy's thoughts flashed to when M. Easy saved his life in Joey's, 'I got a message on good faith from my boss.'

"You son of a bit..." Bo tapped, Boggy on the shoulder bringing him back to reality. "Boss there is nobody here now, but they left this." Boggy grabbed the piece of paper out of Bo's hand and read it, "I taught you better than to be caught with your pants down. Assalam Alaikum."

"Where did you get this?"

"It was taped over the two holes cut into the movie screen. They were just the right size for a barrel and a scope to fit through."

"Beef up the security everywhere and get the rookie to start up my car. Something big is about to go down, I just wish I knew what it was."

21

A hundred miles off the Gulf of Mexico on a leveled off mountain there was a 9,500 square foot piece of land with a thirty-room, two swimming pool mansion. Divided into three shifts, one hundred armed men secured the compound. They changed positions every two minutes to make sure Diego El Sovida was well protected at all times, standing in the middle of his living room looking through the installed glass wall that opened up into his backyard, the calm blue sea.

A knock interrupted his thoughts; he eased his hand onto his 9 mm Beretta and released it from his waistline. For anyone to be a member on Diego El Sovida's compound, they had to pass over two hundred extraordinarily difficult tests given by the top FBI agents in Mexico. But Diego El Sovida still didn't trust hardly anyone.

With his gun pointed at the closed doorframe, he slid the door open with his free hand. "Rafael, I told you to have the men and the plane gassed up and ready for take off."

"I know sir but Senor M. Easy is on the phone and he said he needs to speak with you."

A smile appeared on Diego's face hearing the message, for his once houseguest now turned friend for over two years was on the phone.

~ · ~ · ~ · ~

They met at a party given by the Mexican tourism foundation in the Ritz Carlton hotel in the back of the VIP section, where for the show of entertainment, two men would fight to the death or knock-out whichever came first. The gambling was at high stake and Diego El Sovida loved the chance to win or lose so he took every–and-any bet that came his way.

The word moved around the room making it to the ears of an on-the-run M. Easy. Once he located Diego El Sovida, he started to approach him only to be stopped by five armed guards. "Be easy, I'm just trying to place a bet," said M. Easy, looking the men up and down as Diego El Sovida asked, "What's your name?"

"M. Easy."

"No, your real name," Diego questioned as he handed M. Easy a glass of champagne.

M. Easy thought to himself before answering. *"Who is this man? I know he has class from his high-priced gear with no name because this nigga smells like money. But I'm not going to give this nigga my real name."*

Diego interrupted M. Easy's thoughts by taking the empty glass and passing it to Rafael while handing him a fresh one.

"No disrespect main man, I'm not giving you my real name. I don't know you…I'm just trying to make some money."

"But you don't get it, you already have. Within another minute or so, I will know everything about you, from where you went to school, why you're in my country, and how you have the balls to approach me and not go through my several betting agents. This moment can become very good for you but if there's anything in your past, I mean anything, even a questionable parking ticket…I must kill you for your disrespect."

M. Easy looked around, now realizing that Diego El Sovida had the whole left side of the VIP section to himself except for him and his bodyguard. Rafael returned and handed Diego a computer print out sheet and said, "Boss."

"I know already Rafael."

"How boss? As soon as it came back I brought it straight to you?" asked Rafael.

"Because he never moved, sitting there like he didn't have a care in the world and I like that. But you made the trip so I'll read it," said Diego.

"You're right boss, he's a criminal also wanted in the States for double murder."

"How the hell do you know all this shit?" questioned a puzzled M. Easy.

Diego El Sovida said, "Let me explain something to you. When you come through the door, you see those red lasers moving around the room as if they are lights to entertain?" He pointed out the red lights flying around the room and continued, "Well, that's an eye scan that goes straight to a friend's computer in the DEA's office." Diego paused to look at M. Easy's champagne glass and said, "And your finger prints."

"Well I'll be damned, and I gave them to you," M. Easy replied.

"Yes you did. Now what about this money you're talking about making?"

"I heard you like the Mexican going up against the Columbian in the next fight."

"You hear correctly," Diego answered.

"Well…I'd like to bet fifty on the Columbian."

Diego El Sovida gave a wave of his hand and two men sat two computers in front of them. "You transfer your fifty million."

"Fifty million?" M. Easy said, spitting out his champagne all over the Marla Sher rug.

"Yes, you do know all bets are five hundred thousand or more?"

"No I didn't know that." M. Easy answered, in shock.

"I don't know why, but I like you M. Easy. Maybe it's because I see the heart in you that not too many people have from the U.S. anymore. So I'm going to do this, you said you have fifty thousand. If you can double that I will match it with five hundred thousand."

"Give me the number," M. Easy called Roc and watched as the money appeared on the screen. He then stood up and took off his Ralph Lauren shirt, showing his tank top and then walked off.

"Hey, M. Easy…where are you going?"

"To fight for my money."

M. Easy eased down into the pit and tapped the Columbian on the shoulder. "Watch out Castro, I got this." The puzzled Columbian looked past M. Easy and made eye contact with Diego who waved him out of the cage. Diego El Sovida was impressed with how well M. Easy fought a much more skillful fighter. As the rounds increased, M. Easy showed more heart by the second. The bell rang, sounding the start of the tenth round when a hard body-shot from M. Easy to the exhausted Mexican's rib cage made the man pause. That was all the time that M. Easy needed to rush him. Wrapping his arms around the waste of the Mexican, within a second M. Easy had the man over his head bringing him down hard on his neck.

"Aaaaaaaaaahhh," the Mexican screamed as the blow cracked a bone in his spine.

The crowd went into an uproar as the man lay motionless and they began to shout, "Finish him, finish him!"

M. Easy smiled before exiting the pit and said, "No matter where you're at, they always love a killer." Then he stepped next to Diego El Sovida and stated, "I would like mine in cash." Diego laughed, remembering the moment he'd met a true friend, M. Easy.

~ · ~ · ~ · ~ · ~

Picking up the phone and putting it to his ear he said, "M. Easy, it's good to hear from you again."

"Likewise El Sovida"

"But it's your timing that I can't believe; I too will be in the States with some company in a few hours. Maybe we can get together and I can win back some of that money you took from me as you stayed in my home."

"You're coming to Philly?" M. Easy questioned.

Diego pushed a button that made the glass walls slide back and then he stepped into the backyard to watch the sun set before he spoke, "Do you know the sun is the most powerful entity in life, yet it brings a person like me such relaxation and ease. Do you know why?"

"No El, why?" asked M. Easy.

"Because it is not until it's gone," Diego El Sovida replied as he watched the sun disappear completely and then he continued, "That men such as ourselves, power can truly be maximized. So to answer your question…no my friend, I am not but my company is coming to your part of town to be exact. I myself will be at the cozy Hacienda in Phoenix if you care to join me. There will be a private jet at the Philadelphia airport for the time of 24 hours if you decide to come."

"That's the reason I called El Sovida…about your company. I know the reason they're coming and I need you to put them on reserve so that I can straighten some things out here for Mr. Holmes. Once I'm done, he can tell you all about it."

"Do you know what you just asked me M. Easy?"

"Yes, for a little bit more time."

"No, you're asking about my business. Not only that, you're asking me to change the way I do business."

"I know El Sovida, I'm sorry but I really need this favor," explained M. Easy.

"Say I was to tell my men to stand down until I give the word, what would you do for your friend Roc and his family?" Diego asked.

"So you already know?"

"You wouldn't believe what I know, I'll give you up until the time of the meeting and if Mr. Holmes doesn't appear, how they say in your American movies…you be careful walking the street."

22

At 8:35pm, accompanied by Manny, Raja and Buff, Roc took the stairs to the second floor in a West Philadelphia library to see the table surrounded by most of his trusted soldiers. Roc walked around the room looking each person in the eyes to see if he could spot a weakness. Seeing nothing but determination and loyalty, he began to speak, "The true identity of Solo has been revealed and now the blood of my brother is on the line." At the sound of those words, the whole room became dead silent. Many of them knew the love that Roc held in his heart for Lil Mac, but they all knew what Roc did to anyone that crossed him, making this situation a truly unfair moment for all of them.

Roc continued, "I know…I couldn't believe it either but this is the showing of history at its best; from the time of Kane and Abel or when Romulus killed his twin brother Remus to become the first founder of Rome, to the enviousness of the brothers of Joseph."

"You can't forget about Nino and G-Money!" A voice interrupted, making many grasp for their weapons when Roc motioned for them to stand down.

The man stepped in front of Roc with five of his men at his side along with M. Easy and asked, "Now that you know, what do you have to say?"

"That I misplaced my trust by letting my emotions influence my judgment. As a man I can acknowledge that I was wrong. I'm sorry, but as your blood brother I can tell you it will never happen again." Roc took out his pocket knife and cut a part of his hand in the middle of his palm. He then held it in the air as blood dripped on the rug. Boggy just watched the blood flow for a minute before taking the knife from Roc's hand. In a single quick move he brought the knife up to the pressure point in Roc's neck.

Over forty guns were drawn and aimed at Boggy and those he brought with him in less than a second. Manny's infrared beam was locked on the back of his head as he thought to himself, *"Give the sign and this nigga's a dead man!"*

Just then, the most unbelievable words touched his ears, "Everybody drop your guns, now!" Roc yelled as the knife cut into his neck while he was talking. "If you feel that we need to die together to be even Boggy, go ahead. But if you have it in you to once again connect the dots so that we can put the picture we painted of us on top together, that would be just fine."

Boggy replied, "But you killed my family while I listened to him die."

Boggy pushed the knife in deeper as Roc said," Come on Boggy, you set them two lames up to be put in a box."

"Yeah I did, didn't I? Fuck'em….aaahhhhh," Boggy laughed and then stepped back placing the knife deep into his hand that left a sharp cut. Their hands interlocked while they hugged. Roc slid into Boggy's pocket, a white envelope with a note and a key to a safe deposit box. "What's this?" Boggy questioned.

"Something that I wanted to give you the night the club opened. So when you're alone, read it. Do whatever you want…I'm just glad you're back."

"Me too, but I have one last thing I must handle, my word depends on it."

"Don't worry I got you," Roc replied.

"Okay, what's our next move?" Boggy asked, happy to be back at the side of his friend and ready to put in work with the best gangster in the city.

"I have a plan for Solo; first I will test his foundation. Mohammed," Roc called. Mohammed appeared from out of a door off to the left with a woman at his side. Her hair was out of place and she looked to have been crying as traces of mascara covered her face.

"I found these in the house," Mohammed handed Roc several photos. He raced through them quickly until one caught his eye.

"I'll be damned, Ms. Jones." Roc wrote down NayNay's address, knowing it from the nights that he brought her home. "Haffee, take this and if she's there bring her to me. If not get what you can from the home. Haffee took the photos and then called a few men to follow when Roc said, "Haffee, it's nice to have you back."

"You know, in a way it's like I never left."

Outside, Haffee and a four-men team jumped into a black BMW wagon as several sets of eyes watched their every move.

Special Agent Branson's fingers quickly typed in the plate number while his partner questioned as he saw Haffee backing out, "Are we going to follow them?"

"No, there's something big about to happen with two corporate members in the United States at the same time and we're going to find out just what it is. In order for that to happen, we must stay on Roc…let them have the small fish," Special Agent Branson pointed to Detective Michael pulling out two minutes behind Haffee.

"But who are they after, him or the person he's following?" asked the partner as four Mexicans pulled out after Detective Michael.

"I don't know as of yet, the rental was paid for in LA and transferred to Philly by a Carlos Ramirez."

"Let me guess, a Mexican right?"

"Yes"

"You're right…something big is going down," said the partner as he picked the listening device up and pointed back to where Roc was standing and tuned in.

"What are they saying now?" Special Agent Branson asked.

"I think it's a woman on the phone crying to somebody but I can't hear it's not too clear. They keep moving out of range, do you think we should move in closer?"

"No, I got a better idea." Agent Branson picked up his phone, "Yes Kalman, put me through to Washington."

23

Just a few moments earlier in an Xbox Live arcade booth in the Digital Life Tech show held in New York at the Jacob Javits Center, NayNay let off round after round as Lil Mac covered her. "Top Dollar get the man off the roof that's approaching fast on your left side," yelled Lil Mac through his mouthpiece.

"Don't worry, I got him Top Dollar," said Fox while moving over onto the opposite side.

"No stay in your position Fox and protect the blind side from the right," ordered Lil Mac as he watched their own triangle offense collapse into a ninety degree perimeter as Fox never stopped moving to the left. Fox locked his weapon on the man and fired, when two men appeared on his right.

"Fox watch your back," yelled NayNay while she pointed her gun in the men's direction. Then she continued, "I'll take the one on the right Solo, you get the other one." She battled it out with the man shot-for-shot as the other man a few feet away dropped to one knee and fired, hitting Fox in the back of the head. Then he turned around and fired a shot that connected with NayNay's back, ending their two-hour long game of Call of Duty 4. "Solo why didn't you cover me? This was the final mission?" questioned a confused NayNay.

"Because I'm not going to put my life on the line at any time if it be a game or the real thing for a person trying to prove that he could kill, while he neglects to protect his people from being killed," Lil Mac replied.

"Damn Solo. You just let your man go and shoot me, what's up with that?" stated Fox.

"You're lucky it wasn't me and the next time I give an order and it's not followed to a tee, you will have to prove you can kill me before I let someone get hurt from your mistakes. Now get out of my face and restart the game, we're taking it from the top."

Fox walked off with his head down. "Why do you have to be so hard on him? You know he looks up to you as if you were the Godfather himself," NayNay asked Solo.

"You don't see what I see in him and this isn't a movie. We're actually dying out here…my brother is about to come for my life and he isn't going to be the reason Roc kills me." Lil Mac's sentence was interrupted by his cell phone ringing. "Hello?"

"Lil Mac please save me…they took me from my home," the caller replied.

"Slow down, Ms. Rich please tell me who did this and where you're at?" Hearing the cries from his late best friend D's mother, pained Lil Mac. When no answer was returned Lil Mac thought the worst. "Ms. Rich, Ms. Rich…who did this?"

"Who else but me!"

"Boggy?" asked a furious Lil Mac.

"I'm glad to know that the bed rest I had you on didn't let you forget the voice of the man that put you there," Boggy answered.

"Fuck you Boggy! If you lay a hand on her I'm going to kill you the first chance I get."

"Haaahaaaa," Boggy laughed before saying, "That's without question but don't let your emotions get Ms. Rich here killed before it's her time to die."

"Oh my God, no please stop!"

Lil Mac could hear Ms. Rich pleading in pain in the background as Boggy continued, “But if this is too much for you to handle, you can put the real boss on the phone.”

“What…who?” asked Lil Mac.

“Top Dollar,” said Boggy, knowing that he’d just made Lil Mac even more pissed.

“Enough with the disrespect, what do I have to do to make sure she makes it home safely?”

“Now you’re talking, I believe you have something that’s very dear to our enemy and I need him.”

“Okay.”

“Not so fast, you’ve done well so far as a new soldier so I’m not going to take all of it now. I’ll save some for later but I want 75 of those keys by the day after tomorrow night at pier 51, 9:00 sharp and it has to be that good Columbian coke Roc gets, not that trash ya’ll be selling. It can’t move in my part of the city.”

“But that’s impossible!”

“Aaaahhh, nooooo.”

Lil Mac again heard Ms. Rich screaming.

“Did I hear you say, I got you Boggy?”

“All right, all right,” Lil Mac quickly answered.

“I know.”

Lil Mac was in a daze as he looked at his phone that was now dead. When Top Dollar spotted him he asked, “What’s on your mind young cannon? If it’s too heavy, let it go you dig. I’ll catch it.”

“They just changed the game in the ninth inning,” Lil Mac replied.

“Nah, it’s a go. We’re just waiting on you,” Top Dollar said, not knowing that he was speaking about the wrong game.

“No, Boggy got to D’s Mom.”

“What?”

“That’s what I said, now let’s get her back!”

As Fox pushed the Excursion pass a hundred miles in and out of traffic from New York back to Philly, Top Dollar, NayNay and Lil Mac came up with a plan. Inside the ranch Lil Mac dialed several numbers, "Hello House of Corrections Andrea speaking, how may I help you?"

"Yes I would like to speak with an inmate named Odell Miller please."

"I'm sorry, I can't do that sir visiting hours are from 8 to 5 Monday thru Friday. You'll have to speak with him then."

"Andrea, you don't understand, this is a life or death situation so if you would please put me through to your superior."

"Yes, and you're?"

"His brother," Lil Mac replied.

"Okay, please hold and someone will be right with you."

"Hello, this is Captain Rice. Your brother has spoken so highly of you; we're trying to locate him as we speak."

"Well what's taking so long, he's there right?" A long pause occurred as if the line went dead. Lil Mac looked at the phone as his thoughts ran wild. I know Roc didn't…then the answer came.

"Solo, what do you want? I'm about to get into the shower."

"Is that any way to talk to your brother," Lil Mac questioned.

"Listen, from now on I'm my own keeper, you want to be a man, so be it. Now say what you got to say."

"I'm moving the meeting up to tomorrow at 6pm at the docks pier 47," said Solo.

"You got all these demands and I don't know if Mr. Holmes is alive. Let me speak with him."

"Roc you don't run nothing! You'll hear from him when I get the work!" shouted Solo.

"Well, tell him I tried and when you're done…go tell Dad that room just got a new owner," Roc disconnected the phone as Boggy started the count down, "10…7… 5… 3… 2…1."

Roc's phone came to life, "Yes,"

"Roc he's on the line asking to speak with you again."

"Okay Rice, put him through."

"Yeah?" Roc answered as the phone was connected to Solo.

"Roc?"

"Mr. Holmes? Is anyone listening?"

"No, I'm fine," he answered.

"Watch your top, a double reverse is in play," said Roc.

"No don't give the young punk nothing but shots to the face," responded Mr. Holmes as Solo yelled, "Give me that damn phone," and snatched it away from a shackled Mr. Holmes whose left eye was closed shut from when Top Dollar caught him trying to escape from the yacht.

"You satisfied?" Solo asked Roc.

"Yeah, I will meet you. But for you to get all that butter we'll have to do it like this." Roc filled Lil Mac in on how and where they would meet as he and Boggy made their way out the back door to their car.

Inside, the sound of Tupac's words, "*I couldn't help but notice your pain...my pain? It runs deep, share it with me. They'll never take me alive I'm gettin' high with my four-five cocked on these suckers, time to die. Even as I was a youngster causin' ruckus on the back of the bus. I was a fool all through high school kickin' up dust, but now I'm labeled as a trouble maker who can you blame"* were playing in the background as Roc bobbed his head getting back into his nature that only these streets could respect and understand.

Boggy interrupted his thoughts, "Roc, you know you didn't have to come with me. I got into this one on my own."

"Don't ever think that, I was always with you."

"That's real." Looking through the rearview mirror for the tenth time making sure there was no mistaking what he's just witnessed, Boggy stated, "You still keep a lot of attention on you."

"Where?" asked Roc, leaning his seat back to get a better view of his mirror. Four cars back, the all black – quarter to eight…BMW. It's been on us for twenty minutes but I'm going to lose him right now!"

"Not him."

"Watch."

"No, pull over," Roc said.

"You do know that they're cops right?" Boggy questioned.

"No, this is bigger than that. This fish isn't going to bite the bait; you will have to force it in his mouth."

"If you say so," Boggy looked at Roc while thinking of all the weapons and the time they would get before asking, "Are you sure?"

"Boggy, I know we've been apart for some time but it's me sitting here with you now dawg, Roc…and I have never let you down. So park this thing so that I can show you this game on the next level up close."

Boggy pulled to a stop alongside of the busy highway. Hopping out of the car with Boggy shortly behind him, Roc waved the BMW to keep approaching. "I believe we have been made boss."

"Well let's not keep the young, rich, son of a bitch waiting." The car eased beside Roc as the window dropped halfway.

"Special Agent Branson, I knew that was you back there."

"Oh you did, did you?"

"Yeah, I smelled a little pig…you know being aware of my surroundings at all times. I could tell it was in the air," Roc said.

"That's good, I guess your nose is going to have to get use to my scent because I'm watching you!"

"You know, we really don't have to go through this. I've been thinking about what you said before you set me up."

"Yes, I really underestimated your power dearly in this city. Nobody becomes free until I say and yet here you stand, three months early. But I promise you that it will never happen again," said Agent Branson while locking eyes with Roc.

"I hope it will not come to that, I just need 94 hours to find out what you asked for in order to clear my name. But for me to do that I need for you to give my shadow its space and close your eyes to whatever they see until the end of those hours…then we can talk."

"And what if I said no and decide to bust your ass right now?!" Agent Branson's door came ajar needing to know Roc's answer. Boggy went for his twin 45 automatics, pulling them out from behind his back. Agent Branson stepped out of the car with his eyes on Boggy as his partner did the same. He said, "I wouldn't do that if I were you."

"Why, do you think you're faster than me?" Boggy responded with a smile.

"Roc, tell him to stand down."

"Why would I do that? You asked a question and that's your answer. As you can see, jail is not an option. Plus my friend here needs to keep his word in like…" Roc checked his new Aqua Master watch, "15 minutes right?"

"Twenty, your watch is always fast," corrected Boggy.

Roc continued, "But it's your call Agent Branson."

"Roc you know I can agree and then in ten minutes after you leave, have the FBI, CIA, DEA, and Secret Service on your ass along with your picture on a news update on America's Most Wanted."

"Don't forget about your backup parked three cars back," added Roc.

"You really think you have it all figured out?"

"No, but some of it and that's why I need the time," Roc stated.

"Well you better. Right now you're holding two pair in a game you can't fold with trips showing."

"Well at least I have a boat."

"Funny, just make sure you don't drown because a second after your time…I'm letting the dogs go."

Agent Branson and his partner pulled off with another car following right behind them.

Back in the car Boggy asked, "What was that all about?"

"I think I just bought a piece of the Knicks."

"Man you're still playing mind games with people," stated Boggy.

"If I didn't, it would be no fun. But the question is, are you ready?" Roc asked.

"You know it's ride or die with me."

Roc switched the CD to track one and turned up the volume. As the words echoed through the speakers, *"When I was five years old, I realized there was a road at the end I will win lots of pots of gold."* Roc started to sing along with Kool G Rap on the Road to the Riches, "*They were for kind of fiends bringin jackets and jeans Magazines, anything, just to hustle for beans."*

"What…you not feeling Pac no more?" asked Boggy.

"It's not that, I love Pac, he reminds me of the struggle. But now I don't need to be reminded because it has returned. So I need the music I had when I mastered it," Roc replied.

Boggy witnessed that inflamed look in Roc's eyes that returned with each word he spoke. "Oh shit he's back!" Boggy shouted.

"I never left," Roc smiled before saying, "Make a right on this next corner and then a left at the light and park."

"Roc we only have ten minutes to make it to the spot before we miss him."

"I hear you but sometimes you have to make the hunted come to the hunter." Boggy just shook his head as he watched Roc exit the car smoothing out his Kenneth Cole attire. He felt that Roc of all people should know that to a real man, his word was everything. Thinking to himself, Boggy thought, *"If we're not gone from here in ten, I'm going by myself."*

He followed Roc through the double glass doors. They stopped at the front desk where a man in a black and white tuxedo said, "Welcome to Carlo's gentlemen. How may I help you?"

"Reservations for two under Miller," answered Roc. The man checked the list, a look of surprise showed upon his face because two black men were permitted to be on the VIP list.

"Yes, here it is. Lou, please give these men two blazers. What color would you like?"

"Black," Roc answered.

Carlo's was a five-star restaurant with two of the best chefs on the east coast. Their service was rated by Food World as the best for the last three years. The live entertainment that they provided was singers from all over the world. At Carlo's, it took years to get on the waiting list if you didn't know anyone. So as Roc and Boggy moved through the place to be seated in a large booth in the back, the whispers filled the air from people trying to find out who they were. The waiter placed two bottles of champagne on the table, one in front of them both. "These are the two best we have, enjoy."

As soon as the waiter walked off, Boggy started to talk, "Roc, do you…"

Another waiter appeared at that moment, "Will you two gentlemen be ordering appetizers or are you ready for your meals?"

"Yes, I would like your Chef d'oeuvre pasta and duck with garlic and a little bit of lemon sauce. Make sure that my noodles are al dente," Roc requested.

"And you sir?" the waiter asked Boggy.

"I'll have the same damn thing, now if you don't mind giving us some privacy!" Boggy said, waiting for the man to walk far enough away from the table before he asked, "Roc why did you bring me here?"

"Because I was hungry," he replied.

"Do you know who owns this place?" Boggy said in disbelief that Roc brought him there.

"Yes, Carlo's."

"No, the power…who really owns it?"

"No, who?" asked Roc with a puzzled look on his face.

"Oh my God, help me!" Boggy shook his head as he continued, "This is Martin Castillo's place."

"You don't say…the mob boss!"

"Yeah Roc, let's blow this spot. I know their cameras are on us as we speak. We're the only black people in here!" Boggy once again looked over the entire room.

"Be easy, we don't have any beef with them. And for him to disrespect me while I'm eating, he's going to need his boss's boss to sign off on that." They both laughed knowing that the statement was true.

"But I do have beef with them, when we were on the outs I took over three blocks on their side of town and I don't think they like it too much. The kid Joey tried to bring me a move," Boggy explained.

"I remember because I was there."

"You were? How do you…never mind," Boggy just smiled and then looked at his watch. He pulled out his phone and dialed. "Bo, did our man show yet?"

"No one has come or gone. It's deserted as we speak but if it changes I'll hold it down," Bo answered.

"Well I'm on my way. If he shows before I get there, detain him."

A half hour later Roc and Boggy just finished enjoying their meal when as if on cue, four large Italian men in suits stepped up next to their table. "Excuse me fellas, Mr. Castillo will see you now." Boggy saw them approaching through the corner of his eye but kept looking at Roc not to tip them off that they'd been made. As soon as the words left the man's lips, both of Boggy's palms were filled with steel.

He looked to Roc for a sign to fire but instead he heard him say, "Well I'm ready to see him also."

It wasn't those words that made Boggy become relaxed, it was that look in Roc's eyes. The same look he had before he shot Ron G and many others. Knowing that he had an ace in the cut and when given the chance it always proved to be deadly. Boggy slowly release his guns then exited the booth. He straightened out of his jacket and said, "I know we are." They smoothly moved from the restaurant into the kitchen and then entered a room through a side door off to the right. The area was a large living room with wall-to-wall carpeting. There were several paintings that covered the walls that Boggy couldn't identify but just by their structure and design he knew they were worth a lot. There were four men seated, one on each side of the large round table that sat in the middle of the room prepared for six.

"I'm glad to see that you gentleman could make it this evening. Now come, have a seat and make yourself comfortable," said Mr. Castillo with a smile and his arms open wide. Roc took his seat on the left but Boggy remained standing with his back to the wall right next to Roc's side.

"I guess you prefer to stand."

Boggy never answered, he just stayed quiet.

"Suit yourself. Roc as you may or may not know this is Jimmy 'The butter knife' out of North Philly to my right. On my left is Sammy Frego of West Philly and at the head of the table is my boss the head Capo out of New York, Don Anitgeo."

"Don, nice to see you again, I'm sorry it had to be like this," Roc stated.

"Oh it's understandable, business is business whether it's good or bad. It has to take place for everyone to continue production," Don said.

"That brings us to the reason that I called this meeting," said Castillo, standing to his feet and pacing around the room as he continued, "I do believe there is a situation with my cousin's son Joey and you've taken possession of three blocks on his side of town. May I ask what you have to say about that?"

"Excuse me Mr. Cas..." Boggy started to step up and say it was him that took possession of the blocks but Roc stopped him with the wave of his hand and said, "Do you like to say that?"

"Pardon me?" asked Mr. Castillo.

"I said 'Do you like to say that?'" Roc repeated.

"I don't understand…do I like to say what?" questioned Castillo as he started to become visibly angry.

"Your side of town. You say it with such ease and confidence like you fought to have all those pretty stores, speakeasies and number houses turning all that money hand over fist!" Roc answered.

"Yes, if that is your concern, there were many beloved lives lost in war for us to hold the position we now have in this city," stated Don Antigeo. Roc shot up to his feet as his fist slammed down on the table.

"What? Battle…maybe, but there is no war in the Tri-State until you fight me. Up until now, I felt that it would have been unproductive to have your people be forced to buy from a race they couldn't identify with, which means we wouldn't have their loyalty. So for it to work I would have to make them fear me. That would bring unwanted attention which isn't needed but as I stand here I feel it may be worth it."

"How dare you come in here in front of the Don raising your voice in this disrespectful manner with your foolishness?"

Castillo stepped around the table to face Roc who drop stepped when the Don spoke, "Men this is uncalled for. Roc is a man. He has the right to say what he feels. Of course, that doesn't mean it's true. Plus it's much easier said than done. We must understand that as men, we work under certain rules and if violated, people will die. Castillo you are my boss of this city am I correct?" The Don asked.

"Yes," he replied.

"And there is no way one of your capos would disobey a safety order on his own am I right again?"

"Yes boss," answered Castillo, wondering where this question was going.

"Well, we'll see…Jimmy." On call, Jimmy one of the four men that entered with Roc went to a walk-in closet as another one posted up at the door. Boggy moved his hand into the center of his back when Roc tapped his leg and shook his head no. Jimmy returned with a tied up unconscious Joey strapped in a rolling chair. "Wake him!" demanded the Don.

Jimmy squared off letting a crashing blow connect with Joey's chin. Joey was dazed and asked, "Where am I?" Now Boggy understood why his man didn't show but what he didn't know is what Roc had to do with all of this.

"Seeing that you're now up, I have a few questions for you and please answer them truthfully because I would hate to use this." Don removed a 14-karat gold twelve inch knife from his double-breasted suit jacket. "You know this is the very same knife I killed Al, the last Don with and your blood will cover it next if I hear a lie. Who was it that told you to call the meeting with Boggy?"

"That was my call Don, only me."

"Wrong answer!" The knife made a smooth swish sound as the Don brought it through the air deep into Joey's leg.

"Aaaahhhhhh!"

"Now who gave you the knowledge of how to contact the three assassins you had on site?"

"That was easy, I used them before."

With a smile, the Don pushed the knife into the lower left side of Joey's chest and left it there. He said, "Another lie! This is your last chance to save your life from me."

"But uncle, it's me!"

"I know Joey, that's why I'm giving you this choice, if you don't want to take it…so be it." The Don slowly withdrew the blade as blood dripped from end to end and placed it on Joey's jugular vein.

"Alright, alright…Castillo gave the order! He said ain't no chicken-eating moolie going to own no territory on our side of town, safety pact or not."

Everybody looked at Castillo who was sweating profusely and said, "He's lying Don, don't you see that. You damn near had to kill the bastard for him to say my name!"

"Is that so?"

"Do you have to ask Don, you know I have never questioned your leadership? I follow my orders as well as if not better than anyone," Castillo said while approaching the Don and standing before him. He proceeded, "I can't believe my loyalty is in question from the words of a soldier on his death bed and I won't allow it." Castillo pulled out a chrome 9 mm from his waistline as Jimmy, Sammy, and Boggy drew on him. The Don held out his hand to receive the weapon as Castillo looked from him back to Joey while his trigger hand shook, aimed at Joey's face.

"Give me the gun and I'm only going to ask once," demanded the Don.

Castillo thought, *"I could kill this snitch and that nigger that started this shit before Jimmy could get a shot off."* Castillo cut his eye at Boggy and he saw the look of ambition to bring death. Quickly he let the gun fall into the Don's palm. On a sign of a head nod Jimmy opened fire, followed by Sammy leaving several holes in the frame of Castillo. The Don opened the door and three men rushed in with a large duffle bag. They removed plastic and cleaning products from it and went to work. Boggy recognized them as the three men that held him at gunpoint at Joey's.

"I don't know why it took him so long to tell me something I already know, right gentlemen?" Don asked the three-men assassin team as they finished wrapping up Castillo's body. "I never did lie to you when you were a kid Joey and I'm not going to start now. So, I'm not going to kill you. Boggy, Roc said you're a real man now. Keep your word. He's all yours. There's a room off to the side if you want to have some fun."

Within a second, Boggy had both of his 45 automatics in hand firing one shot after another. The force from each impact sent Joey rolling across the floor, stopping at the back wall lifeless. "That won't be necessary," Boggy replied.

"Well, please follow me," the Don asked as they entered into his office. "Now, that that's out of the way. Roc how is the club doing?" asked the Don.

"Very well"

"I bet it is. You know I named that club right?" The Don asked Boggy, who was shocked to see how friendly the Don has been while talking with Roc. It was like they were old friends.

"No I didn't," Boggy replied.

"Yeah that was me, Soldi is Italian for money. I know you don't think he came up with that?"

"So ya'll know each other?" asked Boggy.

"Who me and Mr. Miller here? Oh yeah, we've been friends for years. Not only that but his father and I used to gang war against each other until we got tired of fighting and we became friends. So when he told me about your situation I promised to get to the bottom of it and you were right. I kept my word and you never have to worry about those two anymore. Now it's your turn!"

"Like I said, my men will be off of your block by tomorrow at sunset," Roc said.

"See, there are still some things in life that all you have to do is ask for." They started to laugh.

24

At 5:54pm, six minutes before drop off time, Fox was moving through a crowd in section C of the 76ers game. As he fought to find his seat he said, "Daz I don't like this at all. With all these people in here we can't tell if it's a set up or not."

"You don't think they feel the same way? That's why Roc had the drop off broken up into different public places."

"It's deeper than that with him," answered Fox.

"Then what is it?"

"I don't know but the first sign of a wrong move and I'm gong to let this thing go wild out in public." Fox flashed his new chrome 9 mm.

"I thought I told you to leave that in the car," Daz asked.

"I must not have heard you because if I did then I would have said you'd lost your damn mind. I don't care if Roc is in jail or in the ground…he's always got a trick in play."

"Fox just sit there, shut up and watch the game!"

"Man, fuck this game. A.I. doesn't even play for the Sixers no more. I don't know why Solo wouldn't just let me go with him."

"Khaled please tell me you see something coming our way because this guy is getting on my last nerve," said Daz.

"Get your hot dog, soda," echoed in the background as Khaled responded.

"There was a couple, three rows behind you on your right with a big enough bag to hold that kind of work but it wasn't them. Don't worry though, I'm on everything." Khaled was positioned directly across from them on the opposite side in Suite A lying on the sofa with a cover over his body, looking through the digital scope of a super power 22 rifle with a silencer.

"Khaled you don't have to tell me nothing, the first wrong move it's on," said Fox.

"Hot dog, peanuts, sir would you like a hot dog or peanuts?" The sales man asked Daz.

"No thanks."

"And you sir, would you like anything?"

"Man do you got any Hennessey in that big ass box that they have you carrying around your neck in this bitch?"

"No sir, but I have Seagram's and classic cola, a lot of coke if you want it."

"Fox tell that salesman to keep it moving, I can't see to cover ya'll!" Khaled screamed into his mouthpiece.

"Did I ask for soda nigga?"

"No sir but…"

"But my ass, now get the hell out of my way I'm trying to watch the game also," as he sat next to Fox. Daz just shook his head in disappointment before he checked his watch. 8:05, thinking to himself, *"These cats better hurry up, Solo will call in five minutes to make sure our side of the deal went through."*

"Man…that was a foul. Referee blow your damn whistle!" screamed Fox as he jumped up out of his seat protesting the no call.

A man asked, "Issuallah young soldier. Would you take your seat so that I can see the game also?"

"Here, get you hot dog and peanuts, sir would you like some popcorn?"

"I said no!" stated Fox while he remained standing before turning to the man. "Issua…what man? I'll stand anywhere I damn well please. So unless you got a bomb on Habib, I'll move when I feel like it."

"Fox who are you talking to, I can't see because the salesman is in the way again," asked Khaled.

"Is that right?" the man questioned.

"Yeah with out a doubt," replied Fox, moving his leather jacket back to let his hand rest on his gun.

Seeing the swift move, the man turned his head while dropping his eyes to the floor. Fox noticed the retreat out of fear and he relaxed and turned his attention back to the game. Just how Mohammed knew he would do, like so many people would take the victory of a small battle only to die in the war. Mohammed was on his feet with his massive thumb and two fingers locked onto Fox's throat. The motion was so quick that it caught Daz off-guard and he screamed, "Oh shit!" as he jumped up to help.

"Daz what's going on?" Khaled asked. Getting no response from Daz, he yelled again, "What's happening…here I come!"

He left the rifle and cocked back his 380 and took off out the door. "Let's not make this into a scene, he's not going to kill him he's just going to teach him a quick lesson." Daz looked down at the gun that the salesman handled that was hidden in his pinstriped vest. Then his phone rang. "Answer that, it's probably your boss…asking about these." The salesman removed the top roll of hot dogs showing over ten sealed keys.

Mohammed eased Fox back down into his seat and said, "Listen killer, Allah promised that every man on his earth must taste death. So the next time you disrespect me I'm going to give you your meal ticket early. Mohammed saw that Fox's eyes were going up into the back of his head then he took his gun from him before releasing him.

"Hello," Daz answered his phone. "Daz how are things on your end?"

"They're in sight and once Fox gets his self back together and tests them we'll be in route. I'll hit you back then!"

Mohammed passed a black latex bag over to Fox that contained five keys. "Hurry up back."

Daz and Khaled locked eyes from a distance as Khaled stood in the section entrance. He caught the message to back off as Fox walked past him as if he didn't know him. Khaled dipped into the crowd going back out the way he came when the feeling that he was being watched came over him. He stepped away from the crowd as his eyes moved around, searching his surroundings. Not noticing anything he headed to his suite.

Fox stepped out from the restroom wearing a pinstriped hat with matching vest and then rushed back to his seat.

"What is it?" asked Daz.

"The best," Fox replied.

"Now you can take this and carry it around your neck in this bitch." Shamone said to Fox. After making sure that the product was all there, they were led out into the parking lot through the service exit to their van when Mohammed checked the time, 8:15.

"Make the call now," he said.

"Solo, mission complete."

"Okay, now do as we planned." Pulling out into traffic, they never spotted the two cars that were following them.

At the same time, forty miles away in a private airport, NayNay sat in the last booth in a café with her back to the wall sipping a fresh cup of vanilla cappuccino. She watched the movement of a fair crowd closely through her Versace glasses while awaiting her next instructions. As the minutes passed, NayNay finished off her third cup as she became impatient. She checked her watch for the tenth time when a man walked by and slid a note onto her table without stopping.

NayNay secured the letter before looking up at the man who seemed to have just vanished. Opening it, she read it in a low whisper tone, "Meet me in five minutes at the entrance of hanger seven alone. This should give you enough time beautiful, to get rid of the two men that are three tables down from you on the left."

"Fatel and AP, that's you, I'll see you in a second."

"Are you sure?" asked Fatel with a newspaper over his face looking as if he was reading it while speaking into the two way receiver that they all had built into their shirts, glasses, and jacket.

"I said leave, you've been made. This is for D's mom and you're not going to mess this up now go!" demanded NayNay before she continued to read the message. "Next, turn your head counter clockwise to your right and stop at seat 16, there is a man in a red hat reading a book, remove him. Then and only then, wait for me."

"Lance, you hear that?" NayNay asked.

"Yeah, I'm out," Lance answered.

"Ayzo I guess that just leaves me and you."

"Don't worry I'm in motion there now." NayNay exited the booth and left a twenty dollar bill. She headed toward hanger seven. When she was about 30 feet away from it, she made eye contact with Ayzo before he disappeared down into the hanger. Now 15 feet away she unbuttoned her coat to give her access to her concealed weapon.

The same man reappeared locking his arm into hers, swiftly changed direction and said, "I knew he was with you, I couldn't really tell but he must have military training in his background. Don't be concerned, he's in good hands now."

"Excuse me; I would like to know where you're taking me," NayNay asked.

"Out to dinner if you would let me, but for now down the hall to your left in hanger two."

NayNay maintained her pace while looking around to see if anyone of her teammates had changed their clothes and were back on her tail for back up. "Excuse me miss, here goes your receipt and your luggage," said a man who was about six feet tall and 185 pounds. He was in a red cap and uniform.

"No there must be a mistake," NayNay replied.

"You're Ms. Jones right?"

"Yes, I mean no…how did you know? What's going on?"

"Just take it," the man insisted, as he pulled on her arm tired of seeing that puzzled look on her face.

"Thank you sir, I almost forgot…they are my bags. I don't know what came over me."

"You're welcome Madam." The man in the red cap left his hand open in the air.

"Oh here you go," NayNay handed him twenty dollars. "It's only right you get money right, why can't I?"

Speechless, NayNay took the large bag on wheels and kept walking until M. Easy stopped at a restroom and released her arm. "Now make sure it's what you came for." Inside, NayNay opened every stall making sure that she was alone and then put the trash can against the door.

"Fatel, I'm in possession of the work, on my way to hanger two. Have someone cover me."

"All right, it's there. They're waiting," he replied.

NayNay went back out into the hallway.

"How was everything?"

"To my liking," she replied. "But there is only twenty here..." NayNay's phone rang stopping her as she was talking.

"If I were you I would answer that."

"Like I wasn't going to," she responded.

"Oh an aggressive one, I like that in a woman," M. Easy said, looking over her whole body once again and slowly licking his lips. "Yeah, I like that."

Rolling her eyes, NayNay answered her phone on the fourth ring, "Hello."

"NayNay you alright?"

"I'm fine."

"And the other thing?"

"The cake tastes good but it's only two thirds of the way done. I'll touch you back in ten."

"NayNay."

"Yes, Solo?"

"You be careful, things are going too good to be true."

"If you only knew the half," NayNay ended the call with M. Easy locking arms with her again as they walked right past hanger two. "Where are you taking me?"

"Anywhere you would like to go. For now make this left." They stopped twenty yards down the hall in front of a man with a black and white suit and Mexican color banner wrapped around his chest and shoulder.

"Pardon me sir, my name is..."

"M. Easy, I know."

"I wasn't going to say that but how..."

"Cut it out, you haven't been in America that long to forget me."

As the man removed his dark sunglasses, M. Easy quickly realized it was his old friend.

"Delacure."

"You know it!" They embraced.

"Man what are you doing on plane post?"

"I lost another bet to El Sovida," they started laughing.

"Is the situation ready?"

"Yes and the crew is waiting on you." Delacure unhooked the velvet rope to let them through.

"After you my pretty lady," said M. Easy as NayNay started down the steps.

Delacure pulled M. Easy to the side, "Watch yourself, there are ten top Le Eme in your city as we speak, waiting on the word. So you must win your bet."

"No worries my friend, I will."

On the all white Jet, M. Easy sat on the cream leather sofa and pulled out the remaining bags from over his seat and passed them to NayNay who sat across from him. She pulled her phone out, "Yeah Solo, I have it."

"There never was a moment of doubt, now meet up with Daz and get that ready for our meeting while I handle my end."

"I'm on it."

After the phone call NayNay packed the product away and started to get up.

"I wouldn't do that if I were you."

Falling back into her seat from the force of the plane taking off she yelled, "I know we're not moving!"

"Yes, do you think we have become the best not to know how to put space between us and the six lames that you have up there waiting on you?" M. Easy said.

"Then may I ask where we're going?"

"Just across town to the Philadelphia airport where my connections at customs will have a van ready with a concealed spot to transport your work."

NayNay slid her hand onto the handle of her 9 mm and said, "You better."

25

At 8:15, outside of pier 54 on a quiet night which seemed to be abandoned, a Chris-craft Catalina cruiser moved through the water approaching the dock.

"Ayzo, take us on in, it's time," said Solo before exiting the control room and stepping down onto the lower deck. "Top Dollar I just spoke with NayNay and they're on."

"Now we must play our part to make sure D's soul rests in peace, you dig. Mall, if you don't stop moving," said Top Dollar as he duct taped the handle of the sixteen-shot pump that was wrapped to the neck of an unconscious Mr. Holmes to the hands of Mall.

"My bad Top, but he's going to die anyway right?"

"He must, for he is too powerful for anyone of us to truly feel safe if he is alive. But for now he is worth more alive." Top Dollar applied the last piece of tape.

"Well, let's wake the money man up. It's time to rewrite the history of this city starting with the death of Boggy," said Solo, checking the ammo on his twin Mack 11. Top Dollar brought the smelling salt to the nose of Mr. Holmes.

"What the hell!" Mr. Holmes yelled.

"Calm down O.G. it's only me. The reason you're like this is due to your last disappearing act and if this deal goes sour you will die sooner rather than later."

"Let's move Top, it's about that time," Solo stated, heading for the steps.

"Listen kid, don't do this. We can find a level of understanding in all of this…you young maggot! I won't let your disrespect for me make my anger override the love I have for Roc. So again, as men I ask you to walk away now and go to college like your brother wants and make something of yourself. If not for yourself then do it so that the blood, sweat and tears that your father and brother dropped in these streets won't be for nothing," pleaded Mr. Holmes.

"O.G. believe me, it could never be for nothing. See, I'm the new beginning of the dying breed with the blood of my brother running through these veins. It's that same blood that refused to let my father then my brother and now me surrender or retreat in these streets. It's just a shame that my time had to overlap into Roc's run."

With that stated, Solo made his way to the upper deck followed by Top Dollar who said, "If we don't call for you within a half hour, something went wrong and you know what to do."

Meanwhile, off in the distance, looking through a pair of binoculars from a third floor office window in a warehouse. Roc was paying close attention to their every move as they exited the boat. Speaking into the wireless mouthpiece Roc said, "Men, our guests have just arrived so let's make sure they feel right at home."

"Are you ready?" Roc asked Mohammed who was looking out of the window next to him.

"Always." he replied.

The sight of Lil Mac double checking his ammo on his two guns before approaching the warehouse entrance forced Roc to finally accept the fact that his once beloved brother had now become his true arch enemy. "How did I not see this before hand?" Roc said to himself before stepping away from the window and taking a seat in the all black leather chair that was posted in front of eight surveillance monitors.

Roc hit the power button just as the vision of Manny and Raja leading Solo with Top Dollar and Ayzo bringing up the rear to watch his back. They stopped at a table lined with 25 keys of cocaine. "Look at this Lil nigga, walking with this look of confidence on his face like he's got it all figured out and he doesn't know the half of it." Roc slammed his fist down on the desktop and stood up quickly. "I've seen enough of this shit!"

Mohammed saw what was about to take place and went into action cutting Roc off at the door. "Move Mohammed, this Lil boy is playing a game he's not ready for!"

"I know that as well as you but telling him wouldn't change anything. His soul needs to see that he's not ready, Issuallah that will be enough."

"Mohammed you were right, I just spotted Mr. Holmes, he's in the cabin in bad shape but alive. I can only see two men from my position. Do you want me to go in for a closer look," Shamone stopped in the middle of his sentence as he eased back into the water. Through the waves he watched a man with a 12 gauge shotgun walk the boat's perimeter.

"Negative, do you copy? Stay still, I'm on my way."

"Mmmmhhh," Shamone moaned. Mohammed turned to face a steamed Roc.

"Listen, I lost my brother in Iraq on a street that I couldn't name and I'll be damned if I let you lose yours in a city that we own. So you sit right there and watch Manny play his part while I bring the Don home." Mohammed placed a black mask over his face that matched his all black wet suit. He opened the window and dropped out the CP 320 safety line and quickly disappeared down the side of the building.

"Issuallah, you're right Mohammed," Roc whispered back at his desk. He turned up the volume hearing Lil Mac say, "Okay, the product is good but where the hell is the rest of it?"

"We met you halfway now you meet us in the middle by putting Mr. Holmes in sight," Manny demanded.

"That's only fair," said Lil Mac.

"Mohammed watch your back, you've got company coming your way," yelled Roc.

Lil Mac slid away from the table and headed for the door. He made eye contact with Buff who turned to unlock the door. In that second, Lil Mac released his guns from his waistline and spun around aiming at Manny's head.

"Oh shit, I didn't see that coming," said Roc looking into the monitor.

"Now that I think about it, that wouldn't be a good idea," said Lil Mac. All five men on the second floor along with Buff and Raja had their guns locked on Solo and his team.

"If I turn over Mr. Holmes, who's to say that you wouldn't just try to take him. We're already overpowered and outnumbered so if it's my time to go…I prefer to go out a shooter. Now you call it!"

Roc watched on in shock at the show of heart that Lil Mac displayed as he and Top Dollar stood back to back with Ayzo at the tip as if they were in a triangle. "Damn that's one of my moves," Roc said out loud.

"Okay, I'll call it. Buff," Manny gave a light head nod and Buff disappeared through two double doors and reappeared with a big duffle bag. He dropped it at Manny's feet and Manny placed it on the table to show the remaining bricks.

"Now if you don't mind lowering your guns that makes me nervous."

"Mohammed you got to make it quick, they'll be there shortly," said Roc.

"Copy that," responded Mohammed while he laid on the deck up against the wall waiting patiently for the man who was twenty feet away and approaching slowly. As the man passed, Mohammed wrapped the black rope tightly around his legs and pulled back forcefully. The man fell to the ground as Shamone came from over the side of the boat placing his Rambo style knife into the back of the man's neck.

Down on the lower deck, Mall asked Mr. Holmes, "Did you hear that?"

"Hear what? I haven't heard anything, I think it's time to stop smoking those brown cigarettes," answered Mr. Holmes.

"Well it better not be anything because if it is, I'm going to love blowing your top off!"

"I bet you would, you young faggot!"

Outraged, Mall screamed, "Shut up and walk!" He then pushed Mr. Holmes up the steps as he pulled his 38 special out with his free hand. On the upper deck Mall heard the sound of splashing water on the opposite side of the boat. "Keith, is that you?" questioned Mall while moving in the direction of the noise.

"Mohammed someone's coming," Shamone said, quickly returning to his hiding spot. Once again bracing himself firmly on the third step of the ladder that hung off the side of the cruiser, Mohammed rolled smoothly back into the shadow of darkness. Mr. Holmes led the way around the corner of the deck. When he didn't see Keith, he remembered the words, "A double reverse." His eyes rapidly searched for any sign of an escape. Shamone eased his face up to the rim of the boat waiting with his knife in hand for Mohammed to make his move.

"Keep it moving old man," Mall screamed to a paused Mr. Holmes while tightening his grip on the handle of the shotgun. They were four feet away coming at a steady pace.

Mohammed opened his eyes slowly sliding his hand out into the path as the sound of Shamone whispering, "Hold your position," entered his ear followed by water splashing off in the opposite direction.

"Now what was that? Keith you better not be out here playing games!" yelled Mall while turning Mr. Holmes around to follow the sound. As soon as Mall's feet were planted facing the other way, Shamone's body was in the air with his eyes locked on its mark. He knew he had to strike at the exact moment his feet touched base or Mr. Holmes was as good as dead. Quiet as the air itself, Mohammed rolled from off the ground as Shamone's left hand sliced apart the duct tape on Mall's right wrist while in the same powerful motion, with just the right precision Shamone cut Mall's neck open from ear to ear.

Mall remained standing for close to four seconds until Shamone told Mr. Holmes, "You can walk now."

Mr. Holmes stepped forward letting Mall's body crash to the ground. Mr. Holmes quickly ripped the remaining tape from his body. He then grabbed the knife out of Shamone's hand, bent down and said, "This is what you were going to do to me." With each stroke, he cut deep into Mall's neck until his head became free. Mr. Holmes lifted it up to eye level. "You always look a man in the eyes before you kill him."

Before tossing him off into the water, he placed the 38 special in his waistline while taking the 12 gauge with two hands, cocking it back and said, "Show me the way, I need to teach a young man a very important lesson."

"Mohammed, are you clear? If not get out of there, they're coming!" demanded Roc.

"Shamone get Mr. Holmes out of here now while I stay and handle the rest of the plan."

"I'm not going anywhere," screamed Mr. Holmes.

"I know, I'm sorry," said Mohammed.

"What are you sorry for?" asked Mr. Holmes. Without warning, Mohammed knocked Mr. Holmes upside his head with the back of his gun. That put him out cold. "For that," he said. Shamone threw Mr. Holmes over his shoulder and went down the ladder. He placed Mr. Holmes softly into the back of a Nitro 911 COC boat with a silent king cobra engine. They raced off into the night.

With Enyce backpacks attached to their backs, they moved in sync with each step enforcing their triangle offense. Top Dollar and Ayzo's guns swung wildly from side to side in the front while Solo secured the rear. Once outside, they quickly dashed for the boat, each following their pre-plan escape route. Solo was the first to reach the cruiser and then Ayzo. "Retract the ropes!" Solo demanded as he took the steps that lead to the captain's box, two at a time. He started the engine with a push of a button. Just then, Top Dollar made it on board.

"What's going on?" Top Dollar questioned Ayzo who shrugged his shoulders. Top Dollar headed for the stairs, "Solo, why are you pulling off. We must keep our end of the deal?"

"Why would I do that?"

"Because you said you would."

"Yes… but when in Rome, we do as the Romans do and they lie to their enemies all the time, and he told me not to let him go."

"Is that so?" Top Dollar said in disbelief.

"Yes, it's his first lesson that a feared enemy must be crushed completely. Meaning he can't stay alive."

Solo pushed the throttle down past half mass making the boat jump forward slicing through the ocean waves.

"If you say so," Top Dollar knew the game. He was just disappointed that his old friend had to leave this world at the hands of him.

Yelling over the rail, Solo said to Ayzo who was watching the rear through his scope to make sure that they weren't being followed, "Go tell Mall to put the old man on that bus to hell with a pillow!"

Five minutes later, Ayzo returned, "Solo, they're gone!"

"Who?" Solo asked.

"Everyone, the boat's clear."

Solo shook his head from side to side knowing that Roc had done it again. A small smile escaped Top Dollar's face as he whispered, "Fight to live soldier, fight to live."

26

"How much time do we have left?" Roc asked M. Easy while he watched Dr. Woods stitch up the inside of an unconscious Mr. Holmes' mouth.

"One hour and fifty six minutes," M. Easy answered.

"And our flight?" inquired Roc.

"I don't know, let me ask the pilot." M. Easy removed himself from the soft cream leather chair.

He quickly returned as a voice came through the intercom, "Gentlemen, our remaining air time is approximately one hour, give or take ten minutes. Thank you."

"That leaves us 46 minutes to make a half hour ride," said Roc.

M. Easy turned to Dr. Woods and asked, "How long will those drugs you have him on, have him out?"

"About another 35 minutes, enough time for me to close the mid-size wound on the back of his neck," Dr. Woods replied.

M. Easy placed his hand lightly on Roc's shoulder and said, "Don't worry we'll make it. But for safety, just in case something does go wrong I placed 20 unseen men at your mother's house and as you know Gizelle is out of town. Lil Mac will be with Boggy at the time of the meeting so we're covered at all ends."

Roc remained silent with a blank facial expression as his soul cried inside for the pain that his mentor endured. Roc looked out the window watching the clouds pass by, hoping that once he got a chance to speak with Mr. Holmes that he could tell him his stay wasn't as bad as it looked. Mr. Holmes rested in a deep sleep from the medication. Relaxed, his mind started to travel to a safer place and time, thinking back to when he was sixteen.

~ · ~ · ~ · ~

The bell at St. Mary's private school had rung, announcing the end of the school day. Mr. Holmes loosened his dark blue tie and dashed for the exit. He was happy that it was Friday, the day that his father did his volunteer work at the local clinic ten blocks from the heart of North Philly. His father always gave him taxi fare but he refused to use it, thinking that he would miss something along the way. St. Mary's was located just outside the hood.

As Mr. Holmes would walk a few blocks, the pretty homes started to turn into abandoned ones. The quiet clean streets with waving neighbors transformed into crowded loud streets filled with prostitutes, pimps, hustlers, and gamblers. Mr. Holmes was captivated by these people because of the way that they talked, dressed, looked, and even down to the way that they moved. Making his way through the last seven blocks, Mr. Holmes would study them as if they were his favorite game, chess. Being that he was the school champion, the first thing he would do is divide the board into sections. Now he applied that same method with the blocks he saw. As he watched the pimps, he associated them with the bishop, they could only move in one direction due to the power of the hustler. But they moved in between everyone. The prostitutes were the pawns; the reason being is that they protected everyone. If the cops raided the block and found one of the hustler's products or tried to take down a pimp, a prostitute knew it was her job to step up and take the case.

The number runners were the rook, for it could move parallel and they knew to stay in their line due to retaliation from the hustlers. In this underworld, Mr. Holmes knew money moved everything, which made the hustlers as valuable in life as the queen. They moved anywhere they pleased. Finally, there was the King, who possessed the characteristics of every one of these individuals and more such as being loved, respected, and feared. Then there was the gangster Mr. Holmes, whose first name was Vernon who knew most of these people from the clinic. His memory relapsed to the day that he approached his sixth block, 5th and Brown.

As always, to him the air smelled different, the atmosphere alone would make his heart beat at a much more rapid pace than ever before. This action came, not from fear but ambition and passion for what he would get to know next. Sticking his chest out as he changed his walk, he dipped down the street. "Hey pretty boy, let me give you a night on the town that you will never forget," said Norma. She was a pretty love toy at 5'7", 120 pounds. She stood next to a parked car in a pair of red fishnet stockings and black spandex shorts that hugged her voluptuous ass tightly. Her white blouse was two sizes too small, which made it hard to conceal her perfectly round size D breast.

"Norma, if you charged by the hour I would take you up on that offer but I hate to see dough boy put his hands on you for coming up short with his coins," Mr. Holmes said.

"Boy, when you get a little older I'm going to make you man up to those words!" Norma teased.

"Yeah I know…one day I'm going to make you pay what you really make and not what you want," Holmes replied, leaving Norma staring back at him with a puzzled expression on her face.

"You dizzy bitch, I know you're not out here messing with the mind of my assistant pimp in training?" asked Dough Boy.

"You know I would never talk to another man without your permission!"

"You know better, now get your money maker on that track and get my money! Let's walk Vernon."

They talked while stopping in the middle of the block where a crap game was taking place. Mr. Holmes stayed off to the side watching everyone closely from their mouth down to their toes. Dough Boy was a smooth, super clean pimp that always matched from his hat to his shoes and actually believed in his heart that he was the second coming of Casanova, but only black. He worked the crowd with his charisma as he pulled out a large amount of money.

"Hey pretty Rome, lay something small then turn it tall and watch me take it all."

"Yeah we'll see, handle this hundred spot."

"What about you Goldie?" Dough Boy asked.

"You know I can't miss no sweet money baby, you digging me?" answered Goldie before placing five crisp twenty dollar bills.

Dough Boy continued to work the crowd. He hit a few numbers but missed mostly all of them. With all the hustlers and players attention, an upset Dough Boy called out, "Vernon!" while waving him over. When Mr. Holmes didn't come, he repeated the call, this time with more of a demand, "Vernon get over here!" People turned and looked to a scared Mr. Holmes who turned his head also, not seeing anyone behind him, he pointed to himself, "Me?"

"Yeah you," screamed Dough Boy when people parted, making a path as Mr. Holmes stopped next to him. "Listen kid, I need you to bring a touch of luck to a player for his buck." Dough Boy passed Mr. Holmes the green dice.

"But I don't know how!" said Mr. Holmes.

"Just shake them up and then throw 'em up against the wall."

"This sucker here can't be true," said D. Brown.

"Be smooth baby, let the lame play himself." said Goldie.

Dough Boy listened to all the whispers from the crowd while watching all his bets nearly double. Mr. Holmes' first shot was a winner along with his next five points. The crowd was shocked as he continued to shoot and win. After twenty minutes of gambling, people walked away from the game with their heads down in disbelief. Dough Boy stood counting $16,000 in profits as Slick Rick approached with a woman on each arm and spoke in a slow smooth tone asking, "Is the kid's arm on pause sucker?"

"Of course not, anything for you baby," Dough Boy answered while licking his lips as he looked at the woman on Slick Rick's arm.

"Nigga you're talking to me, not my bitch and what did I tell you hoe? Keep your gaze down to the ground when another pimp's around."

"I'm sorry Daddy."

"Shut up!" demanded Slick Rick. "Did I tell you to speak?" There was only silence. "That's better. Come now boy and let's shoot this money." Slick Rich pulled out a big knot of money and dropped it to the ground.

"It's Dough Boy nigga, not Boy and don't make me have to show you after I tell you again!"

Slick Rick and Dough Boy hated each other. They were the same high yellow tone with matching green eyes, which kept them in competition. "To hell with all of that, time is bread and I already made my sandwich so bet all that on one shoot."

Dough Boy looked down at the nice sized stack and estimated it to be about three grand, no more than four being that the top bill was a fifty, the rest would get lower. He slowly rubbed his hands together and smiled." Why not?" he patted Mr. Holmes on the back and said in his ear, "This is the very sucker we've been waiting on, so hit this seven in the door and we split the bread sixty-forty."

"Okay."

"Come on, are you going to let that kid shoot?" yelled Slick Rick.

"Yes I am," Dough Boy laughed, knowing that Slick's money was as good as his. A young Mr. Holmes shook the dice rapidly and then let them fly. They bounced off the wall, spinning with his usual touch and then stopped.

Dough Boy bent down and retrieved the money when Slick Rick demanded, "Count that and let it touch my hand as quick as it hit the ground." Slick Rick broke out in laughter. Dough Boy finally looked at the dice and could not believe his eyes as they laid on snake eyes. He quickly looked to Mr. Holmes who, with his head down shrugged his shoulders. Dough Boy started to count the money and then stopped to look Slick Rick in the eyes as he started to laugh even harder.

"It be like that sometimes, baby. You know you always got to count the money first."

Keeping his composure, Dough Boy played it off as if it was nothing. He looked at all the hundred dollar bills hidden behind the fifty dollar bill and said, "Be easy sucker, I make this like the government. You'll get yours." Dough Boy finished counting out Slick Rick's ten G's. Then he watched as he pulled off in his red Cadillac with most of the money he hustled for the day.

Once the car was out of sight, Dough Boy pulled Mr. Holmes to the side and asked, "What happened?"

"The dice got caught on my tooth when I went to switch them, but I just knew I would get him on the next shot."

"Don't worry about it kiddo, we'll get them next week across town. But that mistake will cost you a tenth of your share."

"How, when we still made $6,000?" Mr. Holmes questioned.

"No, I made $6,000 because it's my money on the line lame! So take this fifteen hundred and be happy."

"Thanks Dough Boy." Mr. Holmes continued to walk through his newfound world. About four blocks away from the clinic, he was stopped by a loud car horn.

"Hi Vernon."

Mr. Holmes eased into the passenger seat, "Damn baby, that plan you put together worked like my bottom bitch, brings back nothing but money," stated Slick Rick as he handed over the $17,000 while continuing, "I know that was a quick three G's I made, but ask Pistol Pete if he could do better than 70/30 this time."

Slick Rick pulled to the corner on the next block over. "Slick I'm just going to tell him you want to talk with him."

"Damn, I didn't say that!" Slick Rick said nervously as sweat appeared on his face. "Just slide in a good word Vernon."

"I will, I promise," Mr. Holmes said. The rest he thought to himself, *"If I ever meet him again myself."*

Mr. Holmes knew that in order for his plan to work, he had to use people's weaknesses as his strong point just like in chess. The fact that Dough Boy and Slick Rick hated each other along with them both making money off of him, gave even less of a possibility for them to talk. Then there was the situation of muscle, which was even easier. The pimps were scared of the hustlers but they absolutely feared the gangsters. With that knowledge, Mr. Holmes used the name of the most feared that he knew from the clinic and used it to his advantage. So when Slick Rick saw them talking together, he automatically thought that they were friends, making him the perfect vic.

Now, two blocks away he slowly approached a prostitute speaking to her John. "One more minute baby and I'm going to give you a time you will never forget, but I have to wait on my son."

"Well, he needs to hurry up doll or I'm going to have to float with that nice red bone over there." The John pointed across the street where a group of women stood waiting on work. Norma ran her hand over his manhood as she kissed his left ear and said into it, "Don't worry daddy, here he comes now." Norma broke away and rushed to hug her son.

"Baby, are you all right? I heard what happened at school today," said Norma.

"Yeah I'm fine." Lowering her voice she said, "L-R-F-P"

"Mom who is the man you're with?"

"Oh this is your uncle from down south."

"Nice to meet you uncle." After a handshake and a hard half hug he said, "Okay Mom I'll see you later."

"You got your homework baby?" Norma asked.

"Always!" he replied.

Walking away smiling, Mr. Holmes shook his head while counting the money and thinking of Norma's new special code L-R-F-P which stood for lower right front pocket. He crossed the street to a group of women.

"Betty give this to Norma, she'll be back in five minutes when her John can't pay."

Taking the money, Betty said, "Baby, Norma better keep you close because if she don't I'm going to take you from her. She can't possibly see what I see in you. I don't know what it is but it's there!"

"If you look closer you'll recognize it," replied Mr. Holmes.

"And what's that handsome?"

"A winner," he said before walking off without another word. Mr. Holmes cut through the alley that brought him on the same block of the clinic.

Mr. Holmes moved with a different outlook on his future when his smile returned from seeing his mentor. "How did the test go?" asked Billy D, who was one of the top conmen in the city and the fact that he was also a gangster didn't hurt at all.

"Great, I made five thousand!" Mr. Holmes cheerfully lied.

"I didn't ask you about the money because on a bad day, a dog can get a sucker out of a meal. I questioned your actions, what mistakes did you make?"

"None, I even picked the John's pocket off a half hug instead of the full contact, just like you showed me."

Billy D looked at his student closely to study his face, waiting for any change as he questioned, "So you're telling me there was no fail in your performance?"

"None!"

"You can lie with a straight face, that's good. But let me ask you this, how did you crap out on your biggest bet?"

"The dice just got caught on my teeth that's all," answered Mr. Holmes as he looked to the clinic door.

"Vernon! What did I tell you?"

"To always look a man in the eyes when you're speaking to him"

"And why is that?"

"Because if you're not man enough to look them in the face, then you shouldn't be in their presence," replied Mr. Holmes, now locking eyes with his mentor.

"That's better; do you know what made Ali the best fighter?"

"No Billy D, what?" Mr. Holmes was now all ears, knowing that precious jewels were about to be dropped.

"He is consistent in doing what it takes to win. If his right jab is working in the first round, know that he will continue to use that jab until he's got the sucker where he wants him. Then he would switch it up on the lame." Billy D threw two right jabs at Mr. Holmes who defended himself by knocking them down. Billy D. then faked the third. When Mr. Holmes went to knock it down he landed a semi-hard blow to his rib cage. "See, know this in life; for a good switch to work the change up has to be the same as its prototype. If it's off in anyway, to a real player you're next move will be telegraphic and it may cost you your life." Billy D paused so his words could sink in. "Do you know why I'm telling you this Vernon?"

Mr. Holmes searched his memory but came up empty, "No" he answered.

Billy D. opened his hand and said, "Pay it." Mr. Holmes quickly placed 25 twenty dollar bills in it. Billy D checked to make sure the price for Mr. Holmes missing a lesson was all there before he slid it into his silk jacket pocket and said, "You forgot to blow on the dice."

As the words rolled off of Billy D's tongue, Mr. Holmes closed his eyes and saw himself right back on the ground after Slick Rick dropped his money. As he checked for Dough Boy who was talking to Slick's bottom girl, he pushed back his right shirt sleeve slightly, letting another set of loaded dice drop into his palm before shaking them up and letting them hit the wall. Moving his head side to side in disappointment, Mr. Holmes asked, "So is that how you knew I pulled a move on Dough Boy?"

"Vernon every piece of game I give you is universal. So your move became telegraphic once Dough Boy stopped being consistent with your pay. Only a lame would keep taking that on the chin and I don't speak to lames. I just had to wait until you got the heart, which didn't take you long at all."

They hit fists and laughed before Billy D continued, "On the smooth youngin', you got what it takes to be the best and I would not have seen that flaw if I wasn't looking for it. You have a quick brain that allows you to think fast if something goes wrong while you're on stage. You're also book smart so once you become rich; you'll know what to do with it. Then today you showed me that you have the heart for revenge, that's the most important part. That's when your soul feels it's been dealt with unjustly, it screams to get even. In these three years I've been coaching you, that's one lesson that I couldn't teach you. This is why you are the knight."

"Yeah I'm the knight," replied Mr. Holmes.

"You're what?"

"I'm the knight!"

~ · ~ · ~ · ~ · ~

"What are you saying?" asked Roc while shaking Mr. Holmes back to reality. Upon opening his eyes, Mr. Holmes threw two hard right jabs at Roc's chin that Roc slipped with ease.

"You young punk!" Mr. Holmes faked his next jab that Roc went for as he slammed a left hook to Roc's body and followed it with an overhand right that slammed into Roc's eye. M. Easy quickly wrapped his arms around Mr. Holmes who was still trying to swing.

"Let him go! He's been through enough."

At the sound of Roc's voice, Mr. Holmes stopped fighting as he adjusted his eyes to his surroundings. "Roc, is that you?"

"Who else would come save you and then put you in an Armani suit at the same time?" Roc answered.

Mr. Holmes took in his appearance; the double-breasted drake brown suit with the vest to match went just right with a caramel button up shirt and tie. The elephant shoes were so soft he could fold them up and place them in his pocket.

Raising his head, Mr. Holmes stared Roc dead in the eyes with a look of hate and asked, “Did you kill him?”

Ashamed of his answer, Roc lowered his eyes before shaking his head no.

“Of course not and I wouldn’t want you to, he’s family. But you need to talk to him before someone else does,” said Mr. Holmes. “Don’t worry; I have someone on it as we speak.”

“Oh I’m not.” Roc ran down everything that took place in the last 48 hours. Mr. Holmes, who after a long pause said, “Get my cream hat; I have a meeting to attend.”

27

Solo paced back and forth in a once clean living room. Now there was glass everywhere from the large flower vase that he slammed into the sixty-inch flat screen TV. The two black leather Howard Aldo sofas were flipped over onto their backs which forced Top Dollar, NayNay and several other men to stand. The veins could be seen bursting out of his body as a red-faced Solo screamed, "Can someone tell me how is it possible for us to say we're the best and have people take from us, without us even having a clue who did it?"

"Solo we have every street captain, corner watchman, down to the local fiends with their ears open. We'll have an answer in no time. I promise you!" Top Dollar responded.

"I hear you Top," answered Solo while gripping the keys free from the table. "NayNay, Khaled, let's go!"

They followed right behind him without hesitation when Top Dollar called out, "Solo where are you going? The meeting with Boggy is in a few hours."

"Top if I'm going to be the king of this city, that answer you just gave me can no longer be good enough." With that, Solo stepped outside. He pushed a button that remotely opened the garage door to reveal several vehicles. But Solo knew there was only one for this job. He jumped in the Hummer for the first time and said to himself, "When you hit and miss, you buy something like this."

Top Dollar appeared knocking on the driver's side window and yelled, "I want in." Solo smiled as he unlocked the door.

Riding through another one of Roc's near empty blocks, hidden behind tinted windows, Solo instantly became mad at himself while thinking it was his call to Roc that had him now missing his target. After two packs of Philly blunts and an hour of hearing Top Dollar complain about there being too much smoke in the air, Solo couldn't believe his precious luck as the junky that NayNay informed that they wanted to buy some weight about twenty minutes ago, was now approaching with a top hustler in Roc's crew. NayNay slowly lowered her window as J.D. asked, "What you need beautiful, I got it?" While taking his eyes off of NayNay's MAC lip gloss, he looked pass her to Top Dollar who was counting hundred dollar bills, placing them into thousand dollar stacks on the back seat.

"Yeah I need a half bird soft but we'll take it fried if we have to."

"I told you it was on, baby. I got you a major sale you got to get me; you know what I mean pretty girl. I need mine," said Sam, the junky with his eyes wide open as he rubbed his two hands together, knowing that in a minute he would be high as mars.

"I know honey but it's a shame you will not get it off of me," answered NayNay.

"Shit I'm going to get…" In mid-sentence, Sam's words got stuck in his throat at the sight of Khaled appearing from out of the shadow behind them with his gun rested at the back of J.D.'s ear.

NayNay exited the truck with Khaled forcing J.D. in the back seat. "Ho-ho…hold up, I don't got to get in the car, you can take what I got right here," J.D. quickly braced his foot on the truck's step bar as he emptied his pockets. He dropped two large knots of cash along with a zip lock freezer bag filled with different sizes of weight in cocaine.

"That's nice right there, NayNay pick all that shit up. We need that too," stated Solo before Khaled slammed the butt of his gun into the back of J.D.'s head.

"Aaahhhhhh," he screamed.

"Shut up! Now get the hell into the car," Khaled raced around the truck and jumped into the passenger seat.

Solo started the engine but instead of dashing off he placed the truck in reverse.

"Solo let's go, we just kidnapped a nigga!" Solo dropped his window to reveal his face to the still shocked junky, "Sam, Sam."

Hearing his name brought him out of a daze as he questioned, "Lil Mac, did you see that....we got to tell Roc's people." Just then, like a brick it hit him. "Oh shit, it's true...you're Solo!"

Tossing an ounce from the zip lock out to Sam, Solo smiled and before driving off said, "Why wouldn't I be?"

With a gun to his temple, J.D. sweat profusely as he begged for his life, "Please don't kill me I was just trying to make a few extra grand in the little days we have left to work on the block that's all. You have to respect the hustle." Everyone remained silent hearing this cry for the tenth time.

Solo pulled into a dark alley that was surrounded by mostly abandoned houses and parked. He turned around with his gun pointed to the center of J.D.'s head, cocked it back quickly and asked, "Where is Sun?"

"Sun? Man you almost gave me a heart attack; I thought this shit was about that move I pulled for Pretty Tony."

"So that means you're going to tell me?"

"You damn right, fuck Sun. He's in a spot six blocks from here."

For over twenty minutes, through a pair of digital binoculars, Solo watched the white house from across the street in the cut. The front living room provided the only source of light which Solo believed came from the television. He noticed two different shadows pass by the window since he'd been standing there. One had the shape of a woman so the other had to be Sun.

Feeling that it was now or never, Solo eased out the cut speaking into his mouthpiece, "Top Dollar I'm moving into position." Top Dollar was posted on the right side of the back door with his 45 automatic in hand. "I'm ready, NayNay are you?" NayNay firmly placed her feet on the shoulders of Khaled who was bent down. As he lifted her up NayNay struggled to balance her body while grasping hold of the edge of the roof leaning to the second floor.

Pulling herself up, she checked the first window finding it locked. "Damn!"

"What was that Nay?" Solo questioned. She checked the next window which opened with ease.

"I said I'm ready."

"Khaled let's do it!"

"I'm coming," answered Khaled who was now dashing up the front steps pass Solo and posted at the left side window where he would have the best view.

Solo reached the front door placing his ear to it and knocked with his finger on the trigger. He thought, *"Girl or boy."*

Hearing a soft sexy voice say, "Who is it?" he screwed on his silencer and said, "Girl" before putting several shots through the door. Sun was sitting on the sofa watching the Lakers as Kobe just had the ball stolen by Rip Hamilton when Alicia flopped to the floor.

"What the hell? Baby, are you all right?"

Sun heard no response from Alicia and stood up to see her lifeless body. Alert, he dropped beside the sofa for cover and slid his right hand under the second pillow pulling it back with a 380 in his palm. Sun was watching for any movement behind the now bullet hole filled door. NayNay lowered her mask over the remaining part of her face and then eased down four more steps with her gun locked to the back of Sun's head.

Solo yelled, "Sun I'll give you ten seconds to drop your gun and open this door for me."

"Get the fuck out of here or come get me nigga!" Sun's hand started to sweat as his finger gripped the trigger.

Solo responded, "I know you're mad about that woman but I have three guns locked on your head as we speak."

"Yeah right nigga, prove it!" said Sun.

"As you wish, fellas." On call, three infrared beams lit up the room. Shocked, standing in a triangle of red lights, Sun let his gun drop while thinking, *"How did I not see this coming?"* before he slowly unlocked the door.

On the way to the truck, Top Dollar asked, "Solo why did you kill that girl?"

"Because we made that mistake with Troy," he answered.

Back at the ranch in a crowded basement, Sun sat bloody in a chair with two men holding his arms. NayNay held the Handy Cam HDR camcorder on Ayzo who was jumping up and down shadow boxing. As Solo introduced him, "This is Howard Cosell coming to you live from the basement. In this corner we have Ayzo, a.k.a. A thousand punches." Ayzo threw a combination of blows into the camera. "And in this corner we have Sun, the rat."

NayNay turned the cam on Sun. "Solo what are you talking about, I never told on anyone in my life," protested Sun.

"Yeah right, ding-ding." Solo made the bell sound and then whispered, "That's what they all say." Ayzo rushed to meet Sun, who fought to break free when Ayzo slammed a powerful right hand into his face and followed up with a left hook to the mid-section. The blow forced Sun to double over. Ayzo continued his assault landing a wild punch to the back of Sun's neck, then a right upper cut that set Sun back upright in his chair. Sun continued to fight to get free.

The crowd applause got Ayzo hype. He walked up on Sun until he was only a foot away and quickly hit him with several blows that could be heard clearly on contact to Sun's chest. *Bomb! Bomb! Bomb!* "Time," Solo yelled, but Ayzo refused to stop throwing jab after jab. A wild right hook caught Khaled in the face by mistake while he held Sun. He released Sun to grip his face as Sun went crashing to the floor. Ayzo still refused to quit, he threw a punch, kick, and then an elbow drop to Sun's back.

Several men rushed Ayzo, pulling him off of Sun who was then placed back into the chair with blood now coming from his eye and mouth. Solo once again yelled, "In this corner we have Daz, the bomber."

Daz ducked and swayed while he threw short quick jabs and said, "I'm going to knock him straight out!"

"And in this corner we have a half dead, no good informant. Now Daz, show him what happens when you talk on The Family," stated Solo. Not wanting to die, Sun attempted to kick Daz off. The construction timbs he wore landed hard on the top of Daz's knee cap.

"Aaaaahhhhh…you mother…" Daz backed up letting the pain subside before rushing Sun at full speed with his arm hooked out from his body and clothes lined him. On impact, Sun went flying over the wooden chair head first and crashed into the concrete floor. "Get up and fight like a man, move, let his arms go," Daz said.

Sun looked up from the ground at Daz who was raging and said to himself, *"This nigga is going to kill me."* Sun pushed his way up, making it to his feet when a wooden bat crashed into his mid-section. The blow landed him right back on the floor.

"What the fuck?" Solo said, in shock as he looked for who held the bat. Instantly his blood began to boil. NayNay zoomed in on Fox as he brought the bat back for another swing when Solo entered the picture with his finger in Fox's face. He asked, "What the hell are you doing?"

"Nothing, I'm getting my man," answered Fox innocently.

"Who the fuck told you to do anything?" Solo questioned. Fox was speechless. "I thought so, then why are you always in something? If you want to hit somebody then hit me!"

Seeing what was about to take place, NayNay started to place the camcorder to the side when Top Dollar stopped her and said, "If he's going to be here then he has to make it on his own." Fox refused to make contact with Solo's fire-filled eyes as he spoke, "I don't want to hit you Solo."

'Why not, cause you don't listen to me. Is it because I'm going to fight back?" The whole room looked at Fox's 6'4" frame that was two inches taller than Solo's and 20 pounds heavier. While Solo waited on his response, Fox realized what could happen if he gave the wrong answer. He looked at NayNay who dropped her head before he replied, "No it's not that. He disrespected the team so he disrespected me. You haven't done nothing to me, if you did, that would be different."

At the sound of his words, the feeling of love and pride for her family overwhelmed NayNay's heart. She raised her head to see Fox staring Solo dead in the eyes. "Is that right?" Solo asked.

"Yeah…it is," replied Fox.

"Well, that's understandable." Solo turned and asked Top Dollar, "How much time do we have until the meeting?"

"About an hour and a half."

"That gives me just enough time to take a shower," stated Solo as he turned around and sent a right jab down the pike to Fox's chin. The pressure from the punch caused Fox to release the bat as he fell to the floor. "Now that statement is no longer true."

Fox ran his hand over his mouth and looked at the blood that now covered it and said, "No…it's not," and quickly got up to his feet.

Daz and Ayzo rushed to get Sun out of the way, slamming him into the back corner and Daz said, "Solo saved your ass!" He then rammed his knee into Sun's face, knocking him unconscious. A pair of eyes hidden by the grass, dressed in camouflage felt pain for Sun as they watched from outside through the dirty basement window.

Fox now standing, threw a two-piece combination. Seeing them coming, Solo tucked his chin as he rolled with the punches to reduce their impact a little. Top Dollar just shook his head knowing that Solo could have easily slipped Fox's punches but he needed the pain to get him hyped. "That's all you got nigga? Show me that you belong here or get the fuck out!"

Fox continued to attack, landing another right jab to the face then a short left hook just over Solo's right eye. Solo back peddled a few steps and said, "Now let's make it." He started to bop and weave as he approached Fox who threw several punches to keep him at bay. Connecting none, Solo landed a hard body shot to his left side and then his right.

"Oooohhh," Fox swung back hitting the back of Solo's head and neck to no avail. Solo was planted up too close in his chest, digging deep. After slamming multiple blows to Fox's frame to weaken his structure, Solo could sense Fox's legs were ready to give out when Fox grabbed him with both hands by the neck. Utilizing every drop of power in him, Fox threw Solo across the floor to the ground.

Solo made it halfway to his feet when Fox crashed into him from the side. Solo, being a more intelligent fighter used Fox's momentum as a weapon against him.

On contact Solo drop stepped, leaning his shoulder into Fox's mid-section while he wrapped an arm around his leg and waist. He then flipped Fox over his back, bringing him to the ground with a powerful force that removed all the air from his lungs. Fox witnessed stars floating in his head as Solo sat on his chest pounding his fist into his face. Seeing all the blood, Top Dollar grabbed Solo by his arm. "That's it. He's had enough."

Getting off of Fox, Solo headed for the shower when a voice stopped him. "It's not over nigga, I belong here." Solo turned to see Fox wiping the blood from his eyes before setting his hands in position to continue fighting.

"I know you're just like I was, ready to fight the world and wouldn't let anybody tell you how. But now that I have it, ask me if I want it. Matter of fact, don't…you'll know the feeling one day on your own because it's written all in your eyes."

28

From the comfortable peanut butter interior seat of a classic 1962 black and chrome Lincoln limousine that moved through the high mountain in Beverly Hills, M. Easy checked his watch again, he was nervous and desperately praying that they arrived at their destination on time. “Hey, can’t you drive this thing any faster? Hey…” *Boom! Boom! Boom!* He yelled and banged on the tinted divider.

Roc was too deep in thought to see the panicked look on M. Easy’s face as he listened to the words of Mr. Holmes. On the other hand Mr. Holmes was a different story, he watched M. Easy closely from out the corner of this eye. Sensing that something was wrong he unbuttoned his suit jacket and eased it swiftly to the side to give him quick access to the Ruger on his hip that he now vowed to never leave home without again.

Once content, Mr. Holmes continued his conversation over the smooth tune of Miles Davis playing in the background. “Roc, never again apologize to me for the actions of another man unless you ordered them to commit the act.”

“I know Mr. Holmes but he’s my brother,” Roc answered, ashamed that he couldn’t stop Lil Mac’s ways.

“Look at me, do you know why I took a liking to you so many years ago?” Mr. Holmes asked.

“No…but please tell me.” Roc watched Mr. Holmes, curious to finally know the answer. For it was Mr. Holmes who taught him rule 5 which was to always watch the people that are near to you and say that they love you because in the end they want something and in this game, many times it's your money, power, or your life.

Mr. Holmes began to explain things to Roc, "The reason is that you needed and wanted to better yourself here." Mr. Holmes pressed his index finger to Roc's brain and continued, "And that, I could never teach you son. You demonstrated the motivation to win. You know the day I saw you with that gun in your hand, what your eyes told me was that by any means, you wouldn't be denied a chance at a better life unless forced by death. I made a decision right then and there because after you killed Ron G you became feared. The question was if I was going to let you become an enemy."

Roc looked Mr. Holmes in the face intensely with astonished eyes. Roc knew the rule but he still needed to ask because at the time he was only 14. "You're telling me that if you decided the other way that you would have killed me?"

"You damn right," answered Mr. Holmes.

Roc saw the blaze return in Mr. Holmes eyes while he proceeded to school him, "Don't look surprised, you of all people know we lasted this long in this dangerous society because we follow these rules without any emotional attachment, whether it be me, you, my mother, your brother…anybody."

Roc thought he saw something in Mr. Holmes' eyes when he mentioned Lil Mac, then he brushed the feeling off by thinking, *"I got to be tripping, he said it was over with."*

Several sweat drops rolled down the side of M. Easy's face as his Movado stated that there was only ten minutes left until he would lose his bet. "Man if you don't hurry this car the hell up!"

"M. Easy be cool, El Sovida wouldn't mind if we're a few minutes late…as long as we're there."

"Roc, you don't know him but I'll tell you one thing, if we're late I'm going to empty this clip into the head of that old man driving this car," M. Easy cocked back his 45 as the door opened.

"Gentleman, you've arrived at your destination with five minutes to spare, so you can put that away sir."

M. Easy looked to the gun in his hand and smiled, "Oh this…I was about to clean it that's all."

The three men exited the car, looking open casket sharp from head to toe. "Right this way gentleman," said a man in a new suit and tie that seemed to have come out of nowhere. Mr. Holmes took a deep breath and inhaled the California fresh air into his lungs, proud of this very moment. He remembered back to the day he was brought to this same three-story white and glass home.

~ · ~ · ~ · ~ · ~

The architectural design was very unique and the one point four acre landscaped garden with a swimming pool had not changed. It was 1982, a beautiful summer day. A man dressed in a tailored suit opened the door for him and his mentor also. With each step he placed on the white painted brick walkway, Mr. Holmes could feel his heart coming through his chest as Billy D said, "Son, on this road we walked together, you showed the values of a leader every minute of the way. If a situation called for loyalty you showed it. If it was devotion, you were there before time."

A few tears had escaped Billy D's eye when a young Mr. Holmes said, "It will always be two faces one tear. As one feels pain, so will the other…always. You know that, so wipe your face and let's get to this party that you've been talking so much about because I have my best linen suit on."

"No player, this is your party."

~ · ~ · ~ · ~ · ~

"Mr. Holmes, Mr. Holmes," Roc shook Mr. Holmes, trying to get his attention as he was in an obvious daze. "Mr. Holmes come on, they're waiting on you."

"Yes, they're waiting."

As they approached the ten-foot glass door, "Damn, this spot is major who lives here Mr. Holmes?" M. Easy asked.

"To be honest, I never knew," he replied.

The door eased open with another man in a fresh new suit stepping out from behind it announcing, "Mr. Miller, they will see you now."

"Me?" Roc questioned.

"Yes, you Roc," answered Mr. Holmes.

M. Easy was the first to put the pieces into place from his knowledge of El Sovida as he said, "Oh my God we're on for real now!"

Mr. Holmes pulled Roc to the side, "You know son, I had this long speech ready for you like my mentor did to me when I was brought in but you're better now than I was then so all I have to say is to be the man you are when you're in there and you'll be just fine." Roc wiped away the tear from under Mr. Holmes' eye.

"Come on old head, take it easy on your heart because I'm about to fill it with pride."

"I know you will, now go show them the heart of a man." Mr. Holmes patted Roc on the back and then continued to follow the first man in the suit, with M. Easy at his side, down the path on the side of the house into the back yard.

Before making it all the way there, Roc called out, "Mr. Holmes, wait." He raced over to Mr. Holmes and said, "Thank you for caring, and now with that said I'm complete." Roc gave him a half hug.

Entering the beautiful home, Roc was surprised to see that there was nothing in it but a chair and a glass coffee table with a Sonic computer resting on it in the living room.

"Have a seat Mr. Miller, you'll begin shortly."

Roc sat patiently for several minutes when all of a sudden the computer screen came to life with the vision of a man he had never met but recognized from Special Agent Branson's picture.

"Mr. Miller I'm Diego El Sovida and it is truly an honor to finally meet you after being in the company of so many of your friends that speak very highly of you."

"Thank you, the feeling is indeed mutual," Roc replied.

"Mr. Miller, pay close attention because I will only speak once. By you being in that seat you have assumed full responsibility of Mr. Holmes along with your five closest family members lives from here on out. This corporation is closer to you than your mother; you have now become CEO of it so don't ever disrespect it. In our organization there is not one absolute authority due to other groups' failures. For too much power makes some men arrogant and emotional decision makers. This corporation has five leaders until Mr. Holmes feels that you can handle the whole U.S. on your own, and then we will be back to four."

Roc's eyes widened. "Don't be alarmed, in this world there is always one person at the top in any arena so there are only five people who run the trade in the U.S. and they are who you will control so you can relax." As the words entered Roc's mind, the picture of a smooth Mr. Holmes with him at his side flying in and out of town on so-called vacations as Mr. Holmes would say, all came together. Roc had to laugh to himself because he would have never believed it. El Sovida continued, "In your life you have never been an ordinary man or I wouldn't be talking to you. Now it's official. As we speak your social security number has been changed. You will now have four that will change weekly, any questions?"

"Not at all," answered Roc.

"Then call Mr. Walker to assist you."

"Mr. Walker," Roc spoke aloud. The same man, with a different suit reappeared.

"Right this way sir." He led Roc up the twenty-step stairwell to a hallway past several doors to a back room, where he waited. The room only held a laptop, a chair and desk. Roc paid close attention to the flat screen as the man whose name was spoken in the same sentence as Pablo began to address him.

"Mr. Miller, I am Adrian Cortez and out of respect for your mentor and the great things I know of your actions, I am introducing myself to you this day."

"Thank you"

"Now that, that is done, never speak of that name again, it belongs to a cop. Don't speak it to me, not to yourself when you're alone, never…these are my wishes can you honor them?"

"Yes, but may I ask what should I address you by?" Roc questioned.

"That's the key; you can call me any name you'd like once agreed upon. That name is your code to me and if it should ever pop up with the FBI, CIA, DEA, I will know where it came from."

"Well I will call you the Ghost and Ghost…never disrespect me again by indirectly calling me a cop, that's not in my bloodline."

"Disrespect?" he laughed. "I would never; you have passed our tests with flying colors. What I did was give you wisdom that you know works from firsthand experience."

"I do?"

"Yes, when a name is mentioned, your brain automatically tries to place it with a face but if the name isn't recognized even if you know the face, it will not connect. See, you knew Solo's face the whole time but your brain refused to put the two together but now you will never forget it."

At that moment so many thoughts flooded Roc's mind at once. How did they know and how much did they know. Cortez suddenly put Roc's thoughts to rest, "Please don't trouble yourself, we're the corporation…we know everything."

"You must not because believe me when I tell you, if I knew Lil Mac was indeed Solo, it wouldn't have gotten that far," Roc explained.

"Oh we're well aware of that also, that's why you're here. The question is, once he has reached the level of understanding and if rejected, can you kill him?"

"It won't come to that."

"And how can you be so sure?"

"Because I know," Roc said firmly.

"I hope we don't have to find out, do you have any questions?"

"No ghost, I don't."

"Then call Mr. Walker to assist you."

"Mr. Walker."

"Yes Mr. Miller, right this way."

"Man how many suits you got?" Roc asked, seeing that he'd changed his clothes again.

"Mr. Miller, every room you enter gives you a key to a different part of the world and I never wear the same suit when I travel." Roc was guided to a second floor balcony where the regular computer and desktop awaited him but this time there was a bottle of imported Martell rested in a bucket of ice with a single glass.

"Hello there Mr. Miller," Sunan Kudari said as he bowed. Roc repeated the act. "Mr. Miller, I must say, I don't like Americans too much and it's not because of what they are doing in Iraq or what they did to us. The world was founded off of the survival of the fittest and that's understandable. The reason is that when I was just a ground commander in the 70's I met a colored man with enough heart to travel over here alone to buy product. He was even wise enough to make his own pipeline. For years we made millions together and then the trouble came and in my country you're charter is your life. You only live to honor the soul of your ancestors. Therefore I tell you I would die at this very moment if proving my death would make them more righteous. I couldn't tell you how I felt that a man that I have befriended turned on the same people that entrusted him with their lives."

Sunan Kudari spit on the floor and continued, "The soul of his father's forefather will not rest until the restitution is paid for those actions by the same bloodline. I do understand this doesn't have anything to do with you but I lost a man who I deeply respected, I lost my mentor. He now lies in a U.S. jail cell for the rest of his life. He didn't even talk to his lawyer or write home out of fear that they would change the meaning to entrap more people. This man is continuing to live life through me."

Seeing Sunan Kudari stand to his feet as his face reddened, Roc thought while looking into the most powerful eyes he'd ever seen, "If anything goes bad, God forbid he has to die first." Back seated, Sunan Kudari said, "The U.S. buys 75 percent of the drugs in the world, with those facts I wouldn't be a business man if I let my emotions stop me from enriching my country with more schools, hospitals, tanks and guns. So, until we meet again…do you have any questions?"

"No sir," Roc answered.

"Mr. Miller, you have heard a secret from each one of your corporation members to that you may identify with them personally. Due to what we put you through lately, I'm sorry, but if it means anything to you…you passed with my respect. Now call Mr. Walker to assist you."

"Mr. Walker."

"Now you can come with me." When Roc turned around he couldn't believe his eyes as DEA Special Agent Branson stood in the doorway. Roc lowered his head, shaking it from side to side while thinking, *"Dad get my room ready because I'm jail celled out."* Raising his head back up, Roc looked Branson in the eyes while walking over to where he was and said, "You know I'm not telling you anything right?"

"I figured that much already, that's why I'm here.' Agent Branson stuck his hand out to meet Roc's arm. Roc quickly grabbed him by the wrist, spinning it around backwards while bringing it up to the center of Branson's back.

"Aaaaaahh," he screamed.

"Shut up! I'm about to cash you out."

"Wait, you don't understand," Branson replied.

"What'd I say," Roc wrapped his free arm tightly around the neck of Branson, making it difficult for him to breathe. Agent Branson's head went back wildly as he tried to head bump Roc.

Roc's mission wasn't going to be denied, he forced Branson forward toward the balcony and he kicked the glass table and computer over. The table could be heard in the distance as the glass shattered into thousands of pieces on the marble floor. In the back yard, now dressed in only silk shorts, sitting in the pool while getting a back rub from a beautiful woman, M. Easy asked Mr. Holmes who was relaxing, reading the Robb Report, "What the hell was that?"

"I don't know, but with Roc in there we're going to find out," Mr. Holmes got up to his feet and released his Ruger and raced off into the house with M. Easy right beside him. They headed for the stairs where screams filled the air. M. Easy moved down the hall with caution and his 45 pointed out in front of him when Mr. Walker appeared from out of a side room. He spotted Mr. Holmes and said, "Noooo!" But it was too late; M. Easy opened fire on sight. Roc had Special Agent Branson in the sleep hold as his body hung over the balcony when he heard the shot. "I guess you're back up may get me but I'm going to finish you first," Roc said, releasing his hands. Agent Branson said a silent prayer as he felt Roc's grip loosen. Mr. Holmes pushed M. Easy out of the way just as Roc's hands moved. He grabbed hold of Agent Branson's coat.

"Roc what are you doing, help me get this man up." Roc thought of jerking Mr. Holmes' hand away too so that he could finish what he started. Then he thought better of it, knowing it was too late in the game to have Mr. Holmes as his co-defendant. "Roc, don't just stand there!"

"You're right," Roc replied and turned to walk down the hall pass a shook up Mr. Walker who sat on the floor in shock. M. Easy rushed to assist a struggling Mr. Holmes. Together they got the top half of Branson's body back over the rail when M. Easy recognized the face. "This is the cop that's been on Roc's ass, man get the fuck out of here." Then with a powerful force, M. Easy tried to push Agent Branson back off the railing as Branson held on tightly with his arm interlocked around a balcony post.

"Stop it, that's enough," screamed Mr. Holmes.

"Well you help him by yourself; I'm going to find Roc." Roc sat in the limousine with his hands working under the steering wheel when M. Easy opened the door asking, "Roc what the hell is you doing?"

"I don't know where the hell that driver is at but it hasn't been that long that I can still hot wire this old thing and get us the hell out of here." Roc rubbed several wires together until he saw a spark that brought the car to life.

"No matter where we're at in life, some things you'll never forget, get in." Roc dropped the car into drive as Mr. Holmes and Agent Branson stepped in the way of his exit. A laughing Mr. Holmes tapped on the window that Roc lowered and questioned, "Old head what's up with you and this cop shit?"

"Watch your mouth, I'm going to let that go because I know how much you've been through but this here is Mike. You know him as Special Agent Branson. He's with the corporation. That was your test to see if he took your look and style along with everything that you love but if given a way out would you take it."

"Come on old head, I can't believe you came at me like that. You know that is never an option in life for us."

"I know but it wasn't me you had to prove it to. Now they feel as comfortable with you as I do with their life in your hands. I think it's time for you to go finish your breakfast and once that's complete you can get a piece of the Knicks like you want. Agent Branson here has some important information you need. Tell him…" Mr. Holmes instructed Branson.

"Well for over two years now we've been over seeing the action of an individual by the request of Mr. Holmes, Mack Miller a.k.a. Solo."

Roc's mouth dropped open as he looked to his mentor and asked, "You knew? Why didn't you tell me?"

"Son I love you but there are some things in life we'll never believe no matter how much we respect the deliverer unless we see it with our own eyes. This is one of those things." Roc wanted to be mad that the man he loved like a father would hold something so dear back from him but he couldn't because deep inside he knew Mr. Holmes was right again.

"Please continue Branson," asked Roc. "This is about the time of the second attempt on your life." Roc just shook his head as the words hit hard and cut away at his heart. Agent Branson stated, "A detective Rayfield started his own investigation, taking several important notes before he mysteriously disappeared." Agent Branson smiled, "But not before storing a few at work. We thought to retain them all as we swept his home. Now the problem has become his partner Detective Michael who must have figured out he couldn't win by going at your team so he's now trying a different route and he just asked two of my paid officers in the 39th Station to help him make a bust off record and we believe it's your brother. Roc I can assure you that my men are loyal to the corporation and if it's him and the chance presents itself, they will not hesitate to put Michael down to free him but this is what we have."

Agent Branson handed Roc a folder as Roc replied, "Thank you Mike for everything and I'm sorry for trying to kill you but now I have to get back. M. Easy, call Mohammed and tell him to bring our situation in. Come Mr. Holmes, you can drive."

29

Over a thousand miles away, Boggy waited patiently for Solo's arrival as he laid back on the couch in the back office of Lights on Broadway, a local strip club that he co-owned. He had three sexy topless women with only sheer thongs on, giving him a private show while a tied up Ms. Rich was forced to watch from the corner.

Luscious Chocolate ran her thick lips over Flirtatious' hard nipples as she sat sitting in a chair before taking her breast deep into her mouth.

"China, it looks like our company is getting bored. Why don't you show her a good time," said Boggy to China who sat on his lap playing with herself as she placed three fingers inside of her cum filled pussy before licking it off clean.

"Okay baby," she replied. China seductively moved her body like a snake back and forth in front of Ms. Rich who tried to protest through her duct taped mouth when a scream came from the main floor.

Boggy jumped up to get a better view of the six motions melted into the wall. What he saw made him smile as Ayzo placed his 357 revolver to the side of DJ Raw's head and forced him to cut off the music. "Nigga mix out and the rest of you clowns get the fuck out now." More screams filled the air as people scrambled for the exit. Top Dollar entered the front door, moving to the right followed by NayNay who went left. Solo appeared in the middle with a gun to the head of a man in a pinstriped suit and a bag over his face.

Haffee dashed through the office door and said, "Boggy they're here!"

Boggy looked up from the screen, "I can see that but I got to give it to the kid…his entrance was gangster."

"What the hell's going on here girl, get away from her," Haffee stated as he gripped the arm of China who was making her ass cheeks go up and down on the face of Ms. Rich. Haffee helped Ms. Rich up while easing $5,000 in singles into her side pocket while whispering into her ear, "I'm sorry this was never about you but don't worry it will all be over in a minute."

Boggy fixed his clothes as he took his last look at Luscious Chocolate and Flirtatious going at it on the floor. He stepped out the door, taking in the surroundings of the nearly empty strip club. To the right he noticed Ayzo had secured the side exit while Fox stood on post at the front door. NayNay positioned herself several feet back on Solo's right so that she would have access to covering him on both exits. Top Dollar did the same on the left.

With everything locked in his brain, Boggy thought, *"Double triangle offense…nice. That too, from the kid he stole top game."* Boggy with Bo and Haffee standing on each side of him walked right up to Lil Mac's face. Looking him straight in the eyes the same way he did the day he shot him. Only this time Lil Mac didn't step back, instead he closed the distance between them, determined to save Ms. Rich. "I can't believe your ass is standing here because I missed your heart by an inch. Somebody must like you upstairs but next time I'm going to make sure I do the job with this." Boggy raised his hoody a little to reveal a chrome 45 automatic.

Lil Mac smiled as he said, "Oh how easily we forget that I'm the one who had you on your back with two bullets in your frame, debating if I should have taken your soul first. You know, the only thing that saved your ass was that red ten-speed you bought me on my ninth birthday and the fact that when you caught me and D on the block. You told me you couldn't tell me how to live my life, so you kept it to yourself."

That statement made Boggy furious, "Well take it now then pussy!" said Boggy as he pushed Solo hard in the chest with his right hand and gripped the 9 mm out the center of his back with the left and drew. On cue, four men appeared from the back with their guns out. Solo quickly pushed the man he held to the ground as he raised his gun, locking it on Boggy's head. NayNay with both hands now wrapped tightly around the handle of her Mack 11, slowly closed the space between her and Solo.

While aiming at Haffee, Top Dollar stepped into the line of fire between Solo and Boggy and said, "Now is not the time or the place for this gentleman, you dig. Solo we're here for D only. Fox, get that!" Fox quickly carried two large bags dropping them at Boggy's feet.

"That's your work along with your fallen soldier, now let me see my people," demanded Solo.

Boggy didn't move, he kept his gun locked on Solo as he thought, *"I have to end this now."* As if reading his mind, Haffee covered the barrel of Boggy's gun, lowering it to his side while saying, "He's right, we must keep our word."

"Okay, okay get the bitch!" Bo led Ms. Rich out to the front placing her next to Boggy.

"She's here, now who's that?" Boggy asked, pointing to the masked man on the floor. "Either Mr. Holmes gained 20 pounds or ya'll had him in the gym," Boggy added.

"We're not here for games, that's not Mr. Holmes but I figured, why come empty handed when I don't have to!" Solo pulled the pillow case off to reveal a badly beaten Sun.

NayNay noticed the shock then saddened expression on Haffee's face and altered her aim to Sun. Haffee rushed to aid him, not believing what he saw and for the first time while locking eyes with Solo, he showed his anger and spoke, "You get Ms. Rich and get the hell out of here now and Boggy if he hesitates, kill his ass cause we all can die tonight."

Solo just grinned before taking a scared Ms. Rich into his arms. "Please baby I just want to go home," she cried.

"I know Ms. Rich and I'm the one who's going to take you there." As Solo started up the steps, Fox walked in reverse covering his back. Then NayNay did the same for him, followed by Top Dollar. They all repeated this act until no one remained.

Once cleared, Boggy released his cell phone, "Yeah he just left."

Solo pushed the Range pass 90 rushing to the nearest hospital and after three hours of check-ups at Solo's request, Ms. Rich made her way out to the packed waiting room. Solo jumped up, "Doctor is she okay?"

"She's just fine."

Outside in the truck, Top Dollar asked, "You want me to ride?"

"Nah Top, she's been through so much I think I'm going to stay with her tonight," Solo answered, looking into the rearview mirror at a sleeping Ms. Rich.

"Well I'm coming," stated NayNay.

"Now you know we wouldn't get any sleep," replied Solo.

"You sure?" said NayNay, running her tongue across her lips.

Solo started his engine, "See that's what I'm talking about," and pulled away.

Solo searched Ms. Rich's pockets finding the key he was looking for. He eased her into his arms carefully so that he wouldn't wake her. In route to her bedroom, Solo's heart became overwhelmed with sorrow from seeing all the pictures lining the walls of his best friend. He stopped at one taken of the two of them together. "Don't worry dawg, I got her…I promise." After tucking Ms. Rich in with a kiss on the cheek, Solo returned downstairs and ate two large bowls of Rice Krispies cereal before falling asleep. An hour later, not able to sleep due to the vibration of his phone, taking the stairs two at time and checking each room, Mohammed smiled as he tapped Solo's leg with his gun.

Solo opened his eyes then closed them, thinking he was seeing things but when he reopened them, Mohammed was still there shaking his head. Solo let out a deep breath while being stripped of his gun. "You got me but can you kill me out back so she won't have to see the body."

"You definitely have the same bloodline," stated Mohammed before knocking Solo out with the butt of his gun. The next morning, Solo was awakened from the light that escaped through the drapes. Not willing to give in that easily he pulled the cover over his head and tossed and turned until he made the bed give way to his liking. Suddenly the reality of what happen the night before hit him. Freeing himself, he jumped to his feet and checked out his surroundings as the scent of blueberry pancakes filled his nose.

Lil Mac began to search the room for his gun, "It's not here…damn, wait a minute!" Thinking quickly, he ran his hand under the outline of the bed, "Yes." He pulled out a knife. Feeling safer, he stepped out into the hallway, making sure no one was out there. He slowly started down the stairs and followed the noise he heard coming from the kitchen. Then saw a sight that always melted his heart. Once she noticed him standing there a beautiful smile covered her face as she demanded, “Boy come in here and give your Mom a kiss. You act like you can’t come home anymore. I had you out of my life for a year where I couldn’t talk to you at all and this is how you treat an old woman.”

Even though Lil Mac would never admit it, to him it felt good to be in his Mom’s arms. “Mom I thought you sold this house?”

“No baby, Roc just put the for sale sign in the yard so nobody would try to take our things while I stayed in the summer house that he got me for my birthday. Wait until you see it, it’s beautiful.”

“I bet it is,” Lil Mac said, less emotional. “Mom can you answer a question for me?”

“Yes son, what is it?”

“How did I make it here last night?”

“Your brother carried you in. He said ya’ll was having a great time together at his welcome home party and he gave you a drink that you thought was soda and after you drank it, you passed out.”

I know she didn’t just say Roc. “Mom did you say Roc?”

“Yeah Macky, stop playing.”

“Where’s he at now Mom?”

“Right there,” she pointed off to the living room where Roc lifted his head up from the morning newspaper. On eye contact Roc waved Lil Mac to come in. Lil Mac slid his hand into his pocket, grabbing the handle of the knife as he stopped next to Roc.

“What’s up boss man?” asked Roc.

“Boss man? Where’d that come from?” Lil Mac questioned. “That’s what you are a boss and I respect it. That’s why we’re on mutual ground, you know I wouldn’t do anything with Mom around and I would think you would feel the same.”

Lil Mac put on a smile that was fake while he eased his hand from his pocket. Roc continued, "Now go ahead and finish that lovely breakfast Mom fixed for you. I think it's your favorite. When you're done please meet me in the den because I believe it's where we'll find a level of understanding."

After breakfast, Lil Mac entered the den and stopped in his tracks stepping back to the tip of the doorway. He noticed Roc seated in his hard brown leather Roberto More chair viewing a screen from an old film projector with a picture of him, Roc, and their father playing in the park.

~ · ~ · ~ · ~ · ~

Hearing his father's powerful voice speak again after so many years, sent chills up Lil Mac's spine as he watched him tell Roc as if he knew he would be leaving them 'Odell get over here.' Roc raced to his father as Lil Mac at the age of four raced after Roc. Roc stopped in front of his father with Lil Mac catching up to him and wrapping his arm around Roc's right leg,

"Get off me Macky," said Roc as he tried to pull his leg free from Lil Mac who grabbed a hold of it again.

"No I want to go with you."

Roc went to pull away again when his father stopped him, "Odell."

"Yeah," he responded.

"What did you say?" his father asked.

Roc corrected himself, "Yes daddy."

"Now that's better, and look at me when I'm talking." Roc looked at his father directly in the eyes like he was taught. "That's your brother."

"I know but he always wants to go where I go."

"That's good because the Millers are a family and as long as I'm on God's green earth, I live for you, him and your mother but son I'm not always going to be here."

"Where are you going Dad?" asked a young innocent Roc.

"No where son but if I do, I need you to promise me you'll do everything in your power to provide and look after Lil Mac and your mother if I'm ever not able to."

"That's right player, school the young soldier you dig," yelled Top Dollar, who was holding the camera.

Roc's dad got down on one knee to be at eye level with Roc when he answered, "I promise."

"Always Odell, because it would break my heart no matter where I'm at if you don't."

Roc assured him, "Always dad, I promise!"

"That's my boy; now give your father a hug." As Roc hugged his dad, Lil Mac began to hug Roc.

"Now go play," his dad instructed.

Roc started to run off and then stopped, "Come on Lil Mac let's play."

A sad and upset look instantly turned into a smile as Lil Mac raced off to play with his older brother. Lil Mac watched Roc rewind back to his father's request some several times before he let his presence be known.

~ · ~ · ~ · ~

He shut the door hard enough for Roc to hear. Roc quickly killed the film and acted as if he was watching the Lakers game. Lil Mac took a seat a few feet across from Roc.

"I'm here, what is it you want to talk about?" said Lil Mac as he looked at Roc's eyes that seemed to be cloudy as if he'd been crying.

"Listen, you don't have to be like that with me. I respect you, the whole city respects you but before all this Solo stuff I always loved and respected you. So don't be tough while we talk…please be Lil Mac, my brother." Roc pleaded.

"I hear you Roc, but how can you look me in the eye and say you respected me before when you wouldn't let me do anything to gain my respect?"

With a puzzled look on his face, Roc asked, "What are you talking about?"

"You know damn well what I'm talking about, don't play stupid…you were there, you know how hard you made it for me as your brother growing up."

"No I don't," replied Roc.

"As much as you were overprotective you wanted me to believe that I couldn't fight my own battles, you refused to let me become my own man. Even after I showed you I could win, you still shielded me from becoming the person I need to be, whoever that was." Lil Mac stood and walked around the room as he continued, "You say that you respected me, you didn't, like nobody else did."

"Mac are you listening to yourself, you're telling me that because I cared and made myself powerful enough in this rough city to keep you from feeling the pain of it or better yet having you die in prison for killing someone because of something they did to you means that I don't respect you? You have lost your damn mind. Somewhere along the line your generation has come to believe that this struggle we have been forced to live is the way of life; and they're wrong but they have been living in it for so long, ya'll have lost hope and direction. The fight that once was to better our people as a whole now is to destroy one another for self-pleasure like us. Don't get me wrong, I know my actions weren't right and you shouldn't have had to witness any part of my lifestyle, whether it was the cars, the money or the stories, that was too much and I'm sorry Mac.

"But once I got my education, it was too late. My soul called for the only thing it knew. I'm telling you this from the heart. If I didn't believe that if we took every drug off this planet and put them on the moon, that a black man from the hood would build a spaceship within a few months to get there, I would have stopped. Now my reason has changed, I will give up everything, blocks and all…you name it as long as you go to college this coming year before the life starts to control your soul also."

"How do you know it hasn't already done that?"

"Because when I picked you up into my arms to bring you home, you know what you said?"

"No…what?"

"'Thanks. Mac I know what I'm asking is a lot but as the brother who loves you, listen to me because this is my last chance at talking."

Roc rose from his seat and retrieved a brown file from the safe in the wall and tossed it to Lil Mac. "What's this?"

"Your future," Roc answered. Lil Mac opened the folder and was shocked at what it contained as he looked at a picture of Top Dollar, D, NayNay and himself all getting into different vehicles with several people with them. Lil Mac knew the pictures couldn't prove anything but the date on the bottom of them caught his attention. He thought to himself that this had to be taken hours before he tried to hit Roc in the YMCA parking lot in that damn Hummer. The next few pictures were of his crew leaving the firing range, strip club and a few other places.

Lil Mac quickly moved through the thick stack of photos and stopped, "Oh shit," he whispered as eight repeated shots, all with different dates, showing him and Top Dollar unloading a fake Foot Locker truck, full of boxes of sneakers into a storage place. The ninth shot matched the date on the first photo of the eight and then the tenth matched the second of the eight and so on. They all showed the same thing…that someone was smooth enough to break into the storage space and took the photo of the cocaine that was inside each time, leaving it as if no one had been there.

Lil Mac studied pre-law in high school and he knew how serious these pictures really were. "Where did you get these?" he asked while continuing to go through the remaining photos, seeing Top Dollar and NayNay side by side, shooting at two cops on 13th Street.

Roc paused to light a cigar, giving Lil Mac enough time to take in the value of every photo before he answered, "A drug enforcement agent gave it to me."

At the sound of Roc's response, the pictures fell to the floor freely. Lil Mac questioned in disbelief, "You can't be for real, it's enough stuff to put us away for life." Sweat started to appear on Lil Mac's forehead. Roc picked up each picture, placing them back into the folder.

"Mac this is the reason why I have become a slave…so you wouldn't have to." Roc flipped the switch on the wall to activate the Portuguese limestone fireplace. He started to release the folder into the flame and then stopped. "Oh, I almost forgot, do you want to be a slave?"

"Come on Roc, this shit's not funny…this is my life."

"I know but you're playing with it, why can't I?" asked Roc.

"Come on…you know what I mean."

"No I don't Mac. Yes this time I was able to save Mom from the heartache of seeing her youngest son behind bars doing 40 years in the Feds but what about the day when one of your wild-ass young bulls kills someone or makes the wrong sale and they're presented with the chance to save their own ass. Who do you think they're going to give up?" Roc yelled.

"Roc that's where you're all wrong. My team don't get down like that," explained Lil Mac.

"Tell me how the hell do you know. When I came into this game I was schooled, then tested before I saw a ten-dollar bag, not sold. But who have you tested?"

"Everyone, in case you forgot," Lil Mac's face reddened while stating his crew's loyalty. "Everything we have, we took block by block, enemy through enemy. They put their life on the line for me each time I asked without hesitation. What better test than death?"

"The chance to die breathing," Roc stated, tossing a Sanyo recorder with one hand over to Lil Mac.

"Now what's this?" Lil Mac asked.

"A test," Roc replied.

Lil Mac pushed play to hear the sound of Shamone's voice, "Listen kid, I know it's hard out there for you to live and at times you got to do what you have to just to make it. That's why you're here instead of the station, to give you a chance to help yourself."

"Help myself? Please…you don't have nothing on me, that's why I'm here and not at the station." Lil Mac's eyes grew as he recognized the second voice to be Fatel.

"Are you sure you want to play tough, you know it's hard being a gangster?"

"You damn right and I'm all of it," Fatel had replied.

"That's right Fatel, fuck that cop. Death before dishonor nigga," Lil Mac screamed out as if Fatel could hear him.

"That's fine with me, I just pray that my partner who doesn't like you as much, doesn't find anything in that pretty truck of yours."

"He won't," answered Fatel.

A few moments of just breathing could be heard and then the crackle of a walkie talkie, "Partner cuff the bastard, we got him," said Mohammed.

"With what?"

"A half a key of crack rock and a loaded 380," he responded.

"Copy that. Alright gangster, stand up." A popping noise could be heard from Shamone releasing the button on his holster.

"Okay, okay…how can I help myself?" Fatel asked.

"First you must tell me who you work for, starting at the top of the Get Money Clique and if you lie to me, I'll make sure you do every day of the 25 years you're facing."

Again breathing and nothing else was said for a moment. "Go hard Fatel, don't let them break you, I'm telling you this is *don't* or die!" said Lil Mac, meaning every word of it.

Suddenly Fatel spoke, "Mack Miller."

"Excuse me, what did you say?" Shamone again questioned.

"The head is Solo a.k.a. Mack Miller." Without warning Lil Mac slammed the recorder against the wall, breaking it into several pieces.

"Why did you do that? There were more people on there. One even gave up that lovely ranch home in Valley Forge you got," Roc stated.

"You knew where I lived?" Lil Mac asked. Roc slowly nodded yes.

"Then why didn't you come and get me when you knew I was coming for you?" questioned a confused Lil Mac.

"I guess I was willing to take the loss not to see you lose but…"

Just then, an out of breath Mrs. Miller came rushing through the den door stopping Roc while he was talking and asked, "What's going on, is everybody all right? What was that noise?"

"Everything is okay Mother, I just dropped the recorder," answered Roc, cleaning up the freshly made mess. When he finished he said, "Mac take a walk with me."

Lil Mac closed the door to their lovely brownstone, as he and Roc walked down the steps he heard a window open and looked up to see his Mom in it.

She yelled, "Lil Mac what did I tell you about leaving this house without saying good bye and giving me a kiss?" He looked at her smile and pretty chocolate skin with her hair nicely done. At the age of 55 she looked as though she was only in her thirties.

"Come on Mom, I'm a man now. Don't you think it's time to give that up?"

"Yeah, yeah, I hear you boy but to me you're always going to be my baby Lil Macky," Mrs. Miller said as she kept that smile on her face that always got to Lil Mac's heart. He loved her so much but he needed her to see him as a man. Just like Roc, Lil Mac blew her a kiss.

"You too Odell, don't stand there acting tough because you're with Macky."

"I'm not Mother," Roc blew his Mom a kiss with out hesitation and said, "I love you pretty girl, always."

Lil Mac looked at Roc and then up at Mrs. Miller and said, "I love you too Mom."

"I know ya'll do, you wouldn't let an old woman like me down."

As the continued to walk, Lil Mac thought to himself, "Man I've been tripping; she's been doing that to Roc, too." He then noticed a car parking in front of them. The door opened and Lil Mac recognized the driver as Kim, one of the prettiest girls he had ever met but she never gave him the time of day. As she walked past, Kim spoke to Roc first, "Hello Roc, you look good today." Then Lil Mac, "Hi." On the way up the steps, she did a double take, "Mac, is that you?"

"Yeah, what's up Kim?"

Racing down the steps she said, "Give me a hug baby, I haven't seen you in a while, I tried to speak to you one night I saw you in the club but you had so many people around you like you were the president."

Lil Mac gave Kim a hug when she whispered in his ear, "You know I've been trying to see you baby, you've gotten all big and strong. Knock on my door anytime as long as there's not a blue Benz out front, that's my man's car."

As they separated, Lil Mac said, "If I was free I would smash your frame for all the years I was on you and you fronted, just to show you what you're missing but I'm already committed."

"Who said she has to know?" Kim asked.

"I would know, and real G's don't get down like that," Lil Mac replied.

Off to the side, Roc had to smile with pride while he tossed Lil Mac the keys to the Range with the six TV's sitting on 23 inch rims. Lil Mac turned the engine key and lowered the window for Roc who still stood on the side walk.

"Mac, please think about what I said about giving up the game."

"I will Roc; I know you didn't have to help me."

"As long as you know and here…take this with you," Roc threw a Rambo style knife onto a green duffle bag on the back seat.

Spotting the knife, Lil Mac searched his pocket, "How did you get that?"

"Mac, you of all people should know that I'm aware of everything in my presence. That's why you never wore your gun around me."

Lil Mac could only smile, knowing that Roc's words were the truth. "Hey Roc, whose bag is this?"

"It's yours; take it as a showing of good faith." Roc turned and walked back down the street when a light gray Benz with dark-tinted windows appeared. The car never completely came to a stop as Roc jumped in, "Assalamu Alaikum," then took off down the road.

Lil Mac eased the zipper back slowly and couldn't believe his eyes. "This nigga stays doing some fly shit," Lil Mac said out loud while looking at the money before picking up the note on top. *"If you're reading this letter, by now I have stopped calling you Lil Mac. It is now just Mac because you have definitely proved to be your own man. As one, our word means everything to us. In the bag is $500,000, half of what I promised. If you take the offer, the other half will be waiting for you after your first day of classes. The other million will go to your first born."*

Lil Mac laughed as he pulled into traffic and said, "Top will never believe this."

30

Six months later, inside of his master bedroom at his mini mansion in New Jersey, Roc relaxed in a hot tub when Gizelle eased back the tinted glass divider while approaching the man she loved and cherished with everything she was, happy that her old Roc had finally returned. Roc who out of habit, always faced the entrance in any room he was in, took in her beauty from head to toe. He thought about the passionate vacation they'd just taken to a retreat in Tucson, AZ. Gizelle bent down and placed her soft lips to his. "You came to join me?" Roc asked.

"No."

"Why not?"

"Stop Roc," she laughed, while smacking his hand away that had quickly unfasten four buttons on her blouse as it released her right breast from her Dream Bra.

Gizelle leaned forward giving Roc easy access, as he gently kissed the tattoo of his name that she had on her chest and then took her hardened nipple into his mouth. "You're always starting something you can't finish," Gizelle said in a whisper. Roc removed her bra completely and then placed more kisses on her left breast before taking it into his mouth. Gizelle smiled as she placed the cordless phone to his ear.

"Roc, Roc…you there Roc, I know you hear me," a voice said.

At the sound of Mr. Holmes' voice, Roc stopped and looked up at Gizelle who said, "I told you…but I couldn't let you show love to one of the girls and not the other," and laughed.

Roc motioned with his lips to say, "You know you're wrong," right before he grabbed a hand full of water.

"Roc you better not," Gizelle said as she took off running for the door then suddenly felt her hair and back become drenched.

"Hello Mr. Holmes, I'm sorry. You still there?"

"Yes I'm here. I guess now that you have my spot officially, I don't have a choice but to wait on you."

"Cut it out old head, you know it would never be like that between us."

"I hope not because I haven't shown you all the tricks just yet."

"Without a doubt," said Roc.

"Well I called about that vacation," continued Mr. Holmes.

"Yeah, I'm on, where are you at?"

"Check your monitor." Roc looked to his right at his ten built in wall monitors to see Mr. Holmes alone in his phantom. Roc picked up the remote and pushed a code to release the front gate. "That's better, now get the piece," said Mr. Holmes before driving on to the estate.

An hour later, they were seated in two Baker Bros. hard black leather chairs in Roc's personal office where the only sound that was being made was the movement of the chess pieces. Still, there were also a lot of words being spoken, just not out loud. The score was two-one Roc's way. They were playing the best out of five for 40 G's but the money was only a number for the both of them. The game was really about the respect of the minds, young against old, though neither one of them would ever admit it. The move was on Mr. Holmes who studied the board wisely as he thought, *"If I move my knight, he can call check with his castle and I'll lose my queen. If I move my queen then he can check me with the Bishop and steal a pawn, then recheck me before I can make cover and take my knight."*

Mr. Holmes raised his head to look into Roc's eyes who met his stare as Roc thought, *"I got you off balance, don't I old head. I know."* Roc's face showed no expression as he continued to think to himself, *"I played dead the first game, keeping it close as if I haven't improved so that when you won, you would become comfortable feeling that I'm not a worthy adversary but I have tricked you and you haven't won a game since."*

Mr. Holmes returned his vision back to the board while thinking, *"How did I let myself get down two pieces?"* before he moved his queen back three spaces, taking a pawn in the process. Roc's next move was unpredictable for he didn't take any pieces, instead he moved his queen for better board position that forced Mr. Holmes to remove his King and think, *"Why did he do that!"* Over the past hundred and eighty days, Mr. Holmes schooled Roc on how to elevate his game to master playing on the next level. Roc, like any good student would take in everything that was said but it was what wasn't said that he saw of his mentor that allowed him to be leading this series. He started to notice that Mr. Holmes would never open himself up to reveal any weakness in his strategy, for every move he made in life was a counteraction. With Roc now in possession of this knowledge, he was better able to control Mr. Holmes' movement by how he moved his own piece.

After another quick move, Mr. Holmes started to question himself, *"Why would you leave your king there Roc, knowing in three moves I'll have your queen with my rook."*

"What are you waiting on old head, go on and push the pawn," Roc thought while understanding a good chess player's plan, five moves ahead but by predicting his opponent's moves, he thought seven moves ahead.

"Wait a minute, this can't be right," Mr. Holmes stated to himself before leaving the pawn, refusing to take

Roc's free knight and attack with his rook. Several moves later, Mr. Holmes possessed Roc's queen and castle, going up one piece. Roc made some nice adjustments to fight off Mr. Holmes' assault, ending with little effect and five moves later, Mr. Holmes finally pushed the pawn calling out, "Checkmate. Roc I have to master the art of timing."

Roc reset the piece taking possession of the black ones this time, when he looked up at Mr. Holmes and said, "You're move." He witnessed something he'd never seen before on him, "I know you're not," Roc said out loud and smiling while he pointed.

Mr. Holmes slowly ran his right hand over his forehead, noticing that it was wet. He thought, *"I'll be damned, he got me sweating. I haven't done this in over twenty years. For this is a display of a weak emotion based off an over reaction to an illusion of power and pressure that no strong man should allow another person to possess over him."* Mr. Holmes shook his head and kept thinking as if Roc could hear him, *"I have truly underestimated your power son but as you know Roc, a real man never falls for the same deception twice if he can help it."*

Without hesitation, Mr. Holmes pushed his first piece to start his attack when the door came flying open with Larry Jr. right behind it, moving his legs as fast as he could. "Daaaadddy," he raced up into Roc's arms.

"I'm home, you miss me?"

"Yeah I miss you, always…you know that."

Roc looked at his gold Timex that read 8:00 am. "Why are you back so early?" Roc questioned.

"Because Uncle Ma…"

"I'll tell him myself, because today is my first day at Temple."

At the sound of Lil Mac's voice, a cold chill raced through Mr. Holmes' body as he laid his eyes on Lil Mac for the first time since the kidnapping.

"Daddy, Uncle Mac and Aunt NayNay bought me ice cream and I stayed up all night."

"That's nice Jr. Mac what time will you be done because the people at lifestyle furniture emailed me about your restaurant tables and chairs. They'll be delivering today?" Roc asked.

"My last class is finished at 3:30, tell them we'll be ready around five," Lil Mac said while sensing a funny feeling to the left of him, Lil Mac turned to face it when he locked eyes with Mr. Holmes.

"Mr. Holmes, I didn't see you there. How're you doing?"

"Fine and I'm glad to hear you're doing the right thing," Mr. Holmes replied.

"Yeah I'm trying," Lil Mac answered.

"Mac come on, we're going to be late," screamed NayNay from the bottom of the stairs.

"I guess I better get going, Roc I'll see you later."

Larry Jr. broke free and raced across the wooden floor, "Uncle Mac, Uncle Mac."

Lil Mac turned around just in time to catch Jr. who jumped in the air by the arm. "What's up big man?" said Lil Mac while Jr. wrapped his small hands tightly around his neck.

"When you come back can you, me and daddy play ball again?"

"You bet we can, now let go of my neck."

"Okay."

Lil Mac disappeared down the hall. Mr. Holmes rose to his feet. "Where are you going old head, I'm about to give you an unpleasant dilemma to think about," Roc asked.

"I believe you would have tried but I only came to make sure everything went right with the deal in Phoenix before I head out of town this morning," answered Mr. Holmes.

"You're leaving town, why didn't you tell me…how long will you be gone?" Roc asked a little confused.

"Only a week, that's why I didn't mention it, being that it's my retiring week and I'm just going to say good bye to a few business associates in case I ever need them in the near future," Mr. Holmes explained.

"Okay, contact me when you get to your hotel."

31

At 3:26pm, Lil Mac exited Dr. Harold Rodriguez's forensic science class to be met by NayNay who was awaiting him and said, "There you go baby, I hope you're hungry because all this work has got me craving a cheese steak," before kissing him on the lips and handing him her school books.

"I'll tell you what, you go get the car while I run over to the library and take out these books I need and I'll meet you out front in ten, what you think?" questioned Lil Mac.

"Sounds like a plan to me and while you're there, ask for Mrs. Parker, the black lady…she's nice. She's the one that helped me get them." NayNay laughed as she motioned to the several books that Lil Mac handled while taking possession of the keys to their new silver Benz from his front pocket.

"Girl…you are not right," Lil Mac kicked at NayNay as she took off down the hall.

Once enough space was between them, she stopped and said while giving Lil Mac a great view of her beautiful round heart shape backside, "Now you know you got to be faster than that to hit this."

"We'll see how fast you are when I get you home," he replied.

"There, I'm not going to run," NayNay said.

Moving across the campus, Lil Mac took in the freshly cut grass that was everywhere as students with blankets laid out reading, talking or just relaxing with each other. Many wild flowers outlined each walkway making it a lovely sight of landscape design. A three-level old pueblo water fountain sat in the middle of the campus courtyard; the building's hardwood floor, stained glass windows and original geometric construction made Lil Mac realize that he had finally found peace.

"Hi handsome."

"Hi," he said, returning the greeting of five pretty women who passed. He stopped one and asked, "Excuse me?"

"Ebony," she said with a smile. "Ebony could you tell me where the library is?"

"Yes, go right down there and it's the third door on the right," she answered.

"Thank you."

"That's it? I thought you were stopping me to ask for my number."

"I'm sorry, I just needed that location," he answered.

"Well if you change your mind, I'm in your 10:30 Human Biology class."

Following Ebony's directions, Lil Mac thought, *"Damn I almost missed the chance to live this side of life, thanks Roc. I promise not to let it stop with me."* He entered the library and took notice at the clock on the wall, 4:10 pm. "Oh shit, the restaurant." He quickly checked out the books that he needed and then dashed out the door. Out front and out of breath, Lil Mac scanned the area for NayNay when he spotted two men parked in a car to the right of him. "Are they watching?" Lil Mac started to get a closer look as one of the men in a Temple sweatshirt exited the car before pulling off. "Damn, I'm tripping; this college is not the block." *Beep! Beep!* The sound of NayNay hitting the horn who was parked two cars down on Lil Mac's left, caught his attention.

He jumped into the passenger seat, "You think you're slick," NayNay stated.

"What?"

"Don't play with me, I saw you talking to those hoes. This new beginning and the whole starting over shit, I'm with you baby. But as soon as one of these bitches tries to get too close to what's mine," NayNay rubbed her hand over Lil Mac's manhood and continued, "I'm going to go old on you real quick and bust her ass."

"You'll never have to worry about that. Now let's get out of here, I've got a meeting at five," Lil Mac replied. "I will when this damn car moves, I don't know why he would stop there anyway…blocking us in." *Beep! Beep!* She hit the horn again.

Lil Mac looked up and locked eyes for the third time within seconds with the driver of the same car. On instinct, Lil Mac understood what was about to take place but hoped he was wrong. Hastily he searched for the man's partner; he spotted the man in the Temple sweat shirt approaching five steps behind NayNay as he raised a chrome 9mm. "NayNay get down!" With all the strength he had, Lil Mac pulled NayNay across him using his body as a shield when the driver's side window exploded.

32

In the basement of a three-story home in Upper Darby, Detective Michael sat with a gun on his lap in his favorite chair that was now positioned in the middle of the concrete floor. Staring at the wall, he swallowed the hot liquid of his second bottle of cognac. "Aaahhhh," he said, feeling the burn on contact. At this point, he wasn't drunk but quickly approaching it. For Detective Michael, his night would end like many of the rest…with him out cold. A police scanner locked to several of the local stations bass out calls from a distant corner that kept him up to date on daily events. The cold basement gave Detective Michael the feeling of being in a cave, hunting the wild was nearly pitch black except for the small lamp he placed at the corner of the back wall. On it laid a picture of Detective Rayfield as he was being sworn into the police force as a rookie.

A few inches beneath it were the words written in red print, "I promise to serve and protect your honor by the revenge of your death." and the photo of Top Dollar, Lil Mac, D, and an unknown to him NayNay, Roc and Boggy. A red X covered the face of D's photo. "I don't know how you did it you bastards but when it's your time, all of you will surely pay dearly." Detective Michael took another hard taste of the powerful liquor to re-warm his chest to make the cold bearable. This activity has been his ritual for the past hundred and twenty days after being suspended for six months with pay due to the pressure of Sam Clinton.

He and several other officers raided a Foot Locker truck at the Philly Raw store, on the advice of Detective

Brian that drugs were being brought in, after the two hour search ended with nothing being found. Captain Citric had no other choice but to take his badge and gun, putting him on leave. The upstairs door eased open slowly, "Michael are you down there again?" Detective Michael refused to answer, praying that his wife Shelly of seven years would just go away. The sound of footsteps declining the stairs made him take another drink. *"God why me?"* he thought. Shelly stopped halfway to the bottom and was shocked at the sudden change in room temperature as she quickly wrapped her arms around her body and rubbed them up and down to keep warm. She stared into the darkness, "Michael I know you're down here."

He began to smile as he watched the demonstration of his wife's discomfort.

"Look at you trapped in a lion's den, not aware that you have become the prey."

As the feeling of being watched over came upon her, she yelled "Michael please stop doing this to yourself. I know you love Josh, I love him also but…"

"Stop damn it, stop it," he interrupted. Detective Michael's strong voice escaped from behind the darkness as if it was a roar. "You couldn't possibly know. You didn't have to look into the face of Betty and see the life being stripped from it as you made a promise to bring her closure in the death of her husband. He was my partner, my friend and I swore to have his back at all times."

"Michael, being upset is understandable for anyone. You're human," she replied.

"No Shelly, this is my job…my career and what I get paid to do and I did everything in my power and I still don't have a fucking clue." A sudden loud sound of glass being smashed made Shelly jump nervously. But being the good understanding wife that she was, Shelly delivered the message that she came for.

"Okay Michael, I will leave you but I only came to tell you that Detective Brian called about ten minutes ago saying something urgent has just taken place at Temple University. He wanted to notify you before the word got out so that you could come by and check it out unnoticed."

"To hell with him, if it wasn't for him not rechecking his informant I would still be on the job going after Josh's killer."

Shelly headed back up the stairs and then stopped to say, "You know everybody is not against you Michael. There are a lot of your friends that want to help you through this but they can't if you won't let them and Michael I didn't have to look into Betty Rayfield's face to know how she feels, I just have to look into mine."

For twenty minutes, Detective Michael sat deep in thought and pondering on the reality of Shelly's words when the second call for police assistance came over the scanner and caught his attention. "Dispatch, this is Detective Brian again. Where is that tow truck that I requested over an hour ago?"

"Detective Brian this is dispatch, he said he was on his way. Let me see if I can pinpoint his location."

Hearing the voice of his once beloved friend Detective Brian, Detective Michael became enraged yelling. "I'll be back and when I do I'm going to bring this case to an end by myself if it kills me. I don't need none of ya'll!"

"Billy this is dispatch, do you copy?"

"Copy dispatch, this is Billy."

"What is your 1 2? Copy."

"I'm on the south side of Temple Campus looking for the vehicle, will you repeat the plate number over."

"Detective Brian, you there?"

"I'm here."

"The tow truck is in route on the south side requesting the license plate number."

"Damn, he's on the wrong side. Tell him to hurry over to the west side, north of Broadway intersection. We need to secure this car as evidence. He's looking for an '09 Mercedes Benz, license number G-E-T-M-O-N-E-Y, I repeat that's get money." Detective Michael jumped from his chair knocking over several beer cans before quickly heading up the steps crashing through the door.

Shelly was in the living room watching TV when he raced by. Seeing him speed by she questioned, "Honey what's wrong, where are you going?"

"To the school, Brian may have come through this time," he answered.

"Wait, it's coming up on TV now."

"I don't have time, I love you," Michael slammed the wooden framed door as Shelly said softly, "Be careful." She feared that if Detective Michael kept up his actions, one day he wouldn't make it back through the door. She quickly turned her attention back to the TV wanting to know what brought her husband back to life.

"Ladies and gentleman I'm Molly Weiss and if you're just tuning in to this C.V.T.V. newsflash, moments earlier this quiet peaceful campus that is now closed as you see behind me was full of life as the students enjoyed their first day of the school semester here at Temple University. We have learned at first that the atmosphere was an unrestricted state of relaxation as students tried to ready themselves for a better future. When around four o'clock this afternoon, everything changed as a man in possession of an assault weapon who police believe was accompanied by one or more individuals opened fire on this automobile just to my right."

The camera showed Lil Mac's Benz with the door wide open and yellow caution tape that stopped people from getting near it. "As you can see, the driver's side and front window are blown completely out. Let's hear from a few people that were on the scene at the time of the crime, excuse me sir you are?"

"Kenneth."

"And you were here at the time of the incident Kenneth?"

"Yes, it was unbelievable and I still can't understand it you know. You hear about this type of incident at other schools around the country like Virginia Tech but you wouldn't think it would happen at your school," Kenneth explained.

"Once again, I'm sorry but could you take us through what you saw?" Molly questioned.

"Well I was standing over there about twenty feet away when an African American man about six feet tall or so walked by me like he was taking a normal stroll. Then out of no where, he pulled this big gun from his back and just started shooting, shot after shot until the gun jumped back empty. By the second shot people started running in every direction for any kind of cover. I was over here."

Kenneth pointed to a spot to his right. "About five feet on the opposite side of my car, I was looking as the man retrieved a second gun off his hip and fired it also as he started to exit with most of the bullets crashing into the front windshield. There was glass flying everywhere. It all was just so unbelievable."

"Thank you Kenneth," said Molly as she turned her attention to another man standing on her right. "And sir, you witnessed something also is that right?"

"Well I was ready to cross the street when a blue Ford…wait hold up, is that a camera right there?" he asked.

Molly replied, "Yes sir, you're live on C.V.T.V."

"Well I didn't see shit, bitch is you crazy. What you trying to do, get me killed?" David said while looking from the camera man back to Molly before he ran across the street while covering his face.

"Sorry ladies and gentlemen for that outburst but in these mean streets, his statement is understandable. Here we have Detective Brian who is the lead Detective on this case. Detective Brian can you explain to us what happened and how something in this manner can happen here at this University in Philadelphia?"

"Molly what we believe transpired here today is two unidentified males came onto the campus around noon to surveillance their victim. One of the suspects even sat in the class of the victim, impersonating a student," Detective Brian explained.

"Was he a student Detective?" questioned Molly.

"As of now we have no knowledge of that but what we do know is that these men were professionals and this was indeed a hit."

"And may I ask what made you come up with that conclusion?"

"There are many facts, some of which I cannot disclose at this time but I will say how they avoided campus cameras by watching the route that they chose to enter and exit the grounds. The shooting itself, by witnesses accounts only took between 30-45 seconds and within that short amount of time, there were over 20 bullets released into the vehicle. The getaway car was found only two blocks away so by the time the APB was put out over the air, they were already in a different car for about ten minutes. I have been on the police force for over 20 years so to answer your question, these men were professionals. But the truth in the matter is this could have happened anywhere Molly. Due to the fact of the oppression, loss of jobs and low income community, some of these youth of today feel that selling drugs and other crimes is their only way out of their hard situation which is not true. But when I tell them to stop, they look at me like, 'okay; I'll stop…now what?' I have nothing to offer but emotional and moral support and that can't feed a family which is mostly single parent homes.

"These kids age from 11 and up and by the time most of them make it to 18, they've seen the prison system twice if not more in some way. So by the time they reach adulthood they already have two strikes against them, can't find employment which leads them going right back to what they know…the streets. Giving them not an option but to go hard at any cost because in the end, if they get caught by us with the laws we have now, they will be gone for a very long time, just like their fathers. Leaving yet another single parent home, this cycle is sad and has to stop."

As Detective Brian talked, you could see the disappointment in his face. "Yes it is sad detective, have you heard anything about the victims conditions?"

"Only that it's not looking too good but they're fighting."

"Hey Brian!"

Hearing his name, Detective Brian looked to the left to see what used to be a clean shaven nicely dressed officer, instead stood a rough, dirty looking, full-bearded Detective Michael. "Excuse me Molly, that's all for now," Brian said as he walked over to Detective Michael, smelling the strong scent of alcohol before he even reached him. "Michael what the hell happened to you?" asked a concerned Detective Brian.

"Never mind me, who was in the car?"

"The little one, Mac Miller."

Even though Detective Michael tried hard to hide it, a smile still appeared on his face as he questioned, "Do you think he'll make it?"

"I don't know…it's bad," Detective Brian replied.

"Where did they take him?"

"Temple Hospital."

Detective Michael took off for his Buick with his own plans in mind.

33

Gizelle was in the living room down on the first floor with both hands wrapped around her open mouth as tears flowed steadily from her eyes, over her 4 ct. Laura Munder platinum wedding ring and down her face. She was in shock at the sight of the new car Lil Mac won from Roc in a basketball game, now on TV filled with bullet holes and the interior covered with dry blood. "Once again, I'm Molly Weiss for C.V.T.V and that's all for now, have a good evening. Back to you Chuck."

"Mommy, Mommy what's wrong, why you crying?" asked Jr. coming from the backyard with a small basketball in his hands as Roc brought up the rear.

"Baby, are you okay…" Roc was cut off by the sound of his iPhone, then the house phone and next it was a private phone in the den all ringing at once. Gizelle wiped clear her tear filled eyes and then made eye contact with Roc while awaiting her orders.

"Jr. go get your jacket," she stated before saying a short prayer to God, then prepared herself to do whatever it took to make sure that Roc was successful in making whoever did this pay for hurting Lil Mac and NayNay. In her heart, Gizelle knew they didn't deserve this. She had to fight back her tears to not break her stare as Roc's gorgeous gray eyes turned dark brown right in front of her face. She began telling herself it has been some time but if needed, she could still make smoke appear from her gun.

Roc disconnected the call and calmly headed for the door. When his hand gripped the door handle, he heard,

"Roc." He turned around to see Gizelle entering back into the room wrapping her long beautiful hair into a double ponytail. While her arms were in the air, it made her shirt rise, that's when Roc noticed the 380 on her hip that he'd gotten her many years back for protection. He knew her mind state was ready for whatever the situation called for and that she would be with him in this a hundred percent. Roc wrapped his arms around her tightly. The feeling of Roc's powerful arms always made Gizelle feel safe from the world so she spoke her mind, "Roc I know that I'm always riding you about your lifestyle and telling you how I need for you to stop so that we can move forward. I still feel strongly about that but I know that you did everything in your power to save them. This was so uncalled for. So, what or who you decide needs to go…I'm with you."

"I know baby and on my father's soul, someone will pay for the blood of my brother but I will not make the same mistake twice. It was my intense anger that stopped me from seeing what I needed to see to prevent this whole thing in the first place. That will not happen again. What I need is for you to go be with my mother and I'll get back to you when I know something."

"I will," she replied.

"Roc we're out front, let's move!" Manny's voice came through the intercom. Roc looked to the screen to see him in a black Escalade with Raja and Buff in the back.

Gizelle gave Roc a hard passionate kiss and then said, "Here." She passed him a new 9 mm.

Roc looked into his palm and asked, "Where did you get this?"

"Married to you, I have to stay up to date!"

Manny's foot pressed down hard on the gas, making the heavy truck seem as if it was gliding on air as it bounced through another intersection passing a green Saab. "Raja, what we got?"

"Not much Roc but we have people on the scene as we speak. I notified several of our major connections in the cities closest to us. Most likely the people who did this were imported but in 24 hours, no matter where they are now…they'll be on their knees in front of you."

"And the rest?" Roc asked. Raja knew what Roc was referring to and it pained him to have to be the deliverer of such bad news.

"Dr. Woods said they're in surgery but he's hit pretty bad." Roc understood that there was more to the statement but Raja told him everything that he needed to know. He slowly lowered his head while closing his eyes and spoke through his thoughts, *"I know I have become your enemy in more ways than one. As a youth it was my lust for the power that made me believe in some moments that I could even play you, and when it's time I will stand as a weak man alone in your world before you to answer for my actions. But today I beg of you, me…Odell Miller, the person who believes that begging is forbidden for any person who considers himself a man, to take anything that I ever did good in my life in your vision and pass it on to these two kids. God please! They deserve that much because they learned it by watching me."*

Boom! Boom! Roc was brought out of his deep thoughts to find himself alone. *Boom! Boom!*

"Roc, come on," Boggy screamed after banging on the tinted window. He pushed another reporter back into the crowd by the face who was within the three-feet rule that he, along with Shamone and Mohammed upheld. Buff held the door open wide and said, "They're all awaiting you."

Inside the emergency room waiting area, Manny stood up against the wall on the right side with his hands tightly gripping two Mack 11's as they rested inside his Carheart front hoody pocket. Raja positioned himself in a chair that was in the middle across from Manny and Buff, the newspaper on his lap possessed a tech. Buff quickly placed a clear clamp over the door handle securing it.

Then he slid his hand under his suit jacket until he felt the touch of cold steel. Roc noticed his men were braced for action but didn't know why. Roc then heard the words.

"I don't give a fuck how many times you talked to him, you dig. Tell him again damn it because I need to know what's going on with my family now!" Top Dollar demanded.

"I understand sir and I assure you the operating team is doing their best," stated the nurse. The security guard looked around as Fox, with his hand in his pocket stood on his right, and looked him up and down with eyes that said, "I wish you would move!"

There were several Get Money men present, many with the look of pure rage and the determination to seek revenge upon their faces. Roc moved through the crowd like they weren't there, as Manny closed the distance between him and Roc in case someone still felt some type of way after their truce. Roc approached the nurse while she explained to Top Dollar, "Sir as soon as Dr. Woods gets a minute he will be right with you."

Top Dollar was about to protest when Roc stated, which sounded more like a demand, "I believe he just got a minute."

Top Dollar turned to face Roc as he planted his foot back into position when Dr. Woods walked through the double-swinging doors. The room suddenly became silent as he removed the rubber gloves from his hands and said, "I need you two to follow me quickly." On the way down the hall, Dr. Woods explained, "Gentlemen, usually I wouldn't allow this but Mac has lost a lot of blood and is very weak but his wish is to see you both."

Roc hoped that he wasn't reading too much into Dr. Woods' words but to be safe he closed his eyes requesting to God again to let them live. Inside the small waiting room, Lil Mac was propped up on two pillows. There were several IV's connected to his body, a large towel stained with small blood spots also laid over him. All that could be seen was from his neck up. The sight of the people he loved and mostly respected approaching his bedside forced Lil Mac to crack a weak smile that hurt.

Top Dollar could hold back no longer, as the sight of his unofficial but still son that possessed the heart of a warrior now laid looking so weak and helpless, forced a tear to escape his eye. "Don't you dare cry for me player," Lil Mac said in a raspy low voice. "You owe me more than that....to feel pain for another nigga, that's some weak shit and don't you ever forget it," Lil Mac added. Top Dollar smiled, remembering that those were the very words he'd spoken after he had to shoot Poppin Tags Shorty.

"But..." Top Dollar started to say.

"But what Top? They just fucked the old boy around, they got me. That's it, it happened."

Top Dollar smoothly removed any trace of wetness with the back of his hand. "You're right solider." Roc stepped back a few steps to give them their moment as Top Dollar continued, "I do owe you more than that. Son you brought the willingness to live back into me with that same spark in your eyes that stated you wouldn't be denied. That's what your father possessed and now I'll return the favor, by the time you walk out these doors, the men along with everyone that sleeps in the same home with him will endure a slow and painful death."

Top Dollar unintentionally shook the bed rapidly from the anger he felt as it vibrated the bed rail.

"Believe me, I dig. Don't cry for me, ride for me but you do..."

Top Dollar cut Lil Mac off in mid sentence, "I love you soldier, you just get better and I'll do the rest, dig me...

I promise." Top Dollar bent down and kissed Lil Mac on the forehead, who gave a gentle nod in acknowledgement. Top Dollar took Roc's spot in the shadows as he stepped up.

"Roc you told me there would be days like this but you didn't say they would hurt like hell," Lil Mac lightly laughed but it turned to a deep cough.

"It's okay big man; you're the strongest person I know. You're going to pull through this."

"I don't know Roc," Lil Mac said softly as his body began to tremble slightly. A feeling that was unfamiliar to Lil Mac came upon his body and it put a fear in him like never before, though he tried to remain calm holding onto the little strength that he had left.

"You know you're a Miller right?" Roc asked.

"With all that I am," he replied.

"Then you will be fine!"

"What about NayNay, did she make it?" Lil Mac asked.

"Yes, they said you saved her life."

"Roc, make sure she knows that I have no regrets, I did what any real King would do for his queen."

"Okay," Roc agreed.

"No Roc…I mean it, she must not feel a drop of guilt for living."

"I will handle it until you can tell her yourself," said Roc.

Lil Mac's cough became deeper and longer.

"That's it, I'm sorry Roc you'll have to go, he needs his rest," demanded Dr. Woods as he opened the door to let them out.

"Wait, Roc."

Roc remained still looking at Lil Mac straight in the eyes. "I'm sorry I didn't listen to you sooner but I did listen. So now you and Dad are even."

"What? How did you know?" Roc questioned.

"Come on, you can't be the only Miller that knows everything."

Roc smiled and kissed his brother before saying, "Get your rest big man, I'll be out here in the hall waiting on you. And who said I wanted to be even." Lil Mac smiled and started to cough hard.

"Come on out, time up. Nurse," called Dr. Woods.

Out in the hall Roc asked, "Dr. Woods what are his chances?"

"I'll be truthful, it doesn't look too good but if he makes it through the night, he will have a 50/50 chance."

"And the girl?" Roc inquired.

"She'll be fine. Your brother took most of the impact."

"Okay doctor, I need for you to do this, get her off this floor for 24 hours. Can you handle that?"

With a perplexed look on his face, Dr. Woods answered, "Whatever you need."

Roc walked out into the waiting room as Boggy appeared right beside him asking, "How's he doing, is he alright?"

"Oh he'll be fine," replied Roc and then went into his wallet and pulled photos out that Top Dollar couldn't see. "Get this to Mohammed and tell him to follow it to the tee," Roc ordered.

Watching from the back, Top Dollar called, "Fox!" When he came over, Top Dollar said, "Put a team on him, he's up to something…I can feel it."

34

Two weeks later, dressed in an all black Dior Homme suit and London Fall hat with Gucci Loafers, Top Dollar stepped into the Brickes Funeral Home accompanied by three men.

"Welcome Top Dollar, I'm terribly sorry for your loss," said Calvin, with a light bow who was an old friend of Top Dollar's back in the day when he used to run the streets. Now he was the co-owner of this funeral home. "Like you requested Top Dollar, I had this side of our place cut off for you only."

"And the casket?" Top asked.

"Oh yes, it's right this way." Calvin led them to a pearl white casket with 14 karat gold and marble trim. "Top it is said that this is the same casket that Hitler was buried in."

"How did he die?" ask Top Dollar.

"Who?" questioned Calvin.

"Hitler?"

"Oh it really isn't known," he replied.

"Well, this soldier died on the battlefield and is second to none so until you can say the same damn thing about Hitler, act like this is the only casket ever made until it's in the ground ya dig!"

Top Dollar pulled a super large knot of money from his pocket. He handed Calvin $300,000. Calvin slid them into his pocket and replied, "Thank you."

"No problem." Top Dollar then turned to the casket and said, "This will be your home, so until we meet again, as you came in the game you will leave the game." He smiled while remembering after they robbed Troy, how Lil Mac fell asleep on all the money as he tried to finish counting it.

Top Dollar started tossing the knot of thousands into the empty casket like they were a deck of cards.

Next, Fox stepped up to the casket and stated, "They disrespected family, they disrespected me and I swore to make you proud." He did the same with his knot of money. Calvin looked on in shock because the most money he had ever seen in his life was about to go into the ground.

"Now cover that up Calvin. This is for a reason, not for show and I'm going to leave my man right here," Top Dollar pointed to the third man with him and finished, "With you until this touches six feet you dig, so there will not be any discrepancies with this here."

"Anything you say," Calvin replied. Top Dollar and Fox disappeared like they were never there. The viewing for Lil Mac was scheduled to start at 9:00am but by 8:00 there was already a line of people down the block and around the corner. Inside, a room closed off to the public, stood Roc as he tried to comfort his mother the best that he could while she looked over her youngest son's body for the last time. Her tears were endless and covered Roc's shirt as if water had been tossed on him. As her sounds of agony echoed through his soul, he wanted to be able to take her pain away but for this to truly end, he knew that now was not the time.

Roc knew that it was best to have a separate quiet ceremony just with family present first. He wanted to avoid the live emotions being captured on TV or placed in the FBI files. Lil Mac was dressed in an all white linen B.B. shirt paired with white single pleated pants by Zanetti.

"Mommy why's grand-mom crying?" asked Jr. before he started to cry himself, not knowing what really happened but able to sense that something was wrong.

Mrs. Miller picked her head up from out of the grove of Roc's shoulder and kissed her son on the lips softly. Then with both hands she removed her tears before saying, "Thank you for always being strong for me and your brother after your father died. I know that broke your heart dearly now, because you had that same look that you wear today on your face. That look of determination to keep this family together and now I must be strong."

Mrs. Miller then walked over and eased Jr. out of the arms of Gizelle. "Don't cry baby, it's okay, grand-mom is just happy that Uncle Macky is going to a better place." Hearing the name of his favorite Uncle, Jr.'s face lit up.

"Where's Uncle Mac going, can I go?"

As she wiped away Jr.'s tears she smiled at his innocence, "No, he's going to be with his father. So you stop crying for me okay?"

"Okay grand-mom."

Handing him back over to his mother, Mrs. Miller stepped up to the rim of the casket with Roc right beside her. "Look at my baby. In a way, doesn't he look different to you?"

"No Mom, it's just the make up," Roc answered, holding her close to him.

"I don't know…there's something about him," Mrs. Miller paused as her eyes scanned his body before continuing, "Well if I could bet what an angel looked like; I would say it's this!"

"I know mother."

"He looks so peaceful and handsome." Interlocking hands, she kissed Lil Mac slow and long. "Until I can hold you again my angel, I love you."

Turning to her only remaining son and looking into his eyes, Mrs. Miller questioned, "Have I been a good mother, son?"

"Yes you have Mom."

"Then you wouldn't think any less of me for what I'm about to say."

"Never could I," answered Roc.

"I want to see the people who did this to my son pay with their life just as he did."

At that moment as he watched his mother's eyes darken, Roc found the origin of his bad side. "I promise you," Roc stated.

Without another word, Mrs. Miller walked to the door and paused. "Jr. come on with grand-mom, let's get some ice cream you don't need to be here."

"Yeeeaahhhh," Jr. went quickly over to his grand-mom. Roc gave Haffee a light nod as Haffee turned to follow right behind them.

After the viewing, a 62-car line, accompanied by 21 limousines rode through the streets of North Philly. Showing them the same respect they showed Lil Mac. The sun found its way out from behind the clouds as the leading driver now out of Philly, drove down an old country road at an easy pace watching the trees fly by. He passed through two open steel gates with two men standing on each side. The cars continued to move slowly through the private cemetery and stopped along side a clear road.

While the preacher spoke kind and loving words above the casket, Roc had his team positioned through out the crowd, looking for anyone or anything that they felt shouldn't be there.

"Roc, there's a car here at the front gate saying that they know you but will not lower their window or give a name. They said something about the feds and being one."

"Let them through," Roc said into his earpiece.

Moments later, a black-tinted Maybach pulled to a stop and a 300-pound muscular man with an umbrella, dressed in all black jumped out of the passenger seat. He opened the back door for Mr. Holmes who stepped out to be met by Roc who was standing at the edge of the grass. They embraced. “I’m sorry Roc; I know how much you loved him like a son. I came as soon as I heard.”

“That, I do,” Roc said clearly.

“Have you heard anything about who would dare do something like this?” Mr. Holmes questioned.

“Nothing yet, it’s as smooth as if I did it myself. The way they didn’t leave a trace or trail but we know they were imported.”

“You think?” Roc held Mr. Holmes’ stare.

“Yes…it’s like if I sent them at you, once they served their assignment they would have to be eliminated because they now possess a knowledge that is too powerful to chance ever getting out. That would mean an all out war,” Roc stated as his eyes tightened while still locked on Mr. Holmes.

“You know, if there’s anything within my power that I can do, I will.”

“I know Mr. Holmes but whatever connections you have, I now possess and I will use every single one of them until I get even.”

“I’m sure you will,” replied Mr. Holmes.

“Roc, get Mr. Holmes out of here, the feds got word of his presence and you now have three heading your way,” Boggy said into the earpiece.

“Come on, they know,” Roc held the umbrella to shield Mr. Holmes as the big man reappeared. Safely back in the car, Mr. Holmes cracked the window an inch.

“Roc, I have no doubt that you will find who did this but please make sure you stop wearing your emotions on your sleeve so they don’t see you coming.”

“Thanks old head, but who says I’m trying to hide it.”

Roc walked by and waved at Mr. Holmes’ driver who was another large muscular man. Mr. Holmes raised the window, never taking his eyes off of Roc who stopped near Boggy and said into his earpiece, "Ayzo, get me out of here quick and tell the team from Pakistan that he knows."

"How can you be sure?" Ayzo asked.

"To be truthful, the man just told me." Roc watched the Maybach disappear out of sight before turning to Boggy, "Get everyone together at the old spot on block three."

"Why what happened?"

"I know who spilled the blood of my brother," Roc replied.

"How…who told you, Mr. Holmes?" Boggy asked.

"In a way yes, always know that for a good switch up to work, the change up has to look the same as the prototype and if it's off in anyway, a real player sees right through that bullshit."

"Roc what are you talking about?" Boggy questioned, not fully comprehending what was happening and all that Roc knew.

"Look, he had two new bodyguards and they're men." Roc said.

"And?"

"He hates men; he says he can't to be around anybody he can't fuck. He should have used military women, it would have worked better."

Later that night in a section of North Philly, Roc and another individual sat in the back room watching the screen as it showed the face of his men taking their seats at the large round table in the center of the room. Clockwise from the right was Boggy, Manny, Raja, Buff, Haffee, Mohammed, Shamone, M. Easy, Fox, Top Dollar, Ayzo, Daz, AP, and NayNay. After studying the eyes of their soldiers like they always did to look for weakness and deception, only seeing loyalty. It was evident that they all wanted the same thing…revenge. Roc slowly rose to his feet and stepped out to the head of the table and started to speak.

"I brought you all here for one reason and that is to take out the most dangerous man I know and avenge the blood of my brother…"

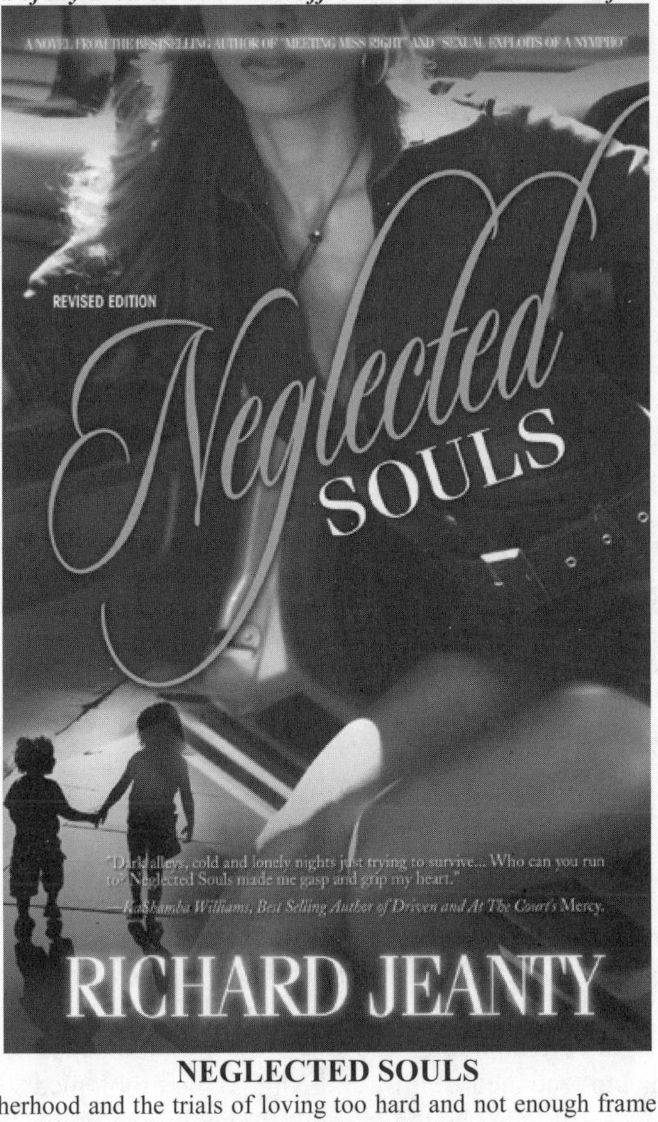

NEGLECTED SOULS

Motherhood and the trials of loving too hard and not enough frame this story...The realism of these characters will bring tears to your spirit as you discover the hero in the villain you never saw coming...

Neglected Souls is a gritty, honest and heart-stirring story of hope and personal triumph set in the ghettos of Boston.

In Stores!!!

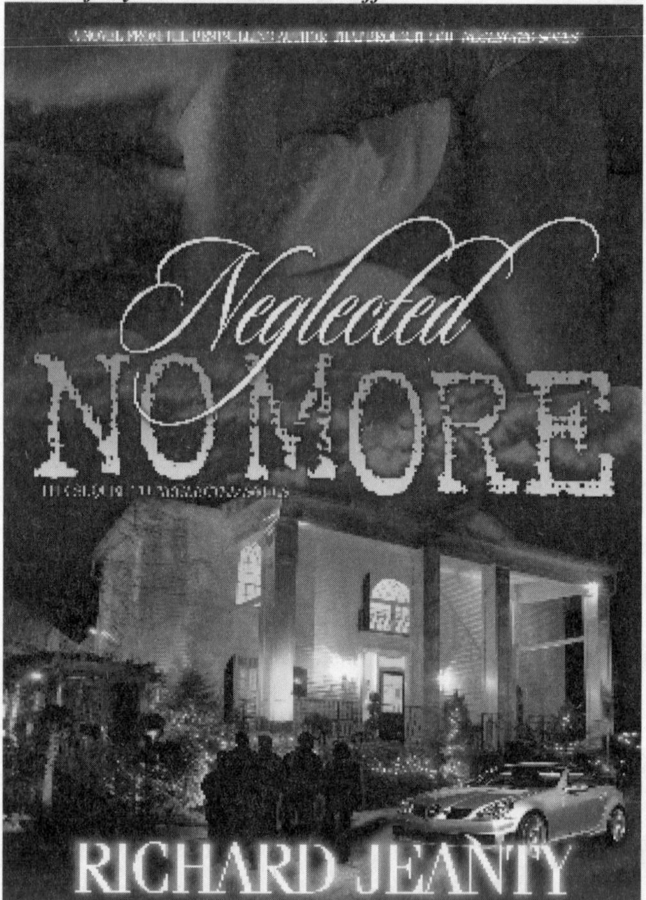

Jimmy and Nina continue to feel a void in their lives because they haven't a clue about their genealogical make-up. Jimmy falls victims to a life threatening illness and only the right organ donor can save his life. Will the donor be the bridge to reconnect Jimmy and Nina to their biological family? Will Nina be the strength for her brother in his time of need? Will they ever find out what really happened to their mother?

In Stores!!!

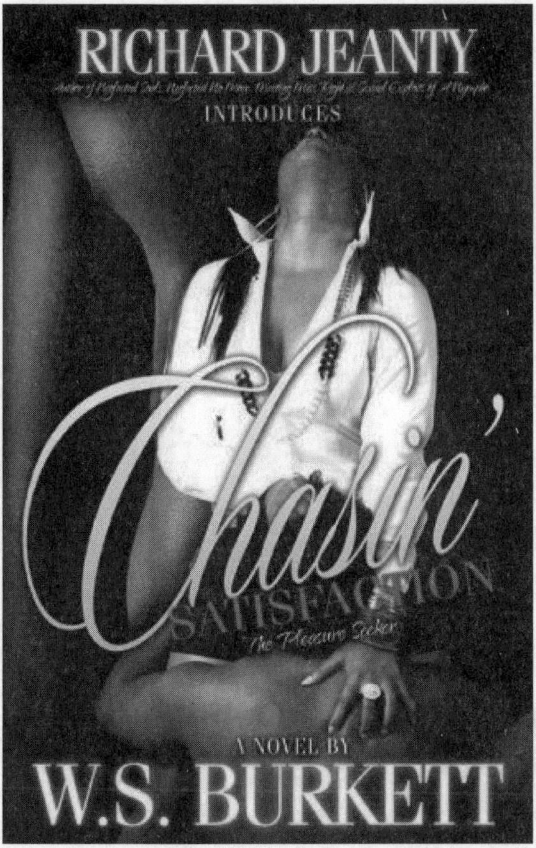

Betrayal, lust, lies, murder, deception, sex and tainted love frame this story... Julian Stevens lacks the ambition and freak ability that Miko looks for in a man, but she married him despite his flaws to spite an ex-boyfriend. When Miko least expects it, the old boyfriend shows up and ready to sweep her off her feet again. Suddenly the grass grows greener on the other side, but Miko is not an easily satisfied woman. She wants to have her cake and eat it too. While Miko's doing her own thing, Julian is determined to become everything Miko ever wanted in a man and more, but will he go to extreme lengths to prove he's worthy of Miko's love? Julian Stevens soon finds out that he's capable of being more than he could ever imagine as he embarks on a journey that will change his life forever.

In Stores!!

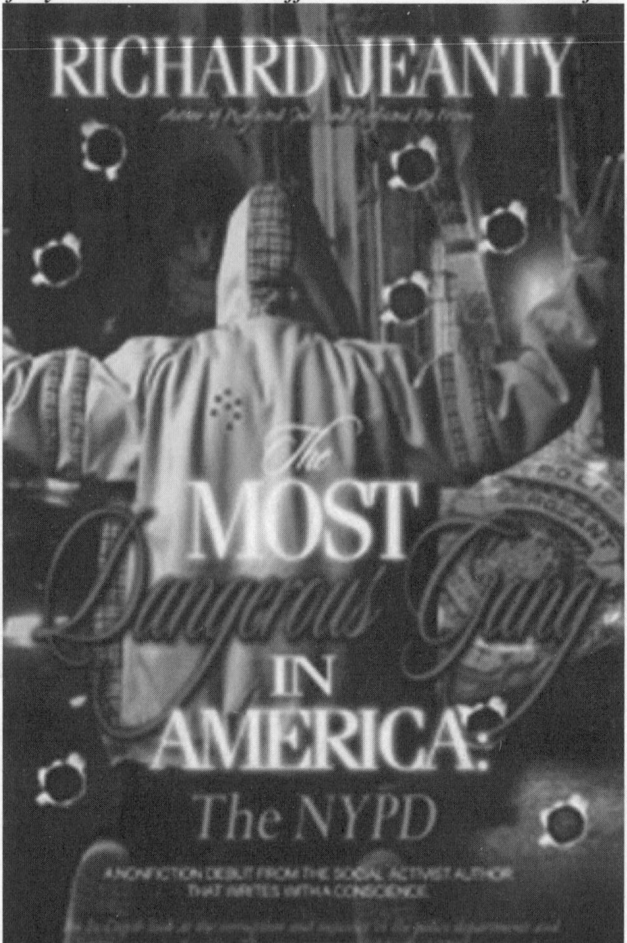

The police in New York and other major cities around the country are increasingly victimizing black men. The violence has escalated to deadly force, most of the time without justification. In this controversial book, noted author Richard Jeanty, tackles the problem of police brutality and the unfair treatment of Black men at the hands of police in New York City and the rest of the country. The conflict between the Police and Black men will continue on a downward spiral until the mayors of every city hold accountable the members of their police force who use unnecessary deadly force against unarmed victims.

In Stores!!!

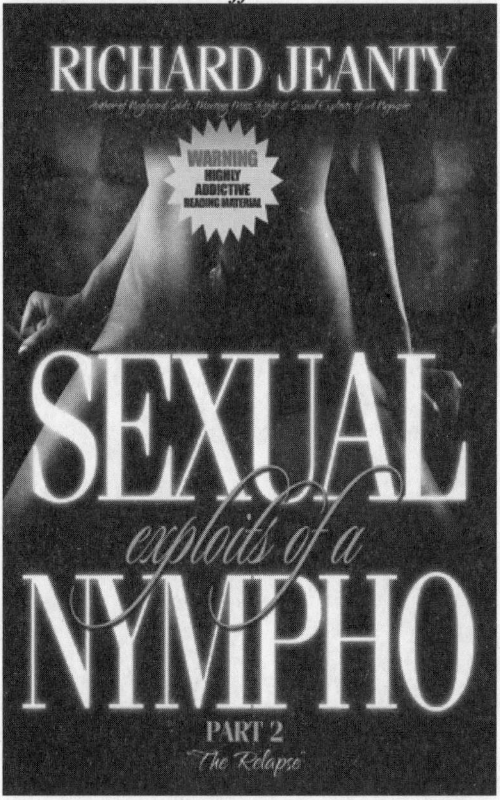

Just when Darren thinks his relationship with Tina is flourishing, there is yet another hurdle on the road hindering their bliss. Tina saw a therapist for months to deal with her sexual addiction, but now Darren is wondering if she was ever treated completely. Darren has not been taking care of home and Tina's frustrated and agrees to a break-up with Darren. Will Darren lose Tina for good? Will Tina ever realize that Darren is the best man for her?

In Stores!!

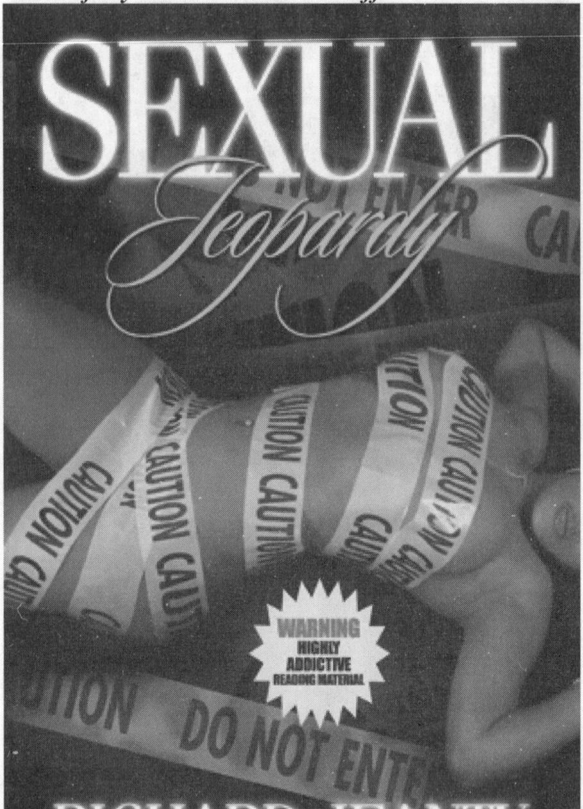

Ronald Murphy was a player all his life until he and his best friend, Myles, met the women of their dreams during a brief vacation in South Beach, Florida. Sexual Jeopardy is story of trust, betrayal, forgiveness, friendship, hope and HIV.

In Stores!!!

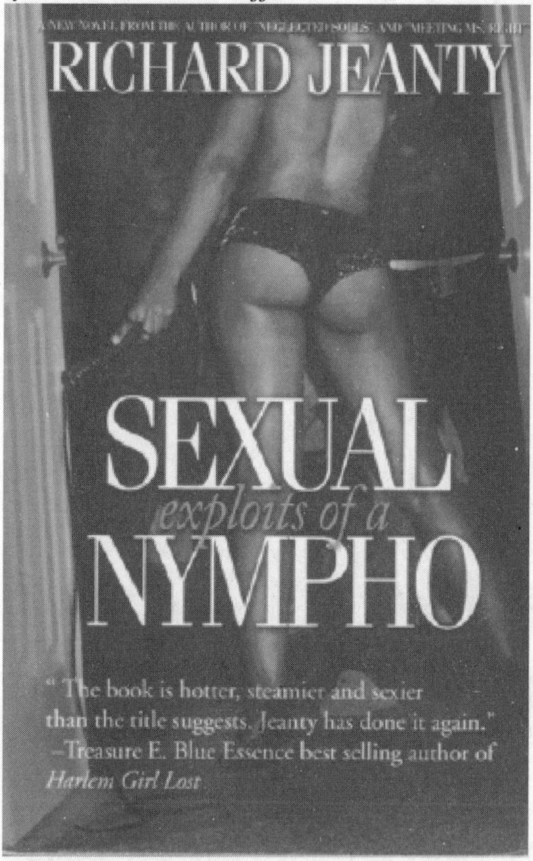

Tina develops an insatiable sexual appetite very early in life. She only loves her boyfriend, Darren, but he’s too far away in college to satisfy her sexual needs.
Tina decides to get buck wild away in college
Will her sexual trysts jeopardize the lives of the men in her life?

In Stores!!!

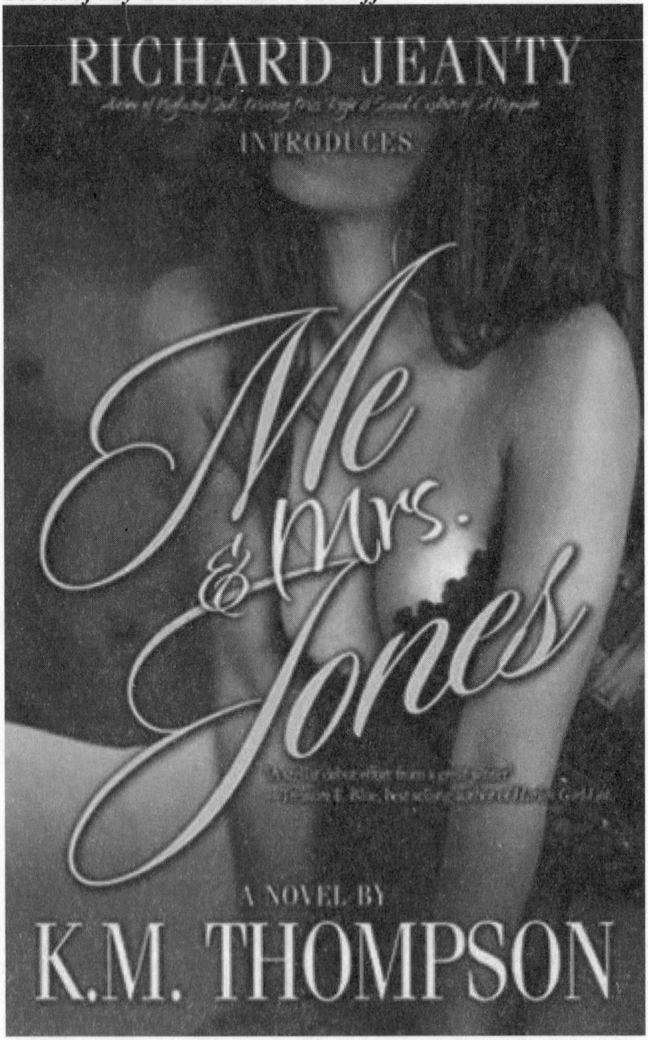

Faith Jones, a woman in her mid-thirties, has given up on ever finding love again until she met her son's best friend, Darius. Faith Jones is walking a thin line of betrayal against her son for the love of Darius. Will Faith allow her emotions to outweigh her common sense?

In Stores!!!

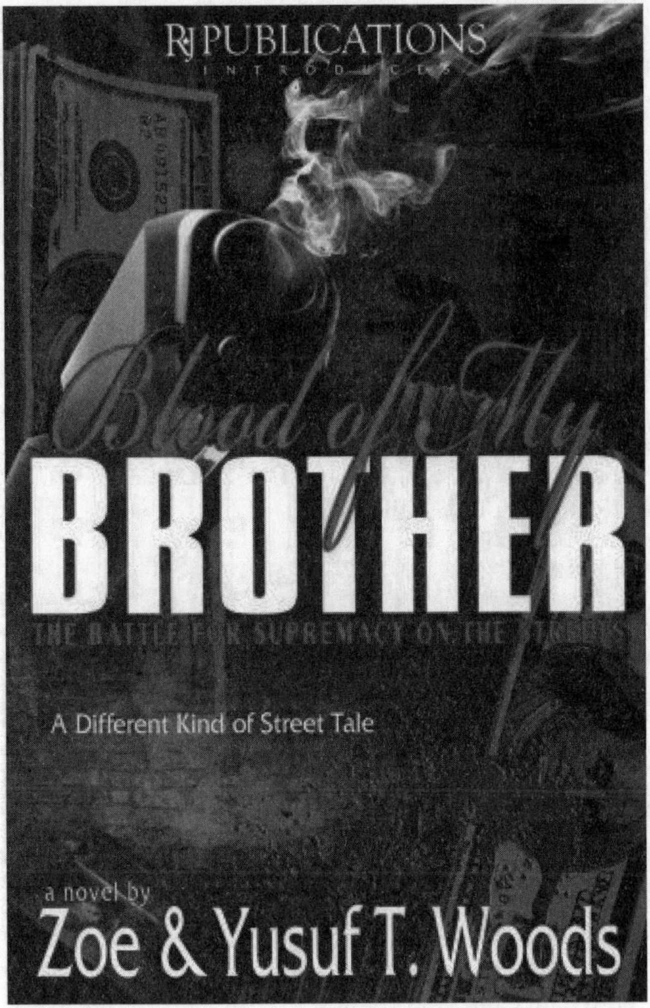

Roc was the man on the streets of Philadelphia, until his younger brother decided it was time to become his own man by wreaking havoc on Roc's crew without any regards for the blood relation they share. Drug, murder, mayhem and the pursuit of happiness can lead to deadly consequences. This story can only be told by a person who has lived it.

In Stores!!!

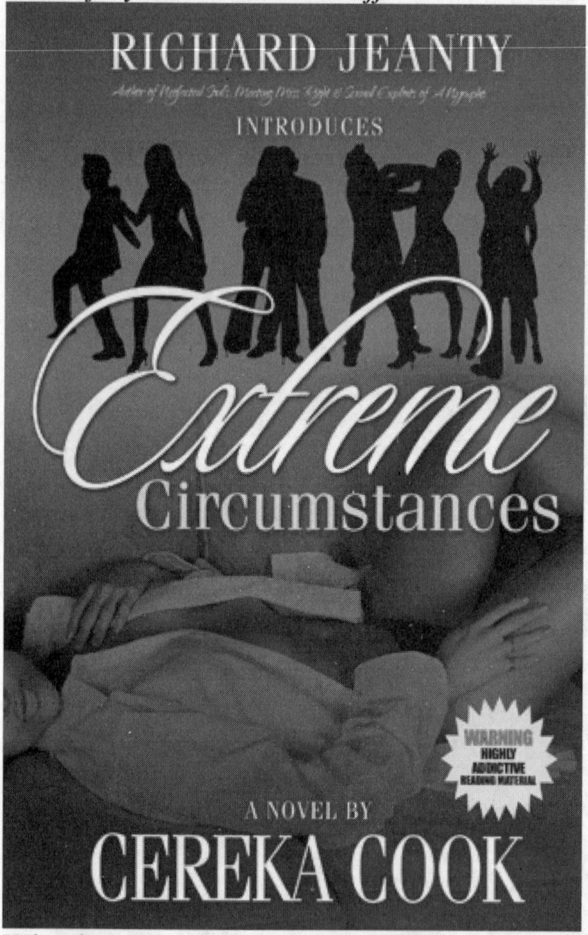

What happens when a devoted woman is betrayed? Come take a ride with Chanel as she takes her boyfriend, Donnell, to circumstances beyond belief after he betrays her trust with his endless infidelities. How long can Chanel's friend, Janai, use her looks to get what she wants from men before it catches up to her? Find out as Janai's gold-digging ways catch up with and she has to face the consequences of her extreme actions.

In Stores!!!

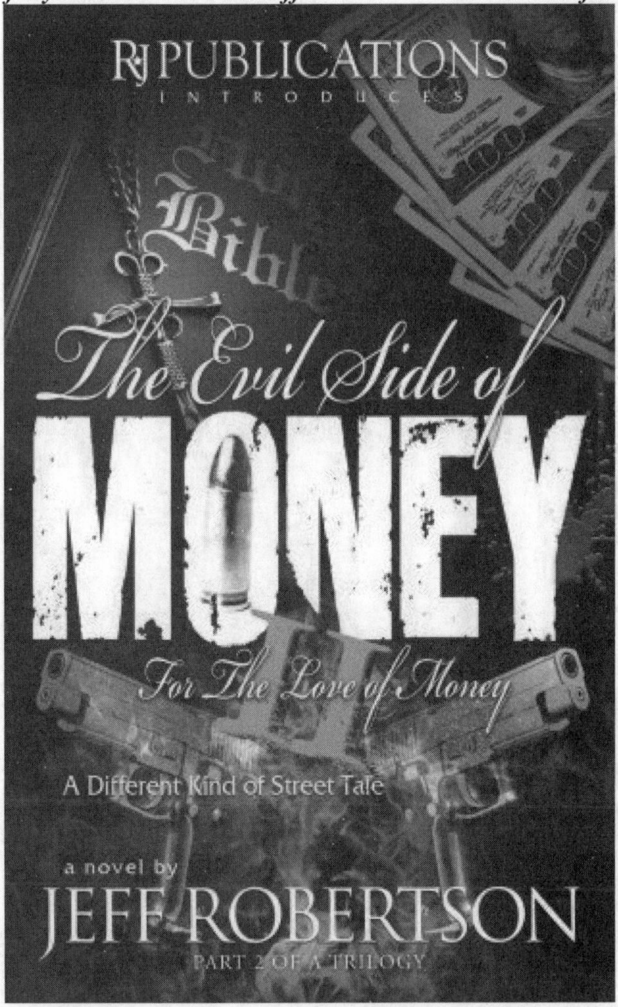

A beautigul woman from Bolivia threatens the existence of the drug empire that Nate and G have built. While Nate is head over heels for her, G can see right through her. As she brings on more conflict between the crew, G sets out to show Nate exactly who she is before she brings about their demise.

Coming in September 2008!!

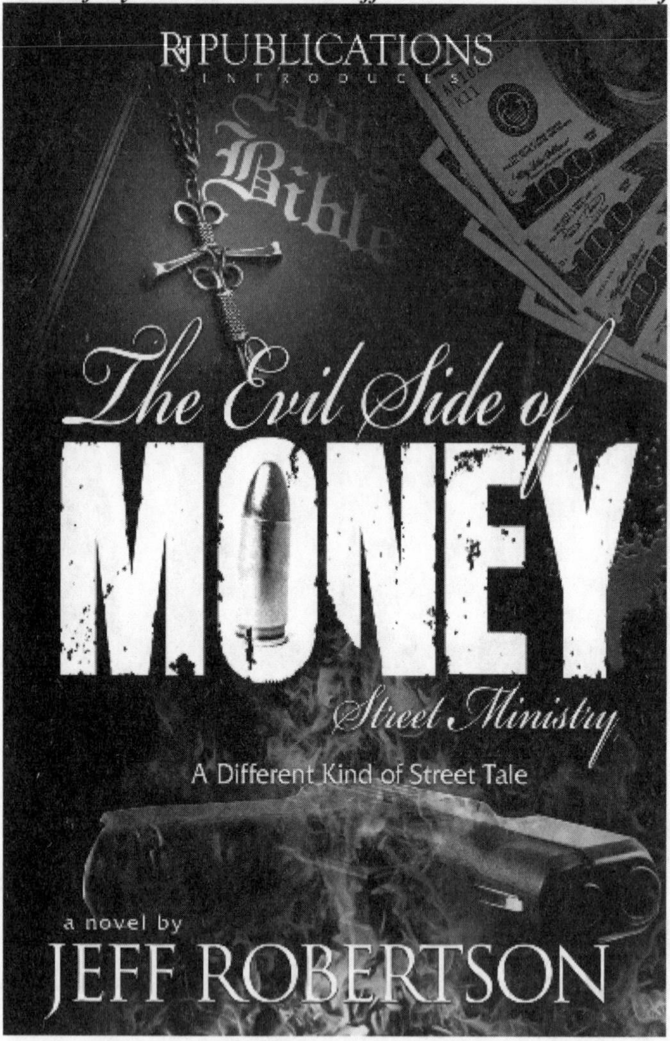

Violence, Intimidation and carnage are the order as Nathan and his brother set out to build the most powerful drug empires in Chicago. However, when God comes knocking, Nathan's conscience starts to surface. Will his haunted criminal past get the best of him?

In Stores!!

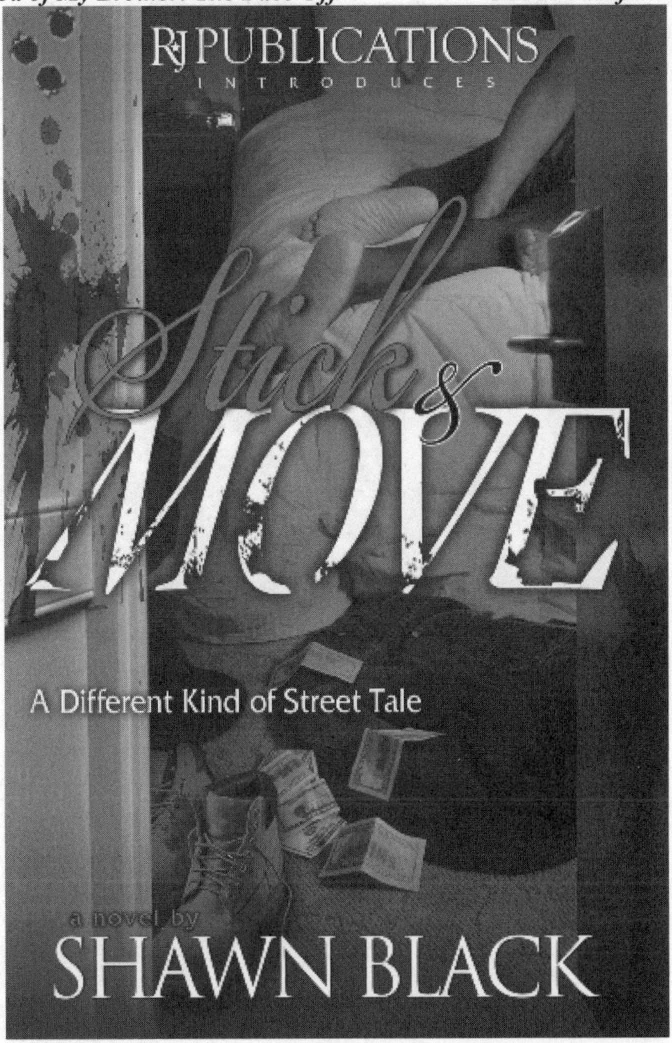

Yasmina witnessed the brutal murder of her parents at a young age at the hand of a drug dealer. This event stained her mind and upbringing as a result. Will Yamina's life come full circle with her past? Find out as Yasmina's crew, The Platinum Chicks, set out to make a name for themselves on the street.

In stores!!

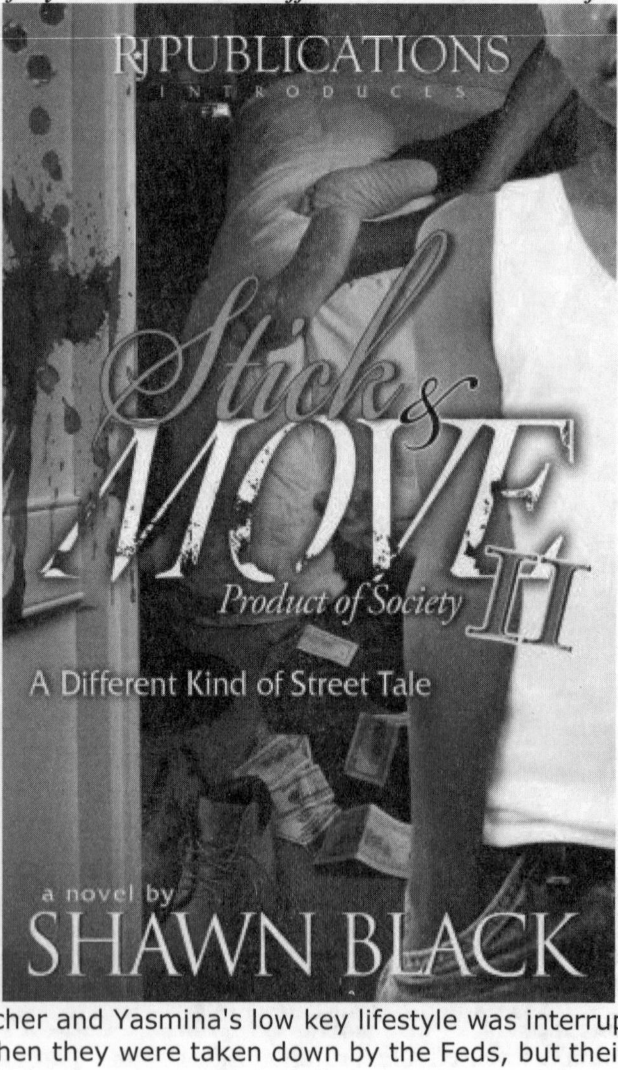

Scorcher and Yasmina's low key lifestyle was interrupted when they were taken down by the Feds, but their daughter, Serosa, was left to be raised by the foster care system. Will Serosa become a product of her environment or will she rise above it all? Her bloodline is undeniable, but will she be able to control it?

Coming soon!!

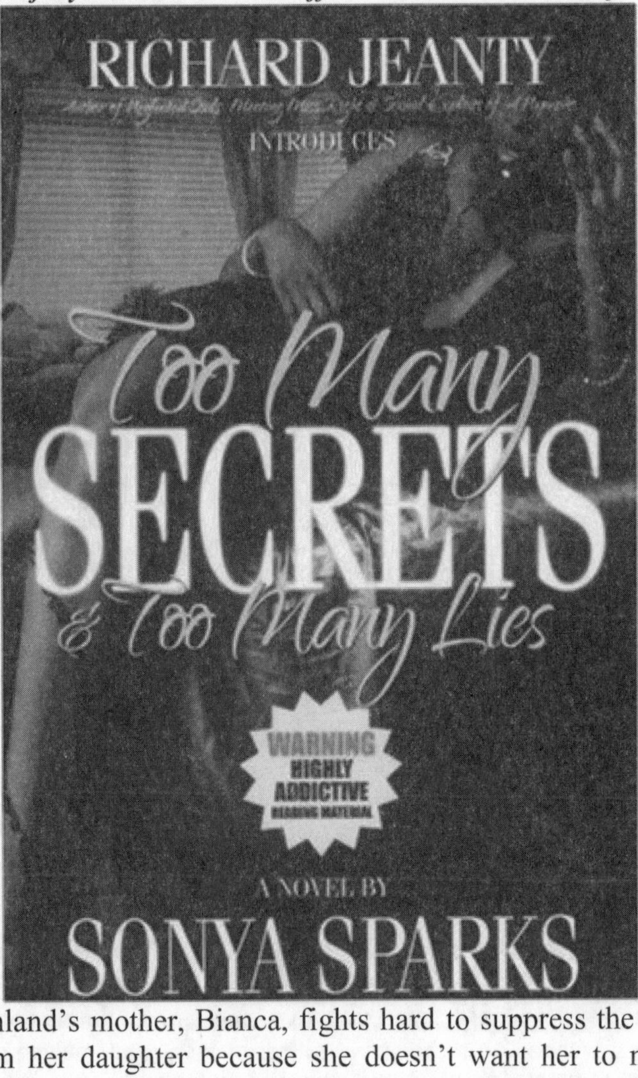

Ashland's mother, Bianca, fights hard to suppress the truth from her daughter because she doesn't want her to marry Jordan, the grandson of an ex-lover she loathes. Ashland soon finds out how cruel and vengeful her mother can be, but what price will Bianca pay for redemption?

In stores!!

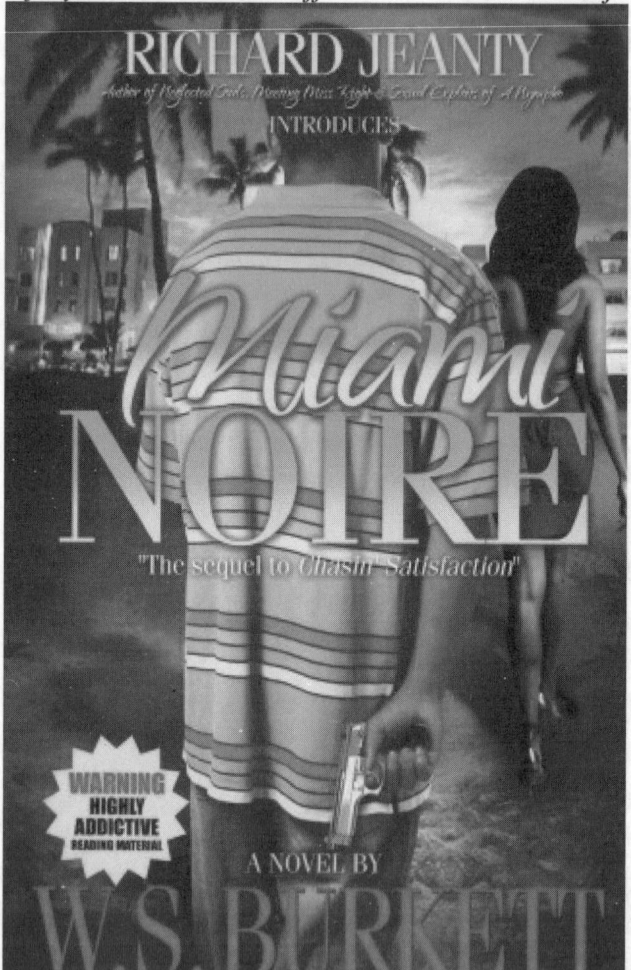

After Chasin' Satisfaction, Miko finds that satisfaction is not all that it's cracked up to be. As a matter of fact, it left nothing but death in its aftermath. Now living the glamorous life in Miami while putting the finishing touches on his hybrid condo hotel, Julian realizes with newfound success he's now become the hunted. Julian's success is threatened as someone from his past vows revenge on him.

Coming November 2008!!

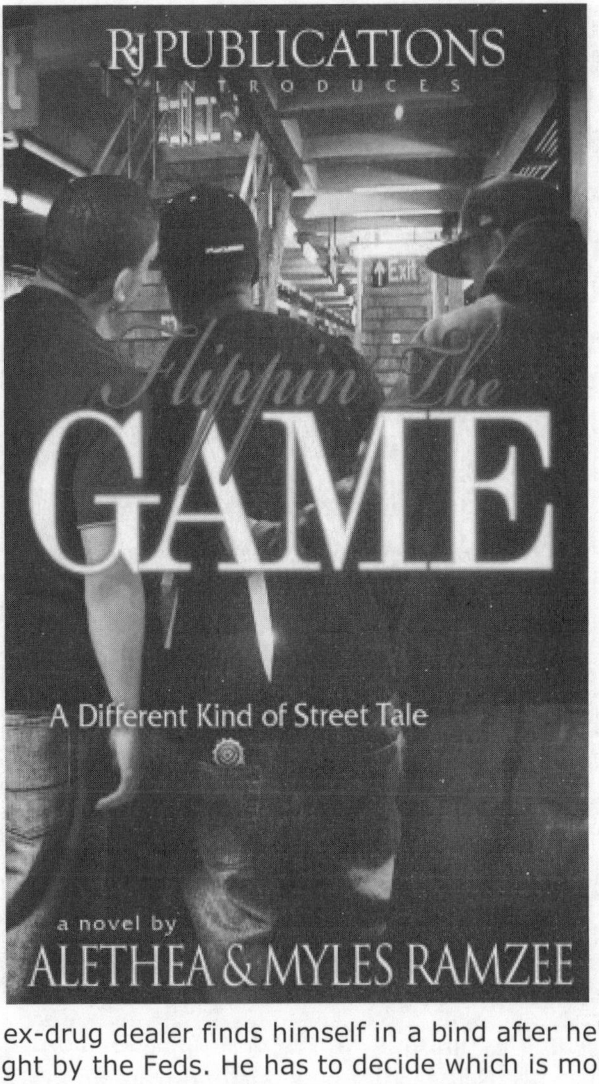

an ex-drug dealer finds himself in a bind after he's caught by the Feds. He has to decide which is more important, his family or his loyalty to the game. As he fights hard to make a decision, those who helped him to the top fear the worse from him. Will he get the chance to tell the govt. whole story, or will someone get to him before he becomes a snitch?

Coming October 2008!!

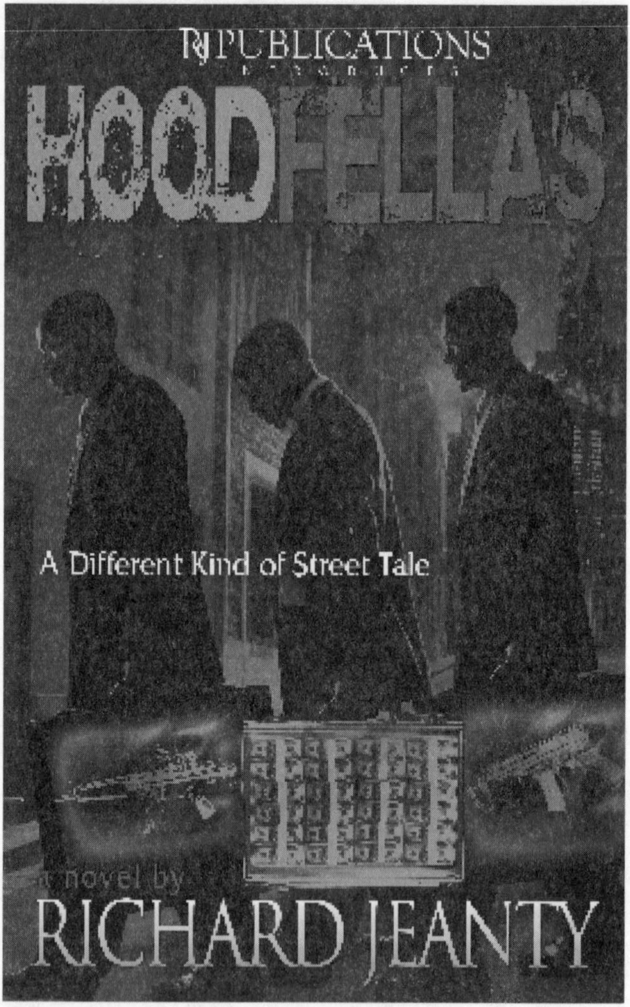

When an Ex-con finds himself destitute and in dire need of the basic necessities after he's released from prison, he turns to what he knows best, crime, but at what cost? Extortion, murder and mayhem drives him back to the top, but will he stay there?

Coming November 2008!!

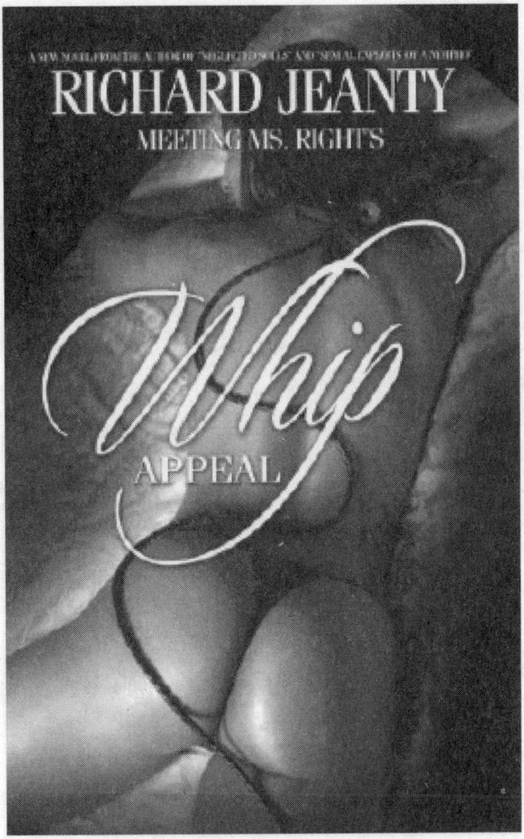

Malcolm is a wealthy virgin who decides to conceal his wealth
From the world until he meets the right woman. His wealthy best friend, Dexter, hides his wealth from no one. Malcolm struggles to find love in an environment where vanity and materialism are rampant, while Dexter is getting more than enough of his share of women. Malcolm needs develop self-esteem and confidence to meet the right woman and Dexter's confidence is borderline arrogance.

Will bad boys like Dexter continue to take women for a ride?

Or will nice guys like Malcolm continue to finish last?

In Stores!!!

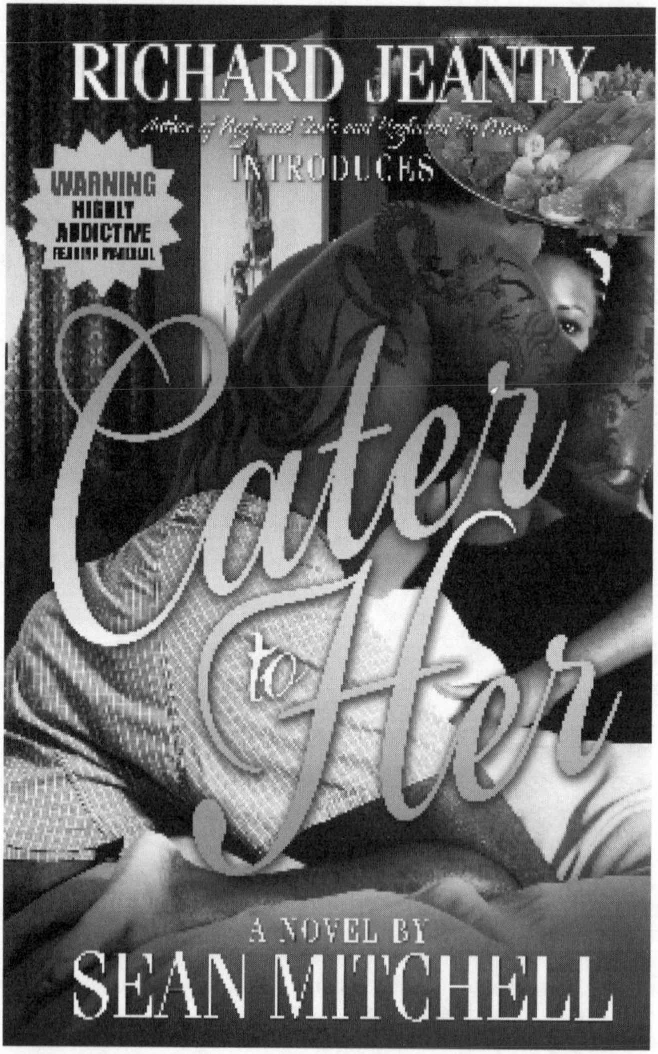

What happens when a woman's devotion to her fiancee is tested weeks before she gets married? What if her fiancee is just hiding behind the veil of ministry to deceive her? Find out as Sean Mitchell takes you on a journey you'll never forget into the lives of Angelica, Titus and Aurelius.

In Stores!!